THE WAR WIDOW

William Kelly Durham

The War Widow

William Kelly Durham

BERLIN CALLING also by Kelly Durham is available at Amazon.com.

Cover design by Kari Lynch

For Yvonne.

He led me back and forth among them, and I saw a great many bones on the floor of the valley, bones that were very dry.

Ezekiel 37:2

Nuremberg, Germany
October 1946

    The wind had picked up, joining the misty rain. A perfect night for an execution, Petersen thought as he peered out the window of the guards' day room. It was just like one of those Hollywood pictures: the dark, stormy night, the guards sitting around waiting, the chaplain in the corner saying prayers. Of course this time, there would be no midnight call from the governor's office staying the sentences. And, truth be told, Chaplain Gerrity wasn't praying. He was still fiddling with the radio, trying stubbornly to pick up stray radio waves from Saint Louis, where his beloved Cardinals were battling the Red Sox in Game 7 of the World Series. Colonel Gaffner, in a rare concession, had allowed one phone call into the prison at the end of each inning. After seven innings, the Cardinals were up 3-1 and Gerrity was happy. He was swapping jibes with Sergeant Gamble, a rabid Boston fan. The phone rang and Gerrity pounced on it. He jotted some notes on a piece of paper on the table. When he hung up, he was frowning. 'Well, damn!' he said to no one in particular, assiduously avoiding Gamble's face. 'Two pinch hits! Two! What are the odds of that?' He tossed the pencil down in irritation.

    'What's the scoop chaplain?' Gamble asked hopefully. Gerrity related that the Sox, after two pinch hits to lead off the eighth, had made two outs. Then, Dom DiMaggio had laced a double off the right field wall of Sportsman's Park to score two runs. Going into the bottom of the eighth, the game was tied at 3 all. 'How I hate to go on duty!' Gamble groused picking up his helmet liner and slapping it down on his head. 'I'm gonna be down there looking through a door watching a guy sleep and you're gonna be up here twiddling the dials on that radio. I bet you pick it up as soon as I leave. Let me know when you get the next call, will ya chaplain?' Gamble pleaded. He left the dayroom and headed down the spiral stairs to take up his post in front of Goering's cell. It was 2200 hours.

    Petersen was reading the *Saturday Evening Post*. Actually, he was holding the *Saturday Evening Post*; he hadn't read a word in several minutes. His eyes were fixed on an article about Broadway's resurgence following the end of the war, but he could not focus. He glanced again at the wall clock. Two minutes had passed since his last look. Half of him wanted the clock to move faster, to get this night over with. The other half wanted to avoid looking into the eyes of Goering and the others as they marched to the gallows. The ringing telephone startled him. Gerrity grabbed it. 'Yes,' he shouted into the handset, 'go ahead.' The chaplain scribbled a note. 'Praise God!' he said. 'Yes, thanks!' he hung up. 'Well, well, well,' he said gleefully, 'I must go inform Sergeant Gamble that the mighty Cardinals now own a one run lead going into the ninth!' Gerrity reported that the Card's Enos Slaughter had scored from first base on a Harry Walker double to left. According to his report, the ball had come back in to Sox shortstop Johnny Pesky, but Pesky held the ball, thinking that Slaughter had stopped at third. 'OK if I break the news to Gamble?' Gerrity asked Petersen.

'OK, sir,' Petersen agreed, 'but keep quiet out there. And chaplain,' Petersen added with a smile, 'be gentle.' Gerrity chuckled and headed toward the door, but he stopped, a puzzled expression on his face. Then Petersen heard it: running footsteps clattering on the metal stairs followed by shouts. It was Gamble, charging up the spiral steps and yelling. 'LT Petersen! Something's wrong! Something's wrong with Goering!' Petersen was on his feet, dashing for the door, where he collided with Gerrity, who had stopped short, and Gamble who had barged in. Petersen pushed Gerrity out of the way and spun Gamble around.

'Go!' he shouted. Together, the two thundered down the stairs toward the cell block where the highest ranking survivors of Hitler's Third Reich sat awaiting their executions.

Chapter 1

John Petersen looked up at the Palace of Justice, the most imposing structure left in the city of Nuremberg. Halfway between Nuremberg's rail yards and the Pegnitz River, just west of the old city, the Palace was both large and largely undamaged after six years of war, making it an oddity in Nuremberg. Most of the sprawling city lay in ruins with thousands of decaying bodies still buried beneath the rubble. Standing five stories tall, the building was capped with a steeply sloping, red tile roof and was protected by a low brick wall topped with wrought iron pickets. At the corner of *Fuertherstrasse*, an armored car covered the west approach to the building. Just off the courtyard, outside the fence, a Sherman tank stood guard. In front of the Palace, jeeps, staff cars and the occasional Volkswagen waited in parallel rows. A warm sun filtered through the trees, leaving a mottled pattern of sun and shade on the dusty brick of the courtyard. A hint of a breeze rustled the leaves and carried a sickly sweet odor of decay from the river just north of the Palace complex.

Petersen stepped through the iron gate, gripping his bag in his left hand. He returned the salute of a soldier, standing in front of his striped sentry box, and entered the building. As his eyes adjusted to the dim hallway, Petersen spotted a building directory posted on the wall to his right. His destination, the Internal Security Detachment, was on the second floor, up two flights of stairs and down the right hand corridor.

Petersen paused outside the detachment office, took a deep breath and opened the outer door. Two Army sergeants glanced up then immediately resumed their work, one pecking out a report on a battered typewriter, the other fiddling with the dials of a radio that was filling the office with static. The room was brighter by far than the hallway, with haze filtered sunlight streaming in through two large windows. Blue ribbons of smoke curled toward the ceiling from unfinished cigarettes. 'Be right with you lieutenant,' said a thin, dark haired corporal, pouring a cup of coffee into a mug. Petersen watched as the corporal dumped a spoon full of sugar, a true luxury in Germany, into the coffee. Holding the mug carefully, the corporal took it to a side office, knocked, entered and pulled the door closed. Within seconds, he reappeared and walked back to his desk. 'Now sir, what can we do for you?' the corporal smiled.

'I'm 1LT Petersen, reporting for duty,' Petersen replied.

'Oh, yes sir. Corporal Wilson, sir. May I get you a cup of coffee?'

'No thanks,' Petersen answered.

'Sir, if you will have a seat, I will let the colonel know you're here. Do you have your personnel folder?' Wilson continued. Petersen handed over the Army's official record of his existence. Wilson obviously knew the routine and Petersen wondered how many lieutenants he had ushered in and out of this place since the war ended.

Petersen sat down in a wooden chair as Wilson knocked on the office door he had exited only a few moments earlier. Again, Wilson disappeared inside. Petersen ran his fingers through his short cropped brown hair. At 5 feet, 10 inches, he was slightly taller than average with a lean build. He considered himself in good health despite having spent five months on the front lines as the war in Europe came to a lumbering close. As he waited, his eyes drifted over the small sitting area of the Internal Security Detachment office. Four wooden chairs surrounded a low table covered with old issues of *Look* magazine and more recent editions of *Stars & Stripes*. Three ash trays, all at capacity, and a tired looking floor lamp with a split shade, completed the furnishings. Petersen's fingers migrated to the short scar above his right eye, an old wound from another place and time. His middle finger traced the scar as he waited. A clock on the plastered wall showed the time as 1100 hours. Petersen was figuring what time it would be in Texas when Wilson returned. 'Lt Petersen, if you please, the colonel will see you now,' he said. Actually it didn't matter in the least if it pleased Petersen or not, as they both knew. His orders had been specific and succinct: report for duty to the Internal Security Detachment, Nuremberg no later than 1 August 1945. No further explanation had been given, nor would Petersen have expected any. The Army did what it did without explanation and

14

most often, it seemed, without reason. Petersen straightened his tie and his green Army blouse, squared his shoulders and proceeded to the inner office door, the two sergeants oblivious to his presence. He knocked on the door and heard a muffled voice from inside, which he took as permission to enter. He pushed open the door and stepped into a large office, quickly noting the location of the heavy, ornate wooden desk and the colonel seated behind it. Petersen stopped short of the desk, snapped to attention, saluted and said, '1LT Petersen reports for duty, sir.' Colonel Douglas Gaffner returned the salute and, standing, extended his hand. 'Welcome to Nuremberg LT Petersen!' he smiled. Gaffner's voice was loud, almost a shout, but his smile seemed genuine. Shaking hands, Gaffner steered Petersen to one of two large armchairs standing next to a small side table. 'Have a seat.' Douglas Gaffner was a stocky man of about 5 feet, 8 inches, weighing nearly 200 pounds. His shoulders were broad and if his gut seemed to lap slightly over his belt, he still appeared more muscle than fat. His leonine head was covered with short, wiry gray hair. He looked tough, battle-hardened, with a creased forehead and squint lines around his eyes. As he sat down, Petersen sneaked a quick look at the uniform blouse hanging over the back of his dark leather desk chair. Gaffner's ribbons included a Purple Heart and Bronze Star. 'So, you were with the 84th Division? I see from your file that you have been in theater for about 10 months,' prompted the colonel, looking up from the file spread across his lap.

'Yes sir. I was part of the division's original complement. We got to France on 1 November and went right on up to the front. We saw some action around Geilenkirchen and then we were pulled off the line for a few days right before the Bulge.'

'And then you went right back into the lines, didn't you?' the colonel suggested.

'Yes sir,' Petersen replied. 'That's the coldest I ever was.'

Gaffner chuckled, 'Those were desperate days.' He leaned forward, set the file on the side table and adopted a more formal tone. 'Lt Petersen,' the colonel jabbed a thick finger in Petersen's direction, 'the work we are doing here is important, not just to the victims of the Nazis or the folks back home, but to posterity, if you

15

know what I mean. The International Military Tribunal has an opportunity to write a new chapter in world history—a chapter that says national leaders are responsible for what they do. I take this opportunity seriously and I expect my officers and men to do so as well. To me, that means a high level of professionalism in everything we do. As staff of the Tribunal, everything we do must be beyond reproach. No impropriety--hell, not even a hint of impropriety,' Gaffner spoke in machine gun like bursts, leaning forward like a sprinter in the blocks. 'Our job is to ensure that these criminal bastards get a fair trial before they're hanged. And I don't mean a trial that just looks fair, I mean one that is fair. You're going to be one of the officers in charge of the cell block. We're going to have VIPs and press in here all the time, not to mention the Red Cross and family members and lawyers. Now, I don't mind the Red Cross and I must confess I am a little curious about what kind of families these monsters may have, but I cannot abide lawyers and I don't trust the press!' Gaffner waved his hand as if swatting away an annoying insect. 'At any rate, the cell block must be maintained in a high state of police at all times. Prisoners must be monitored and protected, fed, bathed, exercised, medicated, supervised, moved to and from the court room and under our control every minute of every day. That's where you come in.'

'Yes sir,' answered Petersen as soon as the colonel drew a breath.

'You will work in the prison facility and will report directly to Captain Stevens. Any questions?'

'No Sir.'

'Eager to get started are you?'

'Yes sir.'

'Now listen son,' Gaffner said as he leaned forward, fixing Petersen with a penetrating stare, 'I am dead serious that we do our part in this deal. No crap Lieutenant. The whole world is going to be watching what goes on here, even the Japanese, 'cause their turn is coming next. We are not going to foul this up. Got it?'

'Yes sir!'

'Good man,' exclaimed Gaffner, slapping his hands on his knees and standing. Petersen sprang up as well. 'Welcome aboard young man,' said Gaffner, smiling and again extending his hand.

'Thank you sir,' said Petersen, as the colonel guided him out of the room.

As the door closed behind him, Corporal Wilson was on his feet. 'LT Petersen, may I give you a hand with your bag?' he said picking up the gray over and under bag Petersen had left in the small waiting area. 'I'll take you to meet Captain Stevens.'

Wilson led Petersen out the rear of the Palace, across *Behrenstrasse* to a complex of sturdy looking three story buildings with tiny windows. The buildings radiated away from the Palace of Justice like spokes from the hub of a bicycle wheel, forming a semi-circle on the north side of the building. The whole complex was surrounded by fencing, topped with rolled barbed wire. Wilson headed toward the building on the far right. 'Captain Stevens will be in the cell block sir. He's been working over here most of the last week trying to get it ready,' Wilson explained. Ready for what? Petersen wondered. How much work do you have to do to get a jail cell ready?

As they approached the building, Petersen saw 'C Wing' stenciled above the door in black paint. Above that, a security light on a metal arm stuck out over a small concrete landing. Petersen stepped inside, his eyes adjusting from the bright sunlight to the dimmer light of the cell block. The oppressiveness of confinement dampened his spirit. He looked up to see three levels of cells surrounding an inner courtyard. Spiral metal staircases at each end of the cell blocks provided access to the different levels. A four foot wide walkway stretched the length of each row of cells. Affixed to the walkways' heavy iron rail was thick gauge chicken wire. The wire reached from one level to the next level and from there to the next level as well. The wire completely enclosed each block of cells, adding to what looked like already formidable security. In addition, the wire fencing formed a metal canopy, hanging above the courtyard, stretching between each level's facing cell blocks. The only passageways through the fencing were the spiral stairs. Though not given to claustrophobia, prisons made Petersen decidedly uncomfortable.

'Go ahead and get started on the numbering,' said a tall, thin man wearing an olive drab coverall to a young buck sergeant. 'We can move the furnishings in after we've inspected them again.' The man turned toward Wilson and Petersen whose approach he had observed. 'Good morning,' he smiled in greeting. 'Good morning sir,' replied Corporal Wilson offering a salute. Petersen quickly followed with a salute of his own. 'Captain Stevens, this is 1LT Petersen. The colonel sent him over.'

'Thanks Corporal Wilson,' Stevens said returning the salutes. 'I'll take him from here. Tom Stevens,' said the captain gripping Petersen's hand with a hard, strong hand. 'Where you from?'

'Texas, sir,' answered Petersen.

'No foolin'?' asked Stevens. 'I had a platoon sergeant from Texas. What part?'

'Quitman, sir.'

'Never heard of it.'

'There ain't a whole lot to it, sir. A couple of stores, two, three dozen churches.'

'Bible belt, huh?' laughed Stevens.

'Yes sir,' grinned Petersen.

'Well LT Petersen, you sure as hell ain't in the Bible belt anymore,' Stevens said looking up toward the higher levels of the prison. 'But I think we're gonna need all the divine intervention we can get. Come on down to the office and let's get you settled in.'

The prison office was a converted cell closest to the ground level entrance Petersen had just used. Stevens walked around behind a metal desk, picked up the telephone and called the billeting office. Stevens seemed the opposite of the colonel. He had dark brown hair and dark eyes. He was taller than Gaffner but Petersen judged he weighed twenty to thirty pounds less. He seemed casual, almost easy-going when compared to Gaffner's intensity. 'I'll get one of the men to show you the way,' Stevens said. 'Get settled in. Learn your way around and report back here at 2000 hours. There's still a lot of work to be done before our

18

guests arrive and we're already getting the men used to working in shifts.'

After a stop at the billeting office, Petersen caught a ride in the back of a jeep to the Grand Hotel where he would be quartered until more permanent accommodations were located. The hotel was less than 4 kilometers from the Palace of Justice, but it might have been in another world. Nuremberg's desolation dwarfed in scale anything Petersen had previously witnessed. In village after village, his infantry company had not only witnessed devastation, but had contributed to it. As the Allies had slowly pushed the German defenders back beyond the Rhine, American industrial capacity had made it far more desirable to fire tank and artillery shells into suspected enemy strong points than to risk the lives of American boys. The result was town after town with few intact structures. Here was Nuremberg, the destruction multiplied a thousand times. The jeep cruised down *Fuertherstrasse*, the main east-west route through the city. Petersen felt the warm sun on his face as he watched the roofless, wall-less ruins pass by. The road was partially blocked in several spots by small mountains of brick and rubble, causing the driver to pull over to allow oncoming traffic to pass. All of the motor vehicles on the road were military, though there were still plenty of horse, mule and even ox drawn wagons and carts plying the streets. A long line of ragged people, many of them German soldiers still in uniform, trudged in both directions along the side of the road. Some carried backpacks laden with belongings. Others pushed small carts. The line seemed endless, stretching both east and west, each weary walker struggling along a never ending road to someplace better. Dust from the rubble swirled in the draft of every passing truck, coating vehicles and people with a fine film of white.

The Grand Hotel had indeed been grand. Located a little more than 100 meters from the *Hauptbahnhof*, or main train station, tucked in among the old city, the hotel had been the most luxurious in Nuremberg, featuring fine accommodations and an attentive, discreet staff. It had survived the Allied bomber offensive, but just barely. Parts of the building were still roofless and large chunks of masonry were missing from the exterior. Wooden scaffolding climbed the wall above the main entrance. The Army's billeting office had quickly commandeered the building in anticipation of the needs of first the civil affairs staff and then the International Military Tribunal. As a result, the hotel enjoyed a high priority for repairs. The building and its adjacent alleys were teaming with workers trying to fix the most obvious damage. Petersen was assigned a small room at the end of the third floor corridor on the *Hopfenstrasse* side of the hotel, about as far away from the lobby as one could get and still be under the same roof. To get to his room, he had to walk over wooden planks stretched across gaping holes in the passageways, some of which plunged three full stories. The room was comfortable, but dingy, the result of years of war and several weeks of Army use. The only light came from the window, as electricity had not yet been restored to this wing of the hotel. Still, all Petersen really needed was a place to unpack and sleep and the privacy and relative quiet beat the hell out of the accommodations Petersen had so far enjoyed in Germany.

Chapter 2

After a short nap, a look around the hotel and a quick bite to eat in the officers' mess in the hotel's basement, Petersen hitched a ride back to the prison complex. Captain Stevens was still working, reviewing requisition forms with an NCO. Stevens quickly introduced Petersen to staff sergeant Hottle, then got back to business. 'LT Petersen will be officer in charge on our evening tour of duty,' the captain explained to Hottle. Turning to Petersen, he elaborated, 'I want you and Sergeant Hottle here to inventory all the furnishings going into the cells. Once you have accounted for all of it, tables, chairs, bunks, mattresses, I want you to inspect it.'

'To make sure it's clean, sir?' asked Petersen.

'Yes and for anything else you can think of too. Look for anything that could be used as a weapon or a signaling device. Anything that doesn't belong doesn't go in. Keep a list of the 'anythings' that you find and we'll go over it in the morning. If you need me tonight, Sergeant Hottle knows how to get in touch with me. Any questions?'

'No sir. We'll take care of it.'

Stevens said good night and left for his quarters, a private home commandeered some weeks earlier by the Army. Petersen and Hottle began their task by taking the requisition forms and counting item by item the furnishings stacked in the wide corridor between the cell blocks. The cells were small, smelling of fresh paint and lit by a single overhead fixture. Each cell would get an iron cot with a mattress, small table to be used as a desk and a chair. Thick, wooden doors sealed each cell from the corridor. The door was equipped with a round peephole as well as a one foot square service panel which folded out toward the cellblock. The opening behind this service panel, cut into the door at chest height, was itself covered with a heavy metal grate. Opposite the door, on the long axis of the cell, was a barred window, which in the daytime allowed a clear view of the prison yards. Nestled into the corner immediately to the right of the door, was the toilet, the only part of the cell that could not be observed from outside the door.

Petersen and Hottle pulled out three cots and two chairs as unserviceable because the legs were of different lengths, causing each to wobble. Two of the mattresses were covered with mold. These were also set aside. By midnight, they had accounted for and carefully inspected each piece of furniture.

Petersen took a break, walking up the spiral steps to the day room on the third level where sandwiches and coffee were available to personnel on the night shift. Climbing the steps he saw guards on duty outside the cells on level 2, where some prisoners were already in residence. Even in the middle of the night, guards rotated among 4 cells each, on a constant watch of their prisoners. No more than 30 seconds were to elapse before a guard peered in to observe his assigned prisoners. Grabbing a ham and cheese sandwich and cup of black coffee, Petersen sat down and watched off duty guards engaged in a card game.

'Good morning.' Petersen looked up to see a round-faced man of about 22 peering down at him. He was wearing a first lieutenant's silver bar on his collar.

'Howdy,' Petersen said, standing and introducing himself.

'Pleased to meet you John. I'm Robert Bentley Simmons. I'm on Colonel Amen's interrogation staff. You are new here, are you not?' Robert Bentley Simmons asked.

'That's right,' replied Petersen. 'How about you?'

'Indeed not,' Simmons said. Simmons had lively blue eyes and full lips framing a perpetual grin. He was slightly shorter than Petersen, but heavier with an almost cherubic appearance. 'I have been here for 2 months already. The Allies knew a couple of years ago that we were going to prosecute the top Nazis and they had all of this,' he waved his arm in a sweeping gesture that took in the prison and the adjacent Palace, 'in the works for months. As soon as the Krauts surrendered and we settled on Nuremberg as the site for the trials, our interrogation team moved in,' Simmons explained, his clipped words reminding Petersen of some of the New Englanders he had served with in the 84th.

'How come you're out here in the middle of the night?' asked Petersen.

'Well, Col. Amen gives us broad latitude in questioning the prisoners. Since none of them has been formally indicted yet, most of them talk pretty freely. There are a couple of them that prefer late night hours.'

'I haven't even seen a prisoner yet,' said Petersen, 'much less talked to one.'

'Well, a couple of them are pretty bizarre,' said Simmons, straddling the back of a chair and leaning in close to Petersen. 'There's Ilsa Koch, she was the wife of the commandant at Buchenwald, one of the camps. She is indescribably strange! If a prisoner had a tattoo, she would have him skinned and lampshades made from the tattooed skin.'

'You're kidding me.' Petersen stopped eating his sandwich.

'I kid you not. You wouldn't believe the stuff these characters did. The amazing thing is they admit to it!'

Petersen shook his head. 'When do the big shots get here? We're fixing up the ground floor cell block for the VIPs.'

'I don't know,' said Simmons. 'It's a big secret. Gaffner and General Watson, the Nuremberg CO, are afraid there might be some big attempt to break them out of here if the Germans know when they're arriving.'

'What do you think?' asked Petersen.

'Well John, you've seen Nuremberg and you've seen the people out on the streets. They don't look all that menacing to me.'

'Yeah,' Petersen said. 'But it's the ones you don't see that you have to worry about.'

'Spoken like a combat soldier!' Simmons laughed, pushing the chair back. 'You've got me on that. The closest I came to combat was when this French whore threw a beer bottle at my head. Back to work for me. I'll see you around, John.'

Petersen spent the rest of the night talking to the soldiers on guard duty. He questioned them about their routine, about maintaining constant vigilance over what could be painfully boring two hour shifts. Following their two hours, they were off four and could sleep, lounge or play cards, billiards or ping pong in the day room. They worked 24 hours on and 24 hours off and nobody much liked the job. The monotony of watching caged men and women move about in a 10 foot by 12 foot cell was exceeded only by the mind-numbing tedium of watching them sleep. Still, Colonel Gaffner had directed that no prisoner was to go unobserved for more than 30 seconds, day or night, and the men were doing their best to carry out their orders. Some of the men were put off by the colonel's 'spit and polish' approach, especially the few remaining combat veterans. These soldiers felt they had endured enough misery for one lifetime and while the quarters, chow, showers and comforts of their current assignment far exceeded those that had been available in combat, they felt they had won the war, done their duty and should be sent home at President Truman's earliest convenience.

Following his shift, Petersen hitched a ride back to the Grand Hotel. He washed his face, stripped down to a t-shirt and boxer shorts and climbed into bed. It was lumpy, but still the most comfortable bed he'd slept in since leaving England. Although the city was now awake and in the routine of another post-war day, the traffic and construction noises were not enough to delay Petersen's slumber. He fell asleep rapidly and slept deeply. And he dreamed. He dreamed of his mother, May, and the small east Texas farm where he had grown up. He smelled the aroma of apple pie baking and felt the sweltering heat in the tiny kitchen. Through the open window he saw clothes hanging limply on the line. He watched from behind as his mother worked, her right arm bent at an odd angle. She was always working: cooking, cleaning, washing, watching over him.

Chapter 3

John was asleep, snuggled beneath a warm, wool blanket. He was dreaming of chasing a rabbit. Every time he seemed close enough to reach it, to grab it, the rabbit darted off in a new direction. The screech of the screen door at the back of the little farm house intruded on his chase. Dim light from the kitchen outlined the closed door of his small bedroom. As his mind awakened, he heard the heavy tread of his father's boots across the kitchen's wooden floor, heard one of the wooden kitchen chairs shoved roughly out of the big man's path. John heard his father's deep voice, muffled through the door, slurred by drink. Quietly, he pulled the covers back and eased his bare feet down onto the floor. John crept to the door and listened. Now he could hear his mother's voice, soft and plaintive. His father sounded angry, his words coming more quickly with an accusatory tone. John put his small hand on the cold metal door knob and listened, trying to work up the courage to confront his father and defend his mother.

The voices grew louder. John heard the sound of a slap and his mother's sob. He stood still, hand on the knob, listening, trying to decide what to do. He needed to pee, but he was afraid to venture out of his room, afraid his father would shout at him, or worse. He crossed his legs. The only way to get to the privy was through the kitchen. The only way through the kitchen was past his drunken father. When he could finally hold it no more, John crept to the corner and peed there. He was afraid his parents would hear the splattering of his urine, but they were distracted by an argument of increasing intensity. John climbed back into his bed, the smell of his shame chasing him back beneath the covers.

Chapter 4

Over the next week, the work to bring the Palace and the prison to a state of readiness and presentability continued. Captain Gifford was in charge of repairing and even rebuilding parts of the Palace in preparation for the world-wide attention expected to be focused on the war crimes trials. Courtroom 600, on the top floor of the Palace of Justice, had been chosen as the main courtroom for the trials, but it was judged too small. Gifford's crew labored tirelessly doubling the size of Room 600, even to the point of raising its ceiling. In addition to the judges' bench and the defendants dock, a large gallery for the expected visitors and a 250 seat press section were constructed. In concert with Gifford's reconstruction team, Stevens, Petersen and their men worked daily, and nightly, to complete plastering, painting, repairs, wiring and the myriad of other tasks related to making the ground floor cell blocks suitable for the remaining 'big fish' of the Nazi regime. Like Hitler, Himmler and Goebbels had committed suicide rather than surrender. But other Nazi chieftains had survived the war and been captured either by the Western Allies or the Russians. They currently were imprisoned at Mondorf, an Army stockade in Luxemburg, but their move to Nuremberg seemed imminent given the level of activity at the prison. The Allies wanted the prisoners and their lawyers in Nuremberg with sufficient time to develop a legal defense strategy prior to the beginning of the trials scheduled for early autumn.

Lieutenant Simmons was busy, interviewing potential witnesses to assist the prosecutors in the preparations of their formal indictments. Even so, he quickly fell into the routine of dropping by for an evening, or, depending on his duty schedule, early morning visit.

'Good evening John. How is life at the Ritz?' he asked on his Friday night visit.

'Robert,' Petersen acknowledged with a nod between sips of his Coca-Cola. 'How's the Clarence Darrow of Nuremberg?'

'Not the Darrow my friend, as I am no lawyer, but rather the artiste that makes the lawyer's perceived brilliance possible.'

Simmons' eyes twinkled, 'Why without my skillful interrogation, without my keen ear and comprehensive knowledge of this harsh language, without my uncanny ability to weigh the tone and nuance of each witness's answers, the lawyer is merely a performer without a script.'

'So you're doing OK?'

'Yeah, not bad,' said Simmons reverting to a conversational tone and pulling up a chair beside Petersen. 'Any idea yet when the bad guys get here?' he asked.

'You mean the badder guys,' Petersen laughed. 'No, but it's got to be pretty soon because everything's ready.'

'And the Army always stays on schedule. Ah John, you have so much to learn! Seriously, my friend, I too have reason to believe they are coming soon, very soon. We received new duty schedules today. As of Monday, we revert to a mostly 8 am to 6 pm work schedule. That's 0800 to 1800 to you,' Simmons teased.

'Interesting,' Petersen nodded.

'Simple really,' Simmons continued the joke, 'you see, John, the military uses what is commonly known as a 24 hour clock. Once we get to 12 PM, we just keep going so that 1 PM is really 1300 hours and so forth.'

'Did I mention that I'm an infantry officer, trained to kill with my bare hands?'

'Actually, I didn't come simply to pass the time, or to explain it for that matter. I visited the billeting office today and collected a couple of favors,' Simmons briefly looked away smiling, then shifted his attention back to Petersen. 'You, sir, are about to receive a new quarters assignment to # 22 *Gartenstrasse* where you will find the accommodations far beyond your present, and, truth be told, previous standards. Not to mention that your housemate will be cultured, intelligent, entertaining and delightful beyond your loftiest expectations.'

'Rita Hayworth is in Nuremberg?'

'No, you dunce! The housemate I refer to is yours truly. Look at this as a God-given, once-in-a-lifetime opportunity for intellectual, cultural and, dare I say it, social growth that, when concluded will make you unrecognizable to other infantry officers—not to mention Texans.'

'Terrific!' Petersen responded with genuine enthusiasm. 'Really. That sounds great, Robert.'

'Don't get maudlin on me boy,' Simmons scolded. 'I may, in the future, have need of your unique skills and abilities,' Simmons continued. 'But that will have to be the subject of future discussions as I am late for my next appointment. Good evening to you John.' And with that, Simmons stood, flipped a casual salute and strode from the room, leaving Petersen slowly shaking his head.

Chapter 5

On Sunday morning, following the completion of his Saturday night shift, Petersen attended Protestant chapel held in a makeshift sanctuary in the basement of the Grand Hotel. Six rows of chairs were split by a center aisle. A wooden lectern stood in front of the chairs, most of which were occupied by Army officers. An occasional civilian suit stood out in the small, olive assembly. Chaplain Gerrity, a Lutheran from Minnesota, had led his congregation through the first two stanzas of 'Blessed Assurance' when the officer next to Petersen passed him a folded note. Petersen quickly opened the paper and read 'LT P report to duty immediately.' It was signed by Captain Stevens. Petersen placed the worn hymnal on his wooden chair and slipped up the side aisle and out the back of the room as the last notes of the hymn faded away.

With little traffic on the Sunday morning streets, Petersen covered the distance to the prison in just minutes. He entered C Wing and reported to Stevens in the office. 'Good morning LT Petersen,' Stevens said.

'Sir.'

'Sorry to drag you back so quickly, but the colonel just informed me that the shipment we have been expecting is coming in early this afternoon,' Stevens explained.

'Yes sir,' Petersen acknowledged the import of the statement as his mind raced ahead to the procedures which had been drawn up for the arrival of the VIP prisoners.

'Colonel Gaffner will be here in 15 minutes to personally brief the men. Sergeant Hottle will be your sergeant of the guard. He is assembling the sentinels right now.'

Petersen took his leave and found Hottle counting heads and checking uniforms. Petersen's platoon formed up in the wide corridor between the ground floor cell blocks and stood at ease awaiting the colonel's arrival. Petersen stood front and center, facing the platoon, but with one eye focused on the entrance through which he expected Gaffner to arrive. Precisely at 1000 hours, the door flew open and Gaffner entered like a bull headed for the matador's cape. His uniform was immaculate, with sharp creases and every ribbon in place. On his head sat a green lacquered helmet liner with the silver eagle insignia neatly centered. In his left hand, he clutched a leather riding crop. Petersen called the platoon to attention in his most authoritative command voice and executed a precise about face. As Gaffner reached the front of his formation, Petersen snapped a perfect salute and announced, 'Guard platoon ready for inspection, sir.' Gaffner returned the salute and barked, 'At ease! Listen up men. This afternoon, a convoy will arrive here containing the prisoners for whom you, and indeed the whole world, have been waiting. These are the worst criminals mankind has ever seen. They have perpetrated crimes which have brought untold misery on tens of millions of people. They have destroyed whole countries, including their own. They have murdered. They have stolen. And now, they will be here under our guard and care until they can receive a fair trial.' Gaffner was wound up, his eyes flashing. As he continued shouting, he began to strut back and forth, slapping his thigh with the riding crop, his face flushing, his eyes darting from one GI face to the next. 'These criminals are scum and they are to be treated as just that. These are not prisoners of war. They are the instigators of war. As such, there will be no exchange of military courtesy, no salutes, no titles or ranks. They are not to speak to you or to each other unless in answer to a question you have directed them to answer. They are not to touch each other. They are not to touch you. Our job is to keep these men alive and well until the court renders its verdicts and its sentences are carried out.' Gaffner paused, seemed to relax for a moment and continued in a more casual tone of voice, 'Now men, you've been reading *Stars & Stripes*. You know how big these trials are and how the whole world is watching what we do here. This is a chance to show why the United States of America is different and by-God better than any other country in the world. We came over here, we kicked ass and we won this damn war and this time we're going to make sure it stays won by taking the bad guys all the way out. I know each one of you men will do your duty to the best of your ability. You have good officers and NCOs here to lead you. Be professional. Be on your toes. Lord knows these Hun bastards aren't going to give up without a fight. Do your best men! Not for me, not for the Army, but for the good folks back home and for the United States of America!' Gaffner paused, switched his intense focus to Petersen and said in a lower voice, 'That's all LT Petersen. Time to get to work.'

'Yes sir,' Petersen answered and then ordered, 'Platoon, attention!' Petersen's crisp salute was returned by the colonel who turned on his heel and marched back out the door.

After Petersen turned the platoon over to Sergeant Hottle, he met with Stevens in the office. Cells were assigned. A white strip of paper was stenciled with each prisoner's last name and taped to the door of his cell. Guard rosters were double checked. 'John,' began Captain Stevens, 'I'm moving you back to days. Most of the activity, once the prisoners arrive, will take place during the daytime. We will be moving them back and forth for meals, showers, meetings with their lawyers and so forth. As officer in charge of the cell block, it makes more sense that you should be here during the day.'

'Understood sir,' Petersen replied with no hint of fatigue in his voice. Despite having completed a full overnight shift and having returned to the compound directly from chapel, Petersen's excitement at knowing the prisoners would soon arrive was all the motivation he needed.

'Here,' said the captain, handing Petersen a safety razor. 'There's soap in the latrine. Scrape your chin off before the shipment gets here.'

The sentinels, as Colonel Gaffner liked to call them, put on their duty uniforms: jacket, shirt, tie, bloused trousers, helmet liners, web belts and gloves. Sergeant Hottle, meanwhile repeated the cell block standing procedures to the men, peppering them with questions to ensure their understanding of the colonel's orders. Hottle stood the guards at rest in a loose formation inside the ground floor cell block, out of the light drizzle that had begun to fall. Then, they waited.

Shortly after 1430 hours, a convoy of two jeeps flanking three Army deuce and a half trucks, rolled through the vehicle gate and into the prison compound, leaving tracks in the mud. At its appearance, Hottle called the sentinel platoon to order. The convoy stopped just short of C Wing and an Army major climbed out of the front jeep as several military policemen emerged from the rear jeep and the back of each truck. The MPs quickly formed a cordon around the convoy, their backs to the vehicles, their eyes searching the area for anyone or anything that might pose a threat. Colonel Gaffner stepped outside followed by Captain Stevens and LT Petersen. The major saluted and handed Gaffner a clipboard on which was a cargo manifest. Gaffner looked the list over and nodded. 'Alright major,' he said, 'Let's get this done.' The major barked orders and the MPs moved quickly. Their mission was almost complete and they were eager to finish it and make the most famous prisoners in the world someone else's worry. A pair of MPs lowered the tailgate of each truck and pulled back the rear curtain. Then, they began to assist the mostly elderly men down to the ground. The prisoners stood in loose groups, stretching and looking around at their new surroundings, while their eyes adjusted to the daylight. To a casual observer, the group would have appeared unremarkable. They were, most of them, well beyond middle age, haggard from imprisonment, gaunt from stress and fatigue. Their clothing was shabby and ill fitting, as most had lost weight during their incarcerations. Three of the men stood stiffly, with their hands at their sides and their chins up. They wore the remnants of German *Wehrmacht* and *Kriegsmarine* uniforms, from which all insignia of rank and office had been unceremoniously removed. Petersen felt a mixture of awe and anger as he looked at the prisoners. They now seemed so ordinary, yet they had wielded nearly absolute power, had guided the German nation on its suicidal folly, had bled that nation white until it lay utterly defeated and exhausted before its conquerors. These ordinary, old men had destroyed not only their country, but millions of lives. Those who had not been killed outright had lost loved ones and had often been forced to live like hunted animals, foraging for food and fleeing from danger. Like so many other young Americans, the arc of

Petersen's own life had been deflected by these men. /
stood, on a wet August Sunday afternoon, a soldier in a conqu.
land about to inherit responsibility for the perpetrators of the
greatest tragedy in history.

The last prisoner to climb down from the truck looked around
with a smile on his thin lips. *Reichsmarschall* Hermann Goering,
one time head of the *Luftwaffe*, chief of the Nazi economy and
Hitler's number 2 man, looked around and nodded to the prisoners
who had ridden on the other two trucks. He dusted off the light
blue trousers of his uniform. When captured by the Americans in
southern Bavaria, Goering had tipped the scales at a portly 264
pounds. At Mondorf, he had been placed on a strict diet and his
nearly 20,000 paracodeine pills had been confiscated. Under the
watchful eyes of the stockade staff and an elderly German
physician, *Herr Doktor* Schuster, Goering had kicked his drug
habit, regained energy and trimmed down to 199 pounds packed
onto his 5 foot 6 inch frame. 'Show them your dignity!' Goering
bellowed to his fellow inmates, startling them. 'We are the leaders
of the German Reich!' His pale blue eyes ranged from face to face,
nodding, smiling, lifting their spirits. Immediately, the military
prisoners, Doenitz, Keitel and Jodl, braced to attention. The
civilian prisoners stopped milling about and stared at the
Reichsmarschall as if awaiting further direction. It came quickly,
but from another source.

'Quiet there!' Gaffner's voice boomed. Handing the
clipboard to Captain Stevens, Gaffner strode forward and ordered
the prisoners into two ranks. The military policemen began to step
back as Hottle and his men moved forward. Hottle directed his
sentinels to form a large rectangle around the newly arrived
prisoners. By the trucks, additional men, under the direction of LT
Rose, the personal property officer, assisted the MPs with the
unloading of the prisoners' luggage. Gaffner faced the Germans.
'You are now prisoners of the International Military Tribunal.
You will be imprisoned here pending the completion of your trials
and the execution of your sentences.' Gaffner scanned the rows of
infamous faces before him, his lips pressed grimly together. 'You
are not prisoners of war. You are criminals. As such, you have no

rights. You will not speak unless you are spoken to. You will not speak to each other. You will do as you are told, when you are told and without hesitation. That is all.' With that, Gaffner stepped back and turned the formation over to Petersen.

The prisoners were marched inside and into the basement of the cell block. There, they stripped and were herded into cold showers. While they showered, their clothes were searched. Before they were allowed to put their clothes back on, the prisoners were lined up against the wall, told to turn around and lean forward. An Army doctor, accompanied by Dr. Schuster, checked each prisoner's rectum to ensure that nothing was being secreted into the prison. The Allies had learned from hard experience: once in captivity, Himmler had killed himself with a hidden cyanide capsule. Following the medical check, the prisoners trooped up stairs and into their assigned cells. The heavy oak doors were swung into place and bolted. The first watch of guards took up their positions, one sentinel for every four cells. After weeks of preparation, C Wings' guests had finally checked in.

Chapter 6

Petersen was back in C Wing by 0630 the next morning. He intended to make sure that the prisoners' first day went smoothly, according to the routine dictated by Colonel Gaffner. He checked in with Hottle, the sergeant of the guard, who reported an uneventful night. Next, Petersen descended into the basement where the prisoners' mess hall had been set up, the aroma of sausages and potatoes rising up to meet him. Goodman, the mess sergeant, was busily supervising his staff of cooks, but not too busy to grab a white mug and fill it with hot, black coffee for his lieutenant. 'Thanks Sergeant Goodman,' Petersen said. 'Ready for some customers?'

'Ever ready, sir,' Goodman replied with a wink. 'We'll feed 'em better than the rest of their countrymen are eatin' right now, that's for sure.'

At 0700, Sergeant Hottle sent two of his men through the cell block banging on cooking pots. This crude, but effective alarm clock woke those prisoners still asleep, calling them to breakfast. Each guard lined up his four prisoners and marched them down the stairs into the dimly lit basement. They were met by the pleasant aroma of food. They proceeded down a single serving line while white-jacketed mess attendants dished steaming helpings of sausage, eggs, fried potatoes and toast onto their plates. Black coffee and water were the only beverage options. The prisoners sat on wooden benches flanking two long wooden tables. Guards stood behind them, still vigilant, watching for any unusual movements and discouraging conversation. Petersen, coffee in hand, stood off to the side, observing the prisoners and his guard detail. For the most part, the meal proceeded in silence. Except for Goering. The *Reichsmarschall* was animated, almost jovial and despite orders to 'knock it off' from his guard, kept up a running monologue. Petersen watched and after a few moments moved forward to assist his sentinel. 'Quiet sir. No talking.'

'Ah good morning lieutenant,' Goering twisted around to face Petersen and smiled. 'I am sorry if I violated the rules. I am

35

simply enjoying this excellent breakfast. My compliments to the chef!'

'Yes sir,' Petersen said, considering the absurdity of an Army first lieutenant telling Adolf Hitler's chief deputy not to talk with his mouth full. 'But no more talking.'

'Of course,' Goering beamed. He held a fat finger up to his thin lips, 'Not another word. Mum's the word. That's the right expression isn't it?' His blue eyes danced.

'Yes sir, that's fine,' Petersen replied, turning away as he stifled a grin.

Goering turned back to his food, raising his eyebrows and grinning across the table at Keitel and Jodl.

'He likes the food,' Petersen told Sergeant Goodman.

'Course he does sir,' Goodman responded, lifting his chin. 'Best Army mess in Europe.'

While the prisoners breakfasted in the basement, Sergeant Hottle and the oncoming shift of guards were inspecting the cells on the floor above. As a general rule, the cells were to be inspected whenever their occupants were absent. Guards searched for contraband of any kind, particularly anything that could be fashioned into a weapon or any drugs. Colonel Gaffner had made it clear to his officers and men that their duty was to safeguard the prisoners, from external forces which might try to assist their escape as well as from themselves.

At 0735, the prisoners were escorted back to their cells. Each was given a mop and a bucket of cold water with which to swab out his cubicle. PFC Skip Seleck, of Rowley, Massachusetts, had arrived in France in late April, reaching the 1st Infantry Division on May 9, the day after the German surrender. Two months later, he had been assigned to the Internal Security Detachment as one of Gaffner's sentinels. Seleck, at 19 years of age, was typical of the soldiers assigned to guard detail. More and more of the combat veterans had already accumulated the service points needed to return home, leaving the younger soldiers in their place. As Seleck handed the mop to Goering, the *Reichsmarschall* slapped it away. Confused, the young soldier bent down, picked the mop up and again held it out to his prisoner. Goering stepped toward Seleck with his jaw clenched, his fists tightened. 'I am *Marschall* of the Third Reich,' he bellowed, 'not a scullery maid.' His face contorted and red with fury, Goering continued to browbeat the soldier, '*You* clean it!' Switching to German and shouting ferociously, Goering launched invectives at the hapless guard, who backed away from the doorway and into the corridor, as Goering continued to close the distance between them. By now, the racket had attracted other guards and prisoners who had stopped their labors to stare open-mouthed at Goering's brashness. Petersen and Hottle were trotting toward the commotion when they saw Goering stop suddenly, gag and fall to the floor.

'Fetch the doctor,' shouted Petersen as he reached the now prone prisoner. Hottle reversed direction toward the prison infirmary. Petersen rolled Goering over on his back. The *Reichsmarschall* was conscious, but not lucid, his eyes rolling wildly from side-to-side. He was breathing heavily and was flushed and clammy. Within moments, Dr. Schuster had arrived from his basement infirmary, black bag in hand. Schuster was well into his 70's, tall and dignified in his worn black suit. He had attended the prisoners at Mondorf, earning their confidence, and had accompanied his most famous patients to Nuremberg. Schuster quickly took Goering's wrist and checked the *Reichsmarschall*'s pulse. 'His heart is racing,' Schuster said to Petersen. 'It is over 200 beats per minute. He must have a sedative immediately or he could suffer heart failure!' The doctor reached into his bag and pulled out a small vial of medicine and a syringe. With skill borne of decades of practice, the doctor administered the drug. Schuster and Petersen watched anxiously as Goering slowly began to relax. With his fingers pressed to Goering's throat, Schuster looked at Petersen and nodded. 'His pulse is slowing. Help me get him to his bed.'

'PFC Seleck, lend a hand here,' Petersen directed the bewildered soldier. The three of them half carried, half dragged Goering to his bed. Schuster laid Goering's head on his pillow and covered him with his blanket.

At the first alert of trouble from the jail's office, Colonel Gaffner had sprinted from his office, across the street and into C Wing, Captain Stevens right on his heels.

'What in T-total hell is going on here!' demanded Gaffner, skidding to such a quick halt in the cell's open doorway that Captain Stevens nearly ran into his back. Petersen jumped to his feet as Seleck tried to melt into the wall. Schuster remained calmly beside his patient.

'LT Petersen?' Gaffner barked.

'Well sir,' Petersen began, 'the *Reichsmarschall*…'

'Stop right there young man,' Gaffner snapped, red faced. 'There is no '*Reichsmarschall*' here. No generals, no admirals, no deputy assistant Nazi ass wipes! You got that lieutenant?!'

Petersen sprang to attention, his face flushing under the colonel's lashing and looking straight ahead answered, 'Yes sir!'

'Now tell me what the hell happened!' shouted Gaffner, his eyes blazing, his full fury focused on Petersen.

Petersen recounted the incident. Gaffner's stare shifted between Petersen, Seleck, who could only nod, and Goering, who moaned occasionally.

'By God!' shouted Gaffner, slapping his left thigh with his ever present riding crop and shaking his head angrily. 'Damnation!'

Fortunately for Petersen, Schuster cleared his throat, shifted his focus away from Goering and spoke. 'I believe colonel that your lieutenant acted appropriately given the medical situation. The *Reichs*… *Herr* Goering could have suffered a heart attack if not for the immediate attention LT Petersen ordered. If I may request some cool, damp towels for *Herr* Goering's forehead.'

Gaffner looked at Seleck, snapped his fingers and jerked his thumb toward the cell door. 'Get them.' Seleck, eager to escape, dashed out of the cell.

Gaffner's eyes moved slowly around the cell. 'LT Petersen, assign a man to clean this cell. Doctor, I'd like a full report on this prisoner's condition as soon as he is stable.' Gaffner spun around to leave, bumping into Stevens, who was too slow to jump out of his way. Guards and prisoners alike who had drifted toward the uproar now parted to let the seething colonel pass. 'Back to your duties,' he snapped.

'Thank you doctor,' Petersen said once they were alone with Goering.

'You did the right thing lieutenant,' the old doctor nodded. 'Your colonel is high strung, no?'

'Yes sir,' Petersen sighed.

That afternoon, Petersen received his new billeting assignment. The Grand Hotel was slated to be used for the Tribunal staff, the international press corps and the expected VIP visitors. As such, the Army was moving its personnel out of the hotel as suitable quarters were found on the local economy. Petersen was directed to clear his quarters in the hotel and take up residence at #22 *Gartenstrasse*, a more convenient address only three blocks south of the Palace. At 1930 hours, having thoroughly briefed his relief and the overnight sergeant of the guard, Petersen stopped by Captain Stevens' office. Steven's was still there, going over papers on his desk. 'Tough day lieutenant?' Stevens asked noting the hang dog look on Petersen's face.

'You could say that sir. I almost lost our most notorious prisoner and then got reamed out by the colonel in front of the whole company. Not one of my better days, sir.'

'I won't apologize for the colonel,' Stevens replied. 'But keep in mind that he's career Army. He's responsible for keeping these guys alive long enough for us to hang them and he's feeling the pressure. One of these guys croaks and a whole lot of shit is going to rain down on his head.'

'Yes sir, I guess so,' Petersen responded looking down at the floor. 'I just wish he realized that I'm on his team, that's all.'

'Well,' sighed Stevens, 'chalk it up to experience. Then, put it behind you. He doesn't expect perfection. He just expects you to learn and move on. Kind of like in combat. Dwell on your mistakes and you lose your ability to make decisions. Besides, from what Schuster said, you made the right call and you made it quickly.'

'Yes sir. Well, I'm on my way to clear out of the hotel. My new quarters are on *Gartenstrasse*. I gave the address to the duty officer in case you need me. Good night sir.'

'Good night LT Petersen. See you in the morning,' Stevens said as Petersen stepped into the hallway and headed toward the exit.

Chapter 7

A row of small houses lined *Gartenstrasse*. Some were moderately damaged; others appeared to be in relatively sound condition. Fortunately for Petersen, # 22 fit into the latter category. Petersen walked up the two front steps and rapped loudly on the door. Within seconds, it swung open to reveal the round face of Robert Bentley Simmons. Simmons face split into a wide grin as he reached out to take Petersen's bag.

'Welcome to Shangri La!' Simmons exclaimed. 'The most complete accommodations offered by the great city of Nuremberg. *Frau* Kohl, *bitte, ein mehr für das Abendessen*!' he said switching effortlessly to German and calling to a short, squat woman in the small kitchen. 'Come in, come in John.'

Petersen removed his cap and stepped farther into the main room of the house.

'This is *Frau* Kohl. She cooks and cleans for us.' Turning to the woman, Simmons said, '*Erlauben Sie mir, Leutnant Petersen zu präsentieren.*'

Frau Kohl offered a shallow curtsy and a gap toothed smile. She was a thickly built woman of short stature. Her hands were strong and her shoulders broad. She reminded Petersen of his mother, a woman hardened by a life of constant labor and few rewards. '*Ich bin zufrieden, Sie zu treffen,*' *Frau* Kohl said, bobbing her head.

'Ah!' said Simmons. 'Off to a good start! She says she is happy to meet you.'

Petersen, smiling, nodded his head and said, 'Likewise.' Apparently, this needed no translation as *Frau* Kohl beamed and then, chattering away, scurried back to the wood stove where supper was already cooking.

'A delightful woman, John,' Simmons effused. 'Lives just out of town on a farm. Walks into the city every day. An excellent, if basic cook. Plus she keeps the place clean.'

'How much do we pay her?' Petersen asked.

'Peanuts, John, peanuts. I have taken care of the financial arrangements so worry not.'

Over an excellent, if basic, supper, the two lieutenants shared the details of their days. Simmons was eager to hear about Petersen's encounter with Goering, whom he had yet to see. He guffawed at Petersen's retelling of Gaffner's explosive visit, absorbing every detail. 'How I would have loved to see him run into Stevens!' Simmons laughed, his tie loosened and his shirt sleeves turned up. 'Next time you plan fireworks, be a good sport and give me advance notice.'

'Hopefully there won't be a next time,' Petersen answered. 'I think I went straight to the top of Gaffner's shit list—do not pass go, do not collect $200.'

'Gaffner's a strutting martinet,' scoffed Simmons. 'Who else would march around an administrative headquarters with a riding crop and a helmet liner?'

'Maybe so,' said Petersen tentatively, 'but he controls my immediate future and if he thinks I'm a screw up, I might just as well be one.'

'John, my friend,' Simmons responded, feigning alarm and cocking his head to the side. 'Do I detect the sentiments of a lifer?'

'Robert, I don't come from much. It's just me and my mother on a 15 acre patch of east Texas. The Army's been a pretty good deal for me.'

'Except for the combat part?' interjected Simmons.

'Well, that seems to be pretty much over, don't it,' Petersen rationalized.

'John, John, John,' Simmons shook his head. 'I'm just glad I got to you in time. You do realize the purpose of an army, do you not? Its job is to kill people. In the course of said job, members of said army are also inevitably killed. This is not the most promising future for one of your skills and abilities.'

'Look,' Petersen responded, 'the war is over. We dropped two bombs on Japan and wiped out two whole cities. No other country is going to mess with us now.'

'Listen to me, John, seriously. People are already talking about an inevitable confrontation between us and the Russians.' Simmons lowered his voice, leaning forward and staring intensely at Petersen. 'They are as bad as the Nazis. If you don't believe me, ask the Polish officers on the Tribunal staff. This war may be over, but there will be another one. Think about that before you commit to wearing olive drab for the rest of your life.'

Frau Kohl left at 2100 hours for her walk home. She would be out of the city before the sun set and well before the 2230 curfew. Darkness in Nuremberg, with its northern latitude, would not fall until nearly 10 pm. Simmons and Petersen sat at the wooden dining table drinking two warm beers. There was, at present, no electricity in the house and no need to light a lantern. The house was small, but comfortable. It contained two bedrooms separated by a large open room containing a stove and wash basin, table with chairs and a small sitting area with an old, battered cloth-covered sofa. Not much, Petersen thought, but it was a nicer home than most Nurembergers had at the moment.

'Tell me about your home,' Simmons said between sips of his beer.

Petersen leaned back in his chair, resting his beer on his thigh. 'Quitman? A little crossroads market town in northeast Texas. We, my mother and me, we lived on a little farm a couple of miles east of town. We had a few cows and chickens. We had a garden for vegetables. Mother took in washing to raise spending money for the things we couldn't barter for. I haven't seen her in over two years.

'What about your old man?' Simmons probed, 'If you don't mind me asking.'

'Gone. Long gone. He left when I was maybe six. Just took off,' Petersen lied, remembering the times when his father had come home drunk, smelling like hell and acting worse. 'Since then, it's just been the two of us.'

'How has your mother handled your separation?' Simmons asked gently.

'Oh, OK I guess. What choice did she really have. That's the way it is with mothers isn't it? Work their fingers to the bone for their children and then the children leave.'

'I suppose so,' Simmons nodded. He drained his beer and set the bottle on the table. 'All done for me. You take that room,' he said pointing past the stove to a small room on the left end of the house. 'I'm in the master suite.' He jerked his thumb over his shoulder to the equally small room on the right front side of the house. 'Good night John,' Simmons said, standing. He stuck out his hand. 'I'm glad you're here. We'll liven this place up a bit.' Petersen shook his hand, gathered up his things and walked into the bedroom.

Chapter 8

Despite the first morning's outburst by Goering and the subsequent drama, the prison and its occupants quickly adapted to a routine. Goering continued to talk, continued to receive reprimands and continued to shrug them off. After breakfast each morning, the prisoners continued to clean their cells, except for Goering, whose cell was cleaned for him by a German prisoner from D Wing.

On the first Thursday of the prisoners' residence at Nuremberg, LT Petersen was summoned to Captain Stevens' office. 'The colonel has a project for you,' Stevens informed him. 'Don't worry lieutenant,' Stevens said when he saw the concern on Petersen's face. 'It's nothing bad. He just wants us to provide the prisoners with a library.'

'A library, sir?'

'It's a place with books, lieutenant. You borrow the books, read them, then put them back,' Stevens replied, grinning.

'Got it sir,' Petersen smiled, hiding his annoyance at being made the butt of the joke.

Petersen entered the same office to which he had originally reported upon his arrival in Nuremberg two weeks earlier. Corporal Wilson looked up from his desk and said, 'Good morning, sir. I'll let the colonel know you're here.' Wilson disappeared into the colonel's office, but was back a moment later. 'Sir,' he motioned Petersen toward the colonel's office. 'The colonel is ready for you.' Petersen muttered 'Thanks,' then knocked and entered. He strode purposefully to the desk behind which Gaffner was at work. He came to attention, saluted and said, 'Sir, Lieutenant Petersen reports.'

'At ease, lieutenant,' ordered Gaffner, offering none of the hospitality Petersen had received on his only other visit to this office. Gaffner, his personal appearance impeccable as always, leaned back in his chair and locked his blue eyes onto Petersen's. 'My prison staff includes a psychologist, Dr. Richards. He has recommended that the mental state of our prisoners will be improved and their morale maintained by providing them with a library. Put one together. Any questions?' Gaffner was curt, as though he had more on his mind than books.

'How big a library sir?'

'Let's say two or three hundred books. Get it done by tomorrow,' Gaffner said, leaning forward and returning his attention to the papers strewn about the top of his desk. 'That's all lieutenant.'

Petersen saluted, turned about and left the office.

Fearing that his limited linguistic skills were inadequate to the task of stocking a prison library, Petersen convinced Simmons to assist him. They requisitioned a jeep and ¼ ton trailer from the motor pool and, following directions provided by a member of the Grand Hotel's concierge staff, set off through the rubble strewn streets in search of the old city library. The city smelled of sewage and decay. After a dusty hour long drive through winding streets, detouring around downed bridges and bombed out blocks, they finally parked in front of a square red brick building near Zeppelin Field. The words '*Stadt Bibliothek*' were carved in marble above large, twin wooden doors. From the parking area, Petersen could see that the building was disheveled, the back left corner had collapsed and areas of the roof were covered with canvas tarpaulins. Several windows had been replaced with wood or cardboard and where glass was still in place, it was without exception cracked and broken.

The two officers strode up the steps and entered the building. From the spacious foyer of the library, Petersen could see shafts of sunlight piercing the broken ceiling at odd intervals, bathing shelves of books in pools of yellow, dusty light. Petersen and Simmons marched straight ahead to the main desk. At the approach of the American soldiers, a small bespectacled man in a threadbare suit stood nervously and bowed slightly. '*Guten Tag*,' he said, adjusting the knot of his neck tie.

'Tell him we need some books,' Petersen said to Simmons who translated without preliminaries.

'He says you don't have a library card,' Simmons relayed after the little man spoke.

Petersen glanced at Simmons and back to the clerk. 'Tell him I have a .45 and I know how to use it.'

Again Simmons rapidly translated as the clerk's eyes darted back and forth between the two soldiers. 'He says go ahead and shoot him. He'd rather die for the Fatherland than entrust a barbarian like you with the priceless treasures of his library.'

Petersen turned to Simmons as the uncomprehending clerk watched. 'Like me? What about you? Aren't you one of the conquering barbarians as well?'

'You forget my friend that I am a cultured officer and gentlemen, schooled at the finest university of our homeland, specially trained in the high art of civil affairs and that I, sir, unlike you, speak his native tongue with some skill.'

Petersen shook his head and gesturing back at the confused clerk said, 'Tell him we need 300 books, preferably classics, Goethe, Schiller, stuff like that.'

Simmons again relayed the message. 'He says *all* of these books are classics, personally approved by the Fuehrer. The rest have been burned.'

Petersen ignored Simmons and wondered if bringing him along had been such a good idea. 'Tell him that we are willing to sign for them, but that we will not pay for them and that we want them within the next 5 minutes.'

The clerk, unaccustomed to arguing with authority figures, immediately summoned two other staff members, one man and one woman, and set about the task. Working diligently, the library staff assembled double the requested number of books in only half an hour. Petersen had Simmons review each title for suitability before it was packed in a box to be removed.

'Victory In the Great War, Escape from Alcatraz, Fun With the Fuhrer: Hitler's Wild Side. These should be very well received,' cracked Simmons, stuffing volume after volume into pasteboard boxes. By now, several more Germans were assisting the library staff, hoping to hasten the soldiers' departure.

As the last of the boxes was loaded into the trailer, Petersen turned once more to the clerk. 'These books will be returned to your facility when we are finished with them. Thank you for your assistance. *Danke.*'

As Simmons translated, the little man gave a curt bow, turned, went back up the steps and disappeared into the building.

'*Danke?*' said Simmons with raised eye brows. 'I didn't realize you had such a comprehensive grasp of the German language.'

'Oh sure, I learned a lot of it in combat. *Hande hoch, nicht shiessen*, stuff like that. I could have assaulted this place without you, but I didn't know how to check out a book. I was afraid there for a minute that you were going to get that poor little guy shot,' Petersen laughed, 'Thanks for coming with me. I would have had a hell of a time explaining what I wanted. I probably would have scared 'em all to death and then come away with 300 autographed copies of *Mein Kampf.*'

With Petersen at the wheel, they covered the distance back to the prison in half the time of their outbound trip. They pulled into the compound through the vehicle gate and parked next to the main ground floor entrance to C Wing. Simmons departed for duty in the Palace and Petersen headed inside to find men to unload the boxes. 'Mission accomplished sir,' he reported to Captain Stevens. 'I think the colonel will be pleased.'

Chapter 9

Pleased he was. The following day, Gaffner toured the new library, established on the third floor in an empty cell. Doctors Schuster and Richards had arranged the borrowed books into some semblance of order and set up a lined paper tablet to record which prisoner had which book. The prisoners too seemed pleased. They could now read during the dreary hours between their meals and their infrequent visitors. 'Well done LT Petersen,' said Gaffner softly with a satisfied look on his face. His riding crop and a pair of leather gloves were squeezed into his left hand, his helmet liner held in the crook of his left arm. 'Gentlemen,' Gaffner spoke more loudly now, directing his comments to a small group of correspondents he was guiding through the prison, 'you can clearly see that we are operating a humane facility here, concerned not only with the physical safety and security of our charges, but also with their mental well-being. We have established this library of several hundred volumes for the prisoners' use so they will have productive and edifying ways to occupy their time.'

'Very impressive Colonel Gaffner,' said a correspondent from United Press browsing through the titles. 'How are the living conditions for the inmates?'

'You will see for yourself in a few minutes. I will show you the cell block where the chief Nazis are held.'

"Colonel Gaffner?' asked a reporter from the *Herald Tribune*, 'What type of physical fitness activities have you arranged for the prisoners?'

Gaffner turned toward his questioner and hesitated. 'Physical fitness? Yes, of course,' he delayed. 'Sound mind, sound body.' He looked around and the first person he saw was Petersen. 'LT Petersen here is the facility's physical training officer. Lieutenant, why don't you brief these gentlemen on your program.'

'That son of a bitch!' howled Simmons over supper. He was laughing so hard no sound was coming forth except a labored wheeze.

'So I said, "Gentlemen, we exercise the prisoners in the yard 20 minutes daily depending on their visitors and appointments. We also carefully regulate caloric intake and the prisoners receive daily medical attention," just making this up out of thin air, trying to think of something off the top of my head that would sound like a real program,' Petersen explained.

Simmons gasped for breath. 'And they bought it?' he asked.

'They bought it! I was a little nervous when they went downstairs though. I was afraid that one of them would ask Goering or Speer or one of the others about the exercise "program" and ruin Gaffner's parade. Fortunately no one asked.'

'Audacious!' Simmons sighed. 'And the colonel, he was properly appreciative of your marvelous ability to ad lib for the gentlemen of the fourth estate?'

'Well, he winked at me as they headed downstairs. I guess that's a good sign.'

'Or maybe the strain of command has simply become too much for him and he is developing nervous ticks!' said Simmons.

Frau Kohl had departed at 2000 hours and the two lieutenants had finished their meal of schnitzel, beets and potatoes. Simmons started laughing again, which made Petersen chuckle.

'OK, Robert Bentley Simmons,' Petersen began. 'Why three names?'

'Most people have three names,' Simmons answered, cocking his head to the right. 'Why I dare say you have three names, do you not?'

'Yes, but I don't go around introducing myself as John Adam Petersen.'

'I can't say I blame you with such common material with which to work,' Simmons gibed.

'C'mon. Aren't you sort of pompous using three names when two suit most folks just fine?'

'It has nothing to do with pomposity, my friend. It has to do with heritage and pride of family. You see,' Simmons explained, 'both branches of my family have been prominent in New York for generations. Banking, business, higher education, even the occasional foray into government service. Using three names allows me to honor both the Bentley side of our clan as well as the Simmons branch of the family.'

'Well, it seems a little high-brow to me,' Petersen chuckled, pushing back from the table.

After dinner, Petersen replayed the events of the day. He assumed he was back in the colonel's good graces after snatching the fat out of the fire over exercise routines. Still, he was less than certain. He had seen men like Gaffner before, seen them blow both hot and cold, depending upon whose favor they were attempting to curry at a particular moment. He would be careful to keep his guard up in Gaffner's presence.

Chapter 10

John heard his father cursing and shouting, heard glass breaking. When he heard his mother cry out, he flung off his wool blanket, jumped from his bed, threw open his bedroom door and ran straight into the back of his father. His father's drinking had led to a rather large belly, but Tom Petersen was still strong and even in his inebriated condition was quicker than 10 year old John. He slapped the boy on the side of his head, spinning him away and sending a harsh ringing through John's reddened ear. Tom turned back toward his wife, who was cowering behind the square kitchen table. Already John could see the welt under his mother's left eye. It would turn an ugly blue-black, keeping her on the farm and away from town, even church, for two weeks. John sprang again at his father's back, grabbing a fist full of brown hair with his left hand and flailing at his father's face with his right. Tom Petersen reached across his right shoulder with his powerful left hand and yanked John forward flinging him against the corner of the stove. The impact snapped John's right collar bone and split the skin just above his right eye. John's mother cried out and moved toward her whimpering son. A hard back hand to her jaw stopped her. Tom grabbed her by her hair and twisted her arm behind her back. 'Now you just be still missy,' he slurred. He gave her a hard shove and she toppled into the corner of the kitchen, crying, her lip bleeding and her face red and puffy. Then, Tom lost interest. He picked up his deputy's hat, pushed open the door and staggered out into the darkness as John watched helplessly.

Chapter 11

Since the arrival of the prisoners, Petersen's routine did not vary on the weekends. Although the legal and interrogation staffs tended to observe a more regular work week, he reported for duty no later than 0700 on Saturday and Sunday, just as he did the rest of the week. As August gave way to September, the days grew cooler. The inmates seemed particularly to enjoy their daily exercise sessions in the yard between C Wing and the gymnasium. Although the prisoners were still technically forbidden to talk and were instructed to remain thirty feet apart, their walks in the yard provided a limited opportunity to communicate with each other. Generally, the military men, Doenitz, Keitel and Jodl remained apart from the political men.

As he did at meals, Goering frequently flaunted the no talking rules, laughing, joking, cajoling, sometimes scolding, but generally working to improve his colleagues' morale and retain his position of preeminence among them. One morning, during the first week of September, Petersen accompanied the prisoners to the exercise yard.

'Good morning lieutenant,' Goering sang out. 'It is good to see you out in the fresh air!'

'Good morning *Reichsmarschall*,' Petersen replied, glancing around apprehensively, hoping no other officers were in the area.

'I failed to thank you properly for helping when I fell ill the other day,' Goering smiled. 'Dr. Schuster tells me that you may have saved my life.'

'Oh I doubt that sir. The doctor is giving me credit he deserves himself.'

Goering stopped walking and stared at Petersen. His eyes twinkled. 'You are a combat soldier aren't you? I can always tell,' he continued without waiting for an answer. He resumed his stroll around the yard, 'I was once a combat soldier, in the first war. I was an infantry officer like you. Then I became a pilot, an ace,' he smiled at the recollection. 'How are your living arrangements LT Petersen? Better than mine I imagine.'

Petersen laughed. 'Yes sir. I am billeted in a small house just south of here. It is quite comfortable.'

Goering nodded, 'Nuremberg is a beautiful city. It is famous for its toys, did you know this? You should find some Nuremberg toys for your children.'

'I'm not married *Reichsmarschall*. No children.'

'*Keine Kinder*!' Goering clucked his tongue. 'A strapping soldier like you? Well, something to look forward to. I have a daughter, Edda. She is eight. A real beauty, like her mother.'

They walked on a little ways, Goering unusually quiet. As they reached the end of their circuit of the yard, Goering reached into the pocket of his light blue marshal's uniform. 'Here lieutenant. A small token of my appreciation and of my respect. Soldier to soldier.' He held out a black fountain pen trimmed in gold.

'I really can't sir,' Petersen shook his head.

'Of course you can. It is of little use to me now,' Goering said, continuing to hold the pen out.

Rather than provoke a scene by refusing the gift or prolong the risk of being seen accepting it, Petersen quickly pocketed the pen. 'Thank you *Reichsmarschall*,' he said.

Goering smiled, 'We, you and I, we can at least be civil, yes?'

As the days grew both cooler and shorter, activity in the Palace of Justice intensified. Supreme Court justice Robert Jackson and his staff were working with counterparts from Great Britain, Russia and France to prepare indictments of the prisoners. Judges from the four conquering powers crafted the rules of procedure for the trials. This required interrogations, interviews, interpreters, clerks, typists, secretaries and others and the International Military Tribunal's staff continued to grow. With its growth, Nuremberg, or at least the Army community in Nuremberg, began to take on a life beyond the Palace and the prison. Clubs were opened for the enlisted personnel. Sporting events were scheduled between Army units. And a thriving black market offered a variety of goods and services for the right price.

Chapter 12

As Petersen approached # 22 *Gartenstrasse* on a mid-September evening, he heard, or at least thought he heard music. The cool evening air seemed to carry a melody along on a gentle breeze blowing toward the river. Opening the door, Petersen was flabbergasted to hear Glenn Miller's orchestra playing 'Chattanooga Choo-Choo' and to see Simmons busily winding the handle on a record player.

'Good evening John!' Simmons shouted gleefully over Miller's trombone. 'What do you think?'

'Great!' Petersen shouted in return. 'Where'd you get that?' He pointed at the player, a German model made by Siemens.

'You just have to know where to shop,' teased Simmons, lifting the needle arm off the record.

'Seriously Robert, where'd you get it?' Petersen persisted.

'John, there are certain things that you should know about me,' Simmons explained. 'One is that I believe in living life to its fullest and that means having things around that make life more pleasant, such as exhibit A here,' he patted the turntable lovingly. 'The other thing you need to know is that I am an unapologetic, patriotic American capitalist. We fought the war and whipped the fascists to spread democracy of course, but also to open new markets, to create international commerce and to improve the standard of living of peoples around the world—beginning of course with us! Beer?' he asked offering a warm bottle.

'Where's *Frau* Kohl?' Petersen asked, noticing with mild disappointment that there was nothing on the stove and no fire glowing within it.

'I don't know,' replied Robert glancing toward the kitchen. 'Apparently she has been absent all day. Nothing was disturbed between the time I left this morning and the time I got back.'

'Maybe she just got sick or something and couldn't make the walk,' Petersen surmised.

'Say John,' Simmons began, 'what say we go to market this evening since we obviously aren't going to get any decent dinner here.'

'To market?' John asked perplexed.

'Yes,' Simmons nodded. 'You know, a little horse trading, bartering, transacting, etc., etc.'

'Where does one go to do that?' Petersen affected his best imitation of Simmons' clipped, upper crust New York accent.

'I know just the place!' Simmons answered reaching for his jacket.

Just two blocks north of their house, Petersen and Simmons turned onto *Am Plaerrer*, a broad avenue forming the northern border of an open plaza. Simmons carried a small black satchel tucked securely under his right arm. Although darkness was beginning to fall, it was still relatively early and well before curfew. Around the plaza, people lingered in small groups. With fraternization restrictions relaxed by General Eisenhower, soldiers were now permitted to converse with German adults in public places. Here and there, Petersen saw GIs chatting up younger German women. In other spots groups of men stood talking and gesturing.

Simmons and Petersen entered the plaza, pausing by a low, partially demolished wall. Here, though none of the surrounding structures was whole, the local populace had cleared away much of the rubble. A few yards away was a neat stack of bricks, matching those remaining in the wall.

'So, what's in the bag?' Petersen asked.

'Gold, my boy, gold,' Simmons answered. He pulled a pack of Lucky Strikes out of his pants pocket, stuck one in his mouth and lit it with a gold lighter. 'Watch and learn, my friend. Here is American capitalism at work.'

Within a few moments, Petersen noticed a man in tattered clothes walking toward them from across the plaza. As he approached, he glanced around, though Petersen could not tell what he was looking for. Petersen nudged Simmons with his elbow and nodded in the direction of the walking man. Simmons took a drag on his cigarette, dropped it and ground it out with his heel. He exhaled a small cloud of blue smoke and said, 'Watch.'

The man had short gray hair and a deeply lined, care worn face. His eyes were dark, his coat a shabby *Wehrmacht* great coat, ripped at one shoulder and badly stained. He nodded in greeting to Robert and spoke softly and quickly. Robert listened and then answered quietly, shaking his head from side-to-side. Petersen couldn't follow the rapid flow of German passing between the two men, but he clearly perceived Robert was bargaining, either trying to lower the price or increase the quantity of whatever he wanted to obtain. Petersen continued to glance around the plaza, keeping a watchful eye out for MPs. Finally, Robert nodded and said, '*Ja, alles klar.*' He handed the satchel to the man who opened it for a cursory inspection. The man nodded, turned and retraced his steps back across the plaza.

'That's it?' asked Petersen.

'Of course not,' answered Simmons with a hint of impatience. 'A transaction must be mutually beneficial or there is no point in continued commerce.'

'So, maybe I'm missing something here, Robert, but you didn't seem to get anything back from Mr. Personality there,' Petersen gestured toward the man as he disappeared into a park on the other side of the boulevard.

'Ah, but I will,' said Simmons knowingly.

'Why do you think so?'

'Because I have before,' he answered.

When he arrived home the following night, a little later than usual and after dark, Petersen discovered that Simmons did, indeed, know the ropes. He found Robert sitting beside the little table at which they shared their meals—or had shared their meals before *Frau* Kohl went AWOL. Sitting beside the little stove, cold for yet another night, was a case of Russian vodka. 'Where did that come from?' Petersen asked.

'My friend from last night.'

'Wow. What kind of 'gold' did that cost you?' Petersen inquired.

'Ten cartons of cigarettes,' Simmons replied calmly.

'Where'd you get 10 cartons of cigarettes?' asked an incredulous Petersen.

'Let's just say I have my sources.'

'C'mon, you gotta do better than that Robert,' Petersen stood with his hands on his hips clearly expecting a straight answer.

'Calm down,' Simmons said. He looked his housemate squarely in the eye. 'Are you sure, John, that you really want to get into this?'

'Robert, I was there with you. I'm already into this and I think we're close enough that you can trust me with the truth.'

'It's not a matter of trust John,' Simmons explained. 'It's a matter of protecting you, of whom I have become quite fond. If I tell you how I do what I do, you become an accomplice after the fact.'

Petersen shook his head and stared at the bare wooden floor. When he looked back up he said, 'Robert, I'm no lawyer, but believe it or not, I know a little something about the law. I'm already an accomplice and before, during or after the fact don't make a hell of a lot of difference if we get nailed by the MPs or CID.'

'Very well,' Robert sighed. 'I have a contact in the quartermaster's depot. We have a neat arrangement. I make the deals, he supplies the capital, we share the proceeds. He will, for example, end up very shortly with half a case of vodka. Satisfied?'

'Robert,' Petersen began sternly, 'you're my friend. You're the only person on this side of the Atlantic I can share things with. I wouldn't be living here except for your generous hospitality. But you're playing with fire, boy!'

'And you sir do not realize what a hypocrite you sound like,' Robert snapped, his voice rising in volume and pitch. 'Do you think two lieutenants rate quarters like this with all the brass moving into this city? Do you realize how many generals there are around here? Not to mention colonels. Do you understand that there is an associate justice of the United States Supreme Court here? That majors and captains are waiting for months to get out of that moldy, falling down hotel and into quarters like ours? Don't you see John that you are the beneficiary of my commercial activities, just as surely as I am? You have no idea just how many transactions it took to put the two of us in here.' Robert relaxed a little and in a more conversational tone continued, 'C'mon John, we're Americans. This is what we do.'

Petersen pursed his lips and waited before responding. 'You're my good friend, Robert. I work every day in a prison and I understand better than you can possibly know the life a prisoner leads. I don't wish that life on anyone, especially you.' He turned and walked into his bedroom slamming the door closed behind him.

Chapter 13

Petersen moved from sentinel to sentinel, making his rounds through the cell block. Most of the men appreciated working for Petersen. He was even tempered and kept the Army bullshit to a minimum. He made sure the chow was good and that the guards' day room was stocked with the latest editions of stateside magazines, many not more than six weeks old. The men knew what to expect from LT Petersen and they liked knowing what to expect. Sentinel duty was dull, the celebrity of their prisoners having worn off after only a couple of days. Most of the men wondered what the hell they were still doing in Germany with the war nearly five months over. Alternating peaks into four cells every two minutes made their legs sore even as it dulled their minds.

Petersen was speaking with PFC Rogers when he heard a metal pail drop and the sound of booted feet running along the third floor gangway. He patted Rogers reassuringly on the shoulder and headed up the spiral stairs at the north end of the building. He reached cell 62 in time to see a sentinel retching into a bucket, probably the same one that had been dropped. LT Langley, officer in charge of the third floor block was standing in the door way, muttering and shaking his head in disgust. Below, Petersen could see Captain Stevens making his way up the stairs, taking them two at a time and pulling on the railing with both arms. Petersen looked past Langley into the cell to see the lifeless form of Leonardo Conti hanging just inches off the floor. Conti, though not a big enough fish for the Petersen's cell block, was no minnow, having served as director of health of the *SS*. Petersen stepped aside as Stevens entered the cell, saw Conti's body and stopped. Stevens looked at Conti, then at Langley. 'Report lieutenant,' he demanded.

'Suicide sir.'

'Brilliant deduction Holmes,' Stevens snapped rolling his eyes.

'Sorry sir,' Langley regrouped. 'He seems to have fashioned a noose from his towel, tied it to the bars on the window and jumped off his chair.'

'Who's the sentinel?' Stevens inquired.

'Him,' Langley pointed to the soldier with his head in the bucket.

'Alright,' said Stevens, resigning himself to the loss of the prisoner and the hell that would have to be paid, 'get your other guards back on their posts and then you and 'him,'' he pointed to the clammy faced guard on his knees, 'report to my office. I'm going to inform the colonel.'

Gaffner swept into C Wing like a whirlwind, Stevens in his wake. He bounded up the stairs to the third floor and into cell 62. With help from off duty sentinels, Dr. Schuster had stretched Conti's body out on the floor. 'He is, sadly, quite dead, colonel.' Gaffner had seen enough dead men to concur without making his own close examination.

'Get him out of here,' Gaffner directed. 'Take him to the infirmary and fill out the paperwork. You,' he pointed at Stevens, 'Come with me.'

Gaffner stomped back down the stairs and entered Stevens' office. Langley and the guard leapt to attention. Stevens closed the door. For the next 15 minutes, sentinels throughout C Wing had an even harder time than usual concentrating on their duties. Gaffner's bellowing reverberated off the office walls like thunder, at times leaking out into the cell blocks. Unidentified voices mumbled unintelligible words and were interrupted by Gaffner's explosions of angry questions and accusatory charges. Finally, the door jerked open and with it, every head whipped back toward its assigned cells. Gaffner, red faced, riding crop in hand and helmet liner jammed down to his nose, charged out of the building mumbling and slamming the door as he exited to the yard.

Stevens called together the three lieutenants in charge of the cell blocks. 'Gentlemen,' he began, 'Colonel Gaffner is reporting to General Watson the death of prisoner Conti.' Although the Internal Security Detachment supported the International Military

Tribunal, Watson, the Army commander in Nuremberg, was technically Gaffner's superior officer. 'The colonel has issued new guidelines for the sentinels which are to take immediate effect,' continued Captain Stevens. He pulled out a lined pad and began to tick off the new rules. 'One, all prisoners will be removed from their cells taken to the shower room in the basement and strip searched,' Stevens looked up, 'including a rectal check. Two, while in the shower room, all cells will be thoroughly searched. Three, following the search, all prisoners will be reassigned to a different cell, within the same cell block. Four, chairs will be removed daily from all cells between 1900 hours and 0800 hours. Five, Captain Gifford's construction crew will begin making architectural changes to the cells ASAP. Said changes will involve the removal of bars and windows and the replacement with cello-glass. Now hear this clearly gentlemen: we are not going to lose another prisoner.' The lieutenants glanced nervously at each other. 'Gentlemen, I needn't tell you that not a word of this is to leave the building. No comments to friends or colleagues and no statements to the correspondents. If you get an inquiry from a member of the press, refer them to Colonel Gaffner's office. I better not hear a word. Understand?' The three lieutenants nodded. 'Questions?' Stevens asked. The three lieutenants shook their heads.

The other prisoners quickly learned what the officers would not tell them. The disruption of the routine upon which all armies thrive was their first clue that something unusual had happened. As they were marched downstairs to the basement shower room, they surreptitiously spoke amongst themselves, trying to piece together the third floor event which had caused the commotion. While the prisoners were physically inspected downstairs, their cells were being combed through above them. Guards checked furniture for loose pieces and hiding places. They checked the toilets, invisible from the guard ports in the cell doors. They inspected mattresses, looking for tears in the covers which might lead to secreted contraband. The few personal items the prisoners were allowed in their cells, books, family photographs and letters, were scrutinized. The thorough search turned up one nail, a small file and a piece of a broken razor blade. And, in Goering's cell, one more item of interest.

'Hey lieutenant!' shouted Private McKeown from Goering's cell. 'I think I found something here.' He had combed through the personal items on the small writing table against the left wall and found nothing. He had carefully inspected the toilet and its plumbing, running his hand up under the rim of the bowl, then standing on the seat to view the inside of the wall mounted tank. Again, nothing. As he picked up Goering's blue uniform tunic and started turning the pockets out, he heard a small 'clink.' McKeown knelt down and picked up what appeared to be a glass capsule, too large to swallow, but still quite small, only about an inch and a half long.

'What you got Private McKeown?' Petersen asked entering the cell. McKeown handed him the capsule. 'Have you finished checking in here?'

'Still the bed to check sir,' McKeown answered and began stripping the mattress. Petersen pulled an envelope from his pocket and wrote on it where, when, how and by whom the vial had been found. He placed the capsule in the envelope, sealed it and signed his name across the flap. When McKeown finished inspecting the bedding, Petersen had him sign his name across the flap as well.

'Take this to Dr. Schuster in the infirmary. Have him sign for it,' Petersen directed McKeown.

By now, the searches in Petersen's cell block were completed. Petersen reported the results of the search to Captain Stevens.

'And where is this capsule now?' Stevens asked.

'I sent it to the doctor sir.'

'Could you tell what it was?'

'No sir,' said Petersen, 'but I guess it's some kind of poison. The capsule was too big to swallow. It was big enough to choke a man.'

'Anything else of consequence?' Stevens inquired.

'No sir, just some little odds and ends. Moving the prisoners to different cells should prevent them from making use of anything we might have missed,' Petersen said, immediately regretting his choice of words.

But Stevens seemed preoccupied and let the slip go unchallenged. 'Go ahead with the cell reassignments. I'll brief the colonel,' he said, grabbing his cap off the rack by the office door. 'And be ready for Captain Gifford's men to start work shortly.'

By the time the prisoners returned from the basement, they had figured out that Conti had killed himself. They weren't sure how, but most of them didn't care. What mattered was that one of their number had given up hope and without hope, had given up life. Goering seemed particularly addled. 'What a fool!' he exclaimed as he and the others waited to be directed to their new cells. 'In fifty years, there will be statues of us all over Germany. We will be revered for standing up and building our country into a world power.'

'Can it fatso,' one of the guards ordered, causing Goering's face to flush. Petersen kept an eye on the *Reichsmarschall*, eager to avoid another seizure. Goering felt Petersen's gaze and turned toward him. 'Can you at least tell us what is going on lieutenant,' he asked beseechingly.

'Sorry *Reichsmarschall*,' Petersen replied. 'Orders are that no information is to be given out except by the colonel.'

Goering smiled and gave a little nod. 'A soldier must always follow orders.'

Gifford's men spent the rest of the day ripping out the iron bars and windows in each occupied cell. The resulting racket and dust created an uncomfortable environment for prisoners and guards alike. When the work crew entered a cell, the prisoner and his guard had to wait in the corridor between the cell blocks. The work could take as long as an hour, during which both guard and prisoner stood impatiently waiting. Once the demolition was completed and the new cello-glass window was installed, the prisoner was allowed to return to an environment which was dramatically different. Where once there had been a glass window, albeit barred, allowing a clear view out and the sunlight to come in, now there was a semi-transparent rectangle yielding only a blurred view of the outside and reducing the amount of natural light entering the cell.

At 1900 hours, all cell doors were opened and all chairs removed for the night. By 2000 hours, some sense of normalcy had been reestablished in the cell blocks. Gaffner had blown through and pronounced himself pleased with the steps that had been implemented. Dr. Schuster had reported to him that the capsule confiscated from Goering's cell had contained cyanide, a fast acting and deadly poison. 'Good work finding that poison, LT Petersen,' Gaffner commented once he, Petersen and Stevens had completed their walk through the block.

'Thank you sir. Private McKeown made a thorough search. Nothing else was found.'

'That's what worries me,' Gaffner said, rubbing his chin with his right knuckles. 'If he had that, what else are these clowns hiding? Now listen men,' Gaffner continued, his blue eyes shifting between Stevens and Petersen. 'This place has got to be suicide proof. Everyone here is to be on a high state of alert at all times, 24 hours a day. They eat, we watch. They exercise, we watch. They sleep, we watch. Got it?'

'Yes sir,' Stevens and Petersen answered in unison.

'I had a most unpleasant experience this morning informing General Watson of Conti's death. I don't want to have to go through that again. I especially don't want to have to inform the general if one of these big shots kicks the bucket. Conti we can hide. You let one of these other bastards kill himself,' he wagged his thick finger at Petersen, 'and there will be all kinds of hell to pay. And I don't want to be the guy writing the check, if you know what I mean.' He paused waiting for a reply.

'Yes sir!' Stevens and Petersen again spoke together.

'100% alert, 100% of the time gentlemen. Make sure your soldiers get the message and make sure they do their duty.' With that, Gaffner donned his helmet liner and disappeared out the door.

'Sir,' Petersen turned to Stevens, 'how in the world am I supposed to maintain '100% alert, 100% of the time'?'

'You heard the man lieutenant. Orders are orders.'

Chapter 14

Within a couple of weeks, the bruises had faded from May Petersen's face. John's collar bone took a little longer to heal, but the painful memories of that night dimmed with the coming of the warmer, longer days of spring. Dogwoods and apple trees bloomed and flowers sprouted. Tom Petersen never acknowledged his drunken rampage or the pain it had caused. John couldn't tell if he even remembered it and no way was he going to bring it up. The fact that he had his arm in a sling for four weeks never drew notice from his old man who seemed more concerned in maintaining law and order in Wood County than in his own house.

'Mother, why is Daddy so mean sometimes?' John had finally worked up the courage to ask one day when they were alone in the yard. His mother was bent over the wash tub, working on a load of laundry for Mrs. Wilder from town. May looked up and with the back of her hand brushed a strand of brown hair out of her face.

She looked at the boy thoughtfully. 'Well, now son, he don't mean nothing by it. It's just the drink gets into him. Best not worry about it. He's trying to lay off it anyhow.' She went back to her washing and never mentioned the conversation again.

Chapter 15

Petersen and Simmons had hardly spoken since their argument over Simmons' extracurricular activities. Petersen had made a point of departing their shared quarters early in the morning before Simmons was awake, an arrangement simplified by their offset duty schedules. Simmons, for his part, was rarely home in the evenings any more, since *Frau* Kohl had never returned and neither lieutenant had much interest in cooking.

So it was that Petersen was mildly surprised one mid-October evening to find Simmons at home and in a gregarious mood. As he mounted the steps to their shared abode, Petersen heard Harry James blasting away on the record player. Entering the house, Petersen immediately noticed the presence of a young woman and the welcome aroma of food cooking. 'Hello John!' called Simmons from the table where he sat browsing through a month-old *Saturday Evening Post*. He grinned and stood and pointed to the woman in the kitchen. 'Come meet *Frau* Bichler!'

Frau Bichler was much younger and smaller than her predecessor. She was perhaps 30 years of age and she wore a heavy cotton apron over her blouse and skirt, her shoes were old and in disrepair. Her face was lined, with small crow's feet around her pale blue eyes and dark, half- moon shadows below them. She was thin, about 5 feet, 2 inches tall. Her hair was a dirty blonde and was tied back with dark blue scarf. She smiled as Robert introduced her and, like *Frau* Kohl before her, offered a curtsy to John. John nodded back and said 'Pleased to meet you. Do you speak English?'

'Some few words,' she smiled.

'Good,' John smiled in return, 'because my German is very limited.'

'Some few words,' she repeated, holding her smile.

Robert intervened and sent *Frau* Bichler back to her cooking.

'Where'd you find *Frau* Bichler,' John asked as he sat on the small sofa opposite the table, 'the civilian personnel office?'

'Something like that,' Robert winked. 'Listen John, I'm sorry I lost my temper with you the other day. I know I was condescending and, well, I'm sorry.'

'Me too,' John replied. 'I really appreciate all you've done to make my time here in paradise more enjoyable,' he chuckled. 'Now, tell me about *Frau* Bichler.'

'Same arrangement as before,' Robert said. 'I've taken care of all the details.'

'Sure,' John nodded, 'but how did you find her?'

'She comes highly recommended by some of my, well, let's just say some of my friends. Her husband was a *Luftwaffe* pilot who didn't return from a mission one day. She lived here in Nuremberg with her husband's family, but they left during the bombings and she stayed. Hasn't heard from them since.'

Frau Bichler turned out to be an excellent cook. Thick slices of pork loin were accompanied by roasted potatoes and asparagus, all nicely seasoned and served hot. 'Terrific,' John said as he finally pushed away from the table. '*Frau* Bichler,' he called to the cook, '*es schmeckt gut!*' This brought another smile and curtsy from *Frau* Bichler and a laugh from Robert.

'I see your German is getting better,' he commented.

'Yes, I know four phrases now,' John replied. 'Don't shoot, hands up, where is the train station and it tastes good.'

It was already dark by the time the two lieutenants bade good night to *Frau* Bichler. Robert was not engaged in commercial activities on this night and the two young men, friends again, shared a couple of beers and talked.

'Have you thought any more about what you are going to do after this idyllic chapter of your life comes to a close John?' Robert asked.

'No. I'm not real sure how I got here and I'm not sure what happens next. I like to lead men, Robert, but I'm beginning to see a side to the Army that was absent in combat.'

'Yes, like warm, dry quarters, someone to do your cooking and cleaning—she will also do our laundry—' John's mind flashed back to his mother, 'a challenging job in which you meet

interesting people who don't shoot at you, an erudite house mate...
I could go on and on,' Robert went on and on.

John smiled. The apologies and the good meal had put him in
a better mood than he had experienced in weeks--so good that the
suicide had slipped from his mind.

'Do you think,' Robert began, 'that you would have an
interest in the legal profession, or perhaps in the corrections
business, given your experience here?'

'No way,' John replied sitting up a little straighter and peeling
the label off his bottle. 'No, no prisons for me.'

'Tell me about your education, John. We've never really
talked about that. There may be some clues there as to what you
might pursue professionally. For starters, where did you go to
school?' It was a question John always dreaded, but one he had
never had to answer until he was commissioned.

'Gatesville State, in Texas,' he gave his rehearsed answer.

'Where, pray tell, is Gatesville State?' Robert continued his
questioning with a light laugh.

'Gatesville.'

'Oh never mind,' Robert moved on. 'In what field of study
did you major?'

'Most of my work was in agriculture,' John prevaricated.

'John, my family does a lot of business in agriculture. My
uncle sits on the board of the Chicago Mercantile Exchange. My
father has business connections with some of the larger farming
concerns in the Midwest. We might be able to open some doors
for you. Hell, maybe even find something appropriate back in
Texas if you want to be near your mother,' Robert offered.

John took a last long pull from his bottle and set it down on
the floor with a thud. He was eager to change the subject. 'Thanks.
What about you Robert. What will you do once you hang up your
uniform?'

'I lack just two courses to graduate from Yale,' Robert
answered. 'I'll take a little time to relax, maybe sit by a cool lake
for a while next summer and then go back in the fall and finish.
Then, find something interesting in the family business, banking,
trading, I don't know. Maybe reopen commercial contacts here in

Europe. This is going to be a great market once it gets back on its feet.'

'You think the trial will be over by next summer?' Petersen asked.

'That seems to be the prevailing opinion,' Simmons said. 'It's not like we don't know how it's all going to turn out.'

Petersen and Simmons talked on until nearly midnight, catching up on what was happening in the Palace and in the prison. Petersen swore Simmons to secrecy and told him about Conti's suicide and the changes in the jail. Simmons shared the rumor that the formal indictments were soon to be presented to the prisoners. Neither mentioned the black market.

Chapter 16

Simmons' rumor proved correct. On Friday, October 19, a British major, Airey Neave, delivered the formal indictments throughout the cell block. Neave had been selected for two reasons. First, he was a highly decorated, German-speaking, genuine war hero. Captured in France in 1940, Neave had escaped from the Germans only to be recaptured and turned over to the *Gestapo*. The *Gestapo* had worked Neave over and then imprisoned him in the escape proof Colditz Castle, from which Neave escaped in 1942, making his way back to England. He had spent the remainder of the war providing planning, coordination and supplies to the French Resistance. The second reason, and the more important of the two, was that having a British officer deliver the indictments would remove from the International Military Tribunal the 'all American' appearance that had so far prevailed in the press.

Neave, accompanied by a captain from the prosecutorial staff and an orderly pushing a cart loaded with official looking papers, reported to the prison office. Captain Stevens received the visitors, gave them mugs of coffee and briefed them on the security that would accompany them on their mission. Stevens appointed LT Petersen and two guards to assist Neave's party. After introductions were made and the small talk was out of the way, Neave set his mug down with a noticeably shaky hand. Although he had faced down the *Gestapo* and twice escaped from captivity deep within enemy territory, Neave admitted, 'I'm a bit edgy this morning. This is one of those historic days you know. Nothing quite like this has been done before.'

'Yes sir,' Petersen agreed as they stepped into the cell block, the cart following just behind. The indictments covered four fundamental charges: conspiracy to wage aggressive war, crimes against peace, war crimes and crimes against humanity. Not all the prisoners were charged with all crimes. Rudolf Hess, for example, who made his infamous flight to Scotland in 1941 ostensibly on a self-appointed peace mission, was charged only with conspiracy to wage aggressive war and crimes against peace. Others, like

71

Goering, Keitel, Jodl, Rosenberg and von Ribbentrop were indicted on all four counts. Neave began on the west side of the cell block visiting one cell then the next. At each, Neave introduced himself to the occupant and handed him the appropriate formal notice of indictment, which the prisoner signed. Neave also advised each of the now accused men of their right to obtain counsel.

Goering was waiting when the party arrived at his cell, having watched and listened as far as was possible as his colleagues had been formally served. The *Reichsmarschall* stood by his door, chest thrust out, chin up. 'Good morning gentlemen,' he smiled in greeting. 'What jollies do you bring on your trolley?' he laughed at his joke. Neave repeated his carefully rehearsed speech, presenting Goering with an indictment charging him on all four counts. Goering hastily scribbled his signature on the document and handed it back to Neave.

'I am to inform you that you have the right to counsel,' Neave stated.

'You find one for me,' Goering retorted with a wave of dismissal. 'It is always the same,' he continued, his face growing redder by the moment, his nostrils flaring. 'The victor will always be the judge and the vanquished the accused. We are here for one reason and for only one reason: we lost.'

Petersen, sensed another outburst might be brewing, a possibility he was eager to avoid for his sake if not for Neave's and Goering's.

'Thank you *Reichsmarschall*,' Petersen said, touching Neave lightly on the back of his sleeve as a signal to move along.

'Ah, LT Petersen,' said Goering frowning and acknowledging his presence for the first time. 'I am sorry to see you involved in this farce. There will be no justice here. I will not be judged by military men or by my peers. This will be what you Americans call a 'kangaroo court' I am quite certain.'

'I don't think so *Reichsmarschall*,' Petersen replied as gently as he knew how.

'A debate for another day perhaps,' Goering replied his eyes never leaving Petersen's. Then he laughed again, the 'good' Hermann reappearing, 'Good day to you Major, Lieutenant.'

As they backed out of the cell and the door closed behind them, Major Neave turned to Petersen. 'Blimey! That's something I'll never forget. How do you get used to being in here with these scoundrels?'

'Sir, I never get used to being in here,' Petersen replied.

The mood in the prison changed with the handing down of the indictments. The prisoners were now officially defendants and felt that events were moving forward, toward an end they could not foretell. And they realized their ability to influence that end was waning.

Chapter 17

For once, Petersen arrived at the house on *Gartenstrasse* before Simmons. There was no music blaring, but *Frau* Bichler was cooking. From the aroma, Petersen guessed the meal would be delicious. '*Guten abend, Herr Leuntnant,*' *Frau* Bichler greeted Petersen. She smiled and Petersen noticed the shadows beneath her blue eyes were nearly gone. In one hand she held a wooden spoon, in the other, a tattered copy of *Look* magazine, folded in half.

'Reading?' Petersen asked, pointing at the magazine.

'Some few words,' *Frau* Bichler laughed. 'I see pictures,' she said pointing with the spoon to an advertisement of a well-dressed woman smoking a Lucky Strike. Petersen nodded and as she turned back toward the stove noticed that she looked less tired than when she had first arrived at # 22.

He took off his jacket and tie and hung them across the chair in his bed room. He took off his uniform shirt and rolled it up, stuffing it in his laundry bag. *Frau* Bichler would see to that tomorrow, he thought. Petersen picked up a torn and faded sweater. The little stove did a good job of heating the area in its immediate vicinity, but October brought with it shorter days and cooler, wetter weather and to remain comfortable in the little house, a sweater, sometimes even an overcoat, was called for. As he pulled the sweater on and emerged through the bedroom door back into the center of the house, he caught *Frau* Bichler staring at him. She quickly dropped her eyes back to the stove and continued cooking. The front door burst open and Simmons entered surveying the interior like a feudal lord.

'Good evening John!' he hailed. '*Guten abend, Frau* Bichler! I'm not interrupting anything am I?' he teased with raised eyebrows.

'Hello Robert. I can't believe how late you've been working!' Petersen glanced at his wrist watch, returning the gibe. 'Tell me about your exciting day at the worldwide center of justice.'

Robert slid a chair up to the table, loosening the knot in his tie and shedding his jacket, which he casually tossed on the small sofa. 'The Indians are restless, my friend,' Robert began. 'The indictments put them in a whole new class of humanity: criminal defendants. Dregs of the earth. Meal ticket for the despised defense lawyer. They now have a whole new world of worries, not the least of which is finding competent legal counsel in this barren land. Things on our side should really begin to pick up speed now,' he continued.

'By our side, you mean the American side?' John asked.

'Well, actually no. I meant the more professional Palace side as opposed to your more, what's the word, 'common' prison side,' Robert laughed.

The two lieutenants settled into their routine of recounting the day's events. *Frau* Bichler moved back and forth between the stove and the table, serving up fried duck and potato dumplings along with a large portion of some kind of greens that John merely pushed around his plate. Robert attacked his food with gusto, chasing it with a bottle of cold beer. One of the benefits of the change of seasons had been lowering the temperature of the beer, which Robert kept beneath the small back stoop in perpetual shade.

'Justice Jackson's bunch wants to start the trial early in November,' Robert told John in between bites. 'The Russians are dragging their feet because they aren't sure their cases will be ready that soon. You know those SOBs aren't used to trying people. They usually just line them up and shoot. That's what Morgenthau wanted to do here,' said Simmons in reference to the Secretary of the Treasury who advocated summary executions of the Nazi leaders. 'Wiser heads prevailed, I guess.'

'I guess,' John nodded.

Frau Bichler stepped over to clear away the dishes. Seeing that John had barely touched his greens, she placed her hands on her hips and stretched on her tiptoes to a towering and glowering 5 feet, 2 inches. '*Was ist das Problem hier? Mein Kochen gefällt Ihnen nicht?*' she asked, her blues eyes flashing, a strand of blond hair peaking from beneath her scarf.

John looked down at his plate, the tips of his ears beginning to burn. He had never liked greens; mustard, turnip, collard. He just didn't like them, even when his mother had cooked them with a slab of fat back. He looked back up at *Frau* Bichler's pouting lips. Slowly, he took a forkful of greens and stuffed them in his mouth. He chewed and swallowed. *Frau* Bichler stood her ground, maintaining her fierce countenance. John took a second, then a third bite, finally making a noticeable dent in the mountainous helping of greens. *Frau* Bichler relaxed her stance, gave a single nod of her head and walked back toward the sink.

'I think she likes you,' Robert said, stifling a laugh.

'I hope she likes me better than I like this stuff,' John grimaced. 'She seems to be pretty comfortable around here. I mean she's a very good cook, keeps the house and our laundry clean.'

'Oh, I'm sure she likes it here if that's what you mean, old sport. This is a very good deal for a German woman right now, especially one with no family nearby. We, actually I, pay her a pittance equal on the local economy to a small fortune. Plus, I supplement her income with occasional gifts from the commissary. Have you noticed she's gained weight since she came to work for us?'

'Careful friend,' John warned. 'If you get caught supplying groceries to a German citizen your ass will be sitting across from Hermann's!'

'Don't worry. I won't get caught,' Robert grinned.

'Are you really making so much money that it's worth the risk you're taking?' asked John.

'Absolutely. I'm sending home more money than a colonel makes and I'm living off of my salary, which is the same as yours. The finance corps boobs haven't figured out the game. If I made a million dollars, I could send it all home, no questions asked.' Robert said.

'Surely they'll wise up,' said John.

'Don't call me Shirley,' Robert cracked, chuckling. 'John, this is the Army. The turnover here right now is over 100% a year in officers and probably three or four times that high among enlisted men. Nobody's going to be in his job long enough to figure this scheme out. The only things these guys are counting are their service points to see how soon they can go home. In the meantime, I'm counting up dollars. Do you know how much a Russian soldier here will pay for good booze?'

'No.'

'Me neither! I haven't reached the top of the market yet!' Robert enthused. 'These poor slobs love it here. They get paid in script. Unlike us, they can't send any of it home and they can't take it with them when they get shipped back. Their only option is to spend it. They will buy anything and everything and they will pay ungodly prices. This is a seller's heaven!'

'OK Rockefeller. When they bring you over to the big house, I'll make sure we have a comfortable room for you,' John tossed back his beer.

'I won't get caught,' Robert repeated.

Chapter 18

It had been a long time, in fact, John had nearly forgotten about it. He still had the scar over his eye, cutting a narrow furrow through his eyebrow, but his collar bone had healed. He had gotten bigger. The daily chores around the farm and helping his mother pick up and deliver washing were hardening his young muscles. He'd gotten taller too. And though he didn't have time for organized sports, he was in good condition with the hand-eye coordination of an athlete. He would throw rocks at coyotes who ventured too close to the pasture. He had once zinged a stone 20 yards, nailing a coyote in full flight. He'd also become a fair shot with an old .22 caliber rifle his father had given him. Like a thousand other kids, he honed his skill shooting at tin cans, moved on to birds and then small game. Rabbits helped supplement the family diet.

After listening to Jack Benny on NBC, John had picked up a book and headed toward his corner bedroom. His mother came in to kiss him goodnight and he settled in with Tom Swift until sleep over took him. He didn't know what woke him, but he sat up in bed, alert. He saw the light from the kitchen leaking under his bedroom door. Listening intently, his heart threatening to bust right out of his chest, he heard a sharp pop and a muffled scream. He heard sobbing and recognized his mother's voice. Then he heard a low angry voice. John swung his legs over the side of his bed and dropped to his knees. He reached under the bed and grabbed the barrel of his .22. Quietly, he pulled it close enough to lift up. He walked on tiptoe to the door, listening, breathing softly so as not to alert whoever was in the kitchen. He cracked open the door. He could see his mother, her face pressed down on the table, held in place by his father's strong right hand. A glass of milk had spilled across the table and was dripping onto the floor. Holding the rifle in his right hand, he pulled the door open. 'Stop it Daddy,' the boy said. Tom Petersen looked around through unfocused eyes. He reeked of cheap liquor. 'Boy, you get back in your room and don't come out unless I call you.' May was crying softly.

'No sir. Now you let go of mother and you back on out of the way,' John tried to keep his voice from wavering.

Tom pressed down harder on the back of May's head, causing her to moan. John could see his mother's right arm, broken and hanging at an odd angle. She continued to cry, but made no sound.

'Stop it!' John shouted.

With unexpected quickness, Tom lunged at his son. The speed of his movement caught the boy by surprise. Before John could react, Tom had wrenched the rifle loose from his hands and whacked him on the shoulder with its butt. John fell back, rolling. Tom lurched forward, unsteadily, the rifle still in his grasp. John stuck his leg out and kicked, catching Tom at the ankles and bringing him down. John rolled away and jumped on the back of his prone father. He began pummeling Tom's head and shoulders with both fists. Tom swung the rifle backwards wildly, catching John on the mouth with the barrel and splitting his lip. The coppery taste of blood filled John's mouth as he grabbed the barrel and jammed it under his right arm. Using both hands, he wrenched the weapon away from the drunken grip of his father. Tom rolled slightly to the left and then came back full force to the right, unseating John. As Tom came up on his hands and knees, John swung the rifle. The stock landed a glancing blow on Tom's forehead, stunning the big man. He wobbled on hands and knees, dazed. John swung again, this time connecting squarely against his father's temple.

Chapter 19

A loud pounding gradually broke through the haze of sleep surrounding Petersen. He opened his eyes trying to place the noise within some context. The pounding sound came again and this time Petersen realized it was someone beating on the front door of the house. As the pounding continued, Petersen swung out of bed, grabbed a robe and padded across the cold floor on his bare feet. Opening the door, he was greeted by the sight of the very wet Sergeant Newberry. A moderate rain was falling and water was dripping from Newberry's overcoat and cap.

'Captain Stevens' compliments, sir,' Newberry announced with a soggy salute.

'Step inside Sergeant,' Petersen said, pulling Newberry by his arm into the house. 'What's going on that they had to send you out in the rain in the middle of the night?'

'Another suicide, sir,' Newberry replied. 'The defendant Ley killed hisself a little bit ago. I don't know how he done it, but the captain tol' me to come fetch you back.' Robert Ley had been the head of the German Labor Front and had crushed the trade union movement within the Third Reich. Upon receiving his indictment, he had been despondent.

Petersen thought for a moment. 'All right Sergeant. You sit down and give me a minute to dress and we'll head back over together.'

Within 20 minutes Petersen, now wet himself, was back at the prison, crowded in front of Captain Stevens' desk with lieutenants Langley and Rose, the other cell block officers-in-charge. Rose had been on duty at the time the suicide was discovered, but Langley, like Petersen, had been tumbled out of the sack by a messenger.

'Here's what we know,' Captain Stevens began. 'Ley somehow tied a strip of his towel around the water pipe supplying his toilet. He sat down on the toilet and tied the other end of the towel around his neck. Then he jammed his underwear as far down his throat as he could. From there, we think he simply leaned forward until he strangled himself.'

Rose piped up, mainly for the benefit of the other two lieutenants. 'Private Harris was on duty. He got suspicious when Ley went to take a shit and then didn't move for a while. That's when he called me over and we went in.' The toilet was the only part of the cell not visible from the door. It was set in a tiny alcove in the corner of the cell just to the right of the door. All Harris had been able to observe were Ley's feet sticking out of the corner.

'The colonel is over at headquarters briefing General Watson,' Stevens picked up the conversation. 'I expect he will come here when he is done. I don't expect him to be in a very good mood.'

Nor did the three lieutenants.

Shortly after midnight, Gaffner stormed into C Wing and into Stevens' office. The four waiting officers had been alerted to his arrival by the slamming of the door and the rapid tread of the colonel's boots echoing through the otherwise quiet cell block. They were standing when he entered, water dripping off of his helmet liner and overcoat, his boots wet and soiled.

'Sit!' he commanded without greeting.

He removed his helmet liner and coat and set them on a small table in the corner. His face was sprinkled with grey stubble, one side of his collar sticking up, as though he, like the others, had dressed hurriedly. 'This shit stops tonight!' His red-rimmed blue eyes moved from face-to-face, burning the message into the minds of his prison officers. 'We will not lose another prisoner,' he continued, his voice rising in both pitch and volume. 'Is that clear to you LT Rose?'

'Yes sir!'

'LT Langley?'

'Yes sir!'

'LT Petersen?'

'Yes sir!'

'I just got my ass reamed out by a general officer because I had to call on him in the middle of the damn night to tell him that my command had fouled up again and lost another prisoner,' Gaffner's voice was rising again. 'I don't like getting reamed, gentlemen! And it ain't gonna happen again!' Gaffner paused, catching his breath. His face was now bright red, his blue eyes a sharp contrast. 'It's time for you guys to get off your candy asses and start watching these bastards so this kind of crap doesn't happen. Get it? I am going to make this place suicide proof and you boys are going to execute my plans without hesitation and with better results than you have heretofore delivered,' he jabbed a thick finger at the lieutenants. 'If you can't do as you're ordered, if you can't do a relatively simple job, I'm gonna run your asses out of here. Think of this as a combat zone from now on boys,' Gaffner paused for a breath. 'Now I've had some time to think, between my visit to General Watson and here. Effective in the morning, one sentinel per cell, every minute of every day.'

Petersen cleared his throat and asked, 'Sir, will we get additional men?'

'No lieutenant! You will not get additional men!' Gaffner snapped angrily, his red face shaking from side to side. 'This is not about the comfort of your men! You're not here to enjoy civilian working hours! We've got a mission to accomplish here gentlemen,' Gaffner's eyes finally moved off of Petersen's stricken face and around to the others. 'You are officers in the United States Army, the greatest fighting force the world has ever known. Not only the greatest, but the most innovative. Figure it out. One man on each cell all the time! Make it work. I will not lose another prisoner. Now get the lead out and get busy setting up new duty schedules that comply with my orders. Go!' Gaffner shouted.

Rose and Langley escaped the office and their furious commander quickly. Petersen headed for the door right behind them, but was frozen in his tracks by Gaffner. 'LT Petersen, a moment of your time,' he said with a touch of sarcasm in his voice. 'Now you listen to me son,' Gaffner moved in so close that Petersen could smell his breath. Jabbing his stubby finger into Petersen's chest he said, 'I will not accept insubordination from any man under my command, is that clear.'

'Sir, I meant no disre...'

'Is that clear?' Gaffner shouted, spit flying, his eyes bulging.

'Crystal clear, sir!' Petersen responded sharply.

'Good,' Gaffner said, lowering his voice. He stood for another moment, as if trying to burn a hole through Petersen with his stare. Then he grabbed his helmet liner and overcoat and stalked out of the office.

'Shit!' Petersen clamped his jaws tightly and glanced at Stevens. 'What did I do to deserve that sir?' he asked angrily.

'Don't take it personally, John,' Stevens said calling him by his given name for the first time.

'I don't know any other way to take it. One more question, sir,' Petersen plunged ahead. 'Does the colonel always drink at night?'

The three lieutenants spent most of the rest of the night reworking the guard scheme. By 0900, they had put together a schedule with four men standing guard where the previous night one man had worked alone. At 0930, Gaffner returned to the prison to address the prisoners. They were assembled in the basement mess hall. The military defendants sat together at one table, the civilians were scattered among several tables. While the prisoners were downstairs, guards, under the able direction of Sergeant Hottle, were searching every cell, combing for any type of contraband.

'It is my duty to inform you,' Gaffner addressed the prisoners, 'that the defendant Robert Ley took his own life last night.'

'What a coward,' Goering stated loudly enough for the prisoners to hear.

'Silence!' Gaffner barked, glaring at Goering. 'For this reason,' the colonel continued, 'there will now be one guard on your cell at all times. The guard will observe you at all times you are present in the cell, waking or sleeping. His orders are to be obeyed immediately and without question,' Gaffner stared at Goering, who smiled and nodded. 'All other standing orders remain in effect. That is all.' Gaffner turned and walked up the steps.

That afternoon, the colonel was back. His eyes were red and puffy, suggesting that he had enjoyed no more sleep than the rest of the prison's officers. But, his uniform was crisp, sharply pressed and everything in its place. His helmet liner was polished and he carried his gloves and riding crop in his left hand. The reason for his attire, in fact for his presence at all, came through the door shortly after 1500 hours. It was the colonel's public affairs officer with a retinue of correspondents.

'Gentlemen,' Gaffner said hospitably, 'Welcome to C Wing.'

With that, Gaffner gave the newsmen a short briefing on security in the prison. He carefully pointed out that there was now a sentinel on each cell, constantly vigilant. He pointed out the wire mesh strung throughout the cell blocks in order to discourage any prisoner who might contemplate leaping to a premature death. 'These measures,' Gaffner postured, 'now make this prison suicide proof.' As they walked through the first floor block, Petersen's eyes followed the group warily. Gaffner stopped from time to time to point something out. As he did, Petersen saw a dozen pencils scribbling furiously on the pressmen's ubiquitous pads. At some cells, Gaffner would speak to the guards, the kindly commander checking on the welfare of his men. At others, he called in to the prisoner, showing the humane side of the dedicated prison warden. When finally the cell block tour seemed completed, Gaffner led the correspondents toward the door. Petersen turned away to head downstairs in order to inspect preparations for the defendants' evening meal in the basement mess hall. Before he had made it two steps, he heard Gaffner call his name. Petersen reversed course quickly, stopping just in front of the colonel and bracing to attention.

'LT Petersen,' said Gaffner in a voice calculated to be just loud enough for the newsmen behind him to hear. 'Look after the appearance of your men, lieutenant. Several have sloppy uniforms.' Gaffner's eyes left Petersen's and looked up and down the young lieutenant's own uniform which he had now been wearing for more than 15 straight hours. 'While you're at it,' he said locking his eyes on Petersen's once more, 'your own uniform could use a little attention.'

'Yes sir,' Petersen said, feeling his face and ears burn. Two of the closer cell guards hazarded a quick look in Petersen's direction. Gaffner's lips straightened into a barely perceptible grin. He turned toward the door, 'Gentlemen, if you will follow me,' he called to the reporters, guiding them out of the building.

As soon as the prisoners were back in their cells following their evening meal, Petersen checked out at the prison office and headed to his quarters. He was dog tired, with just a couple of hours of sleep during the previous day and a half. Upon reaching the house, he was pleased to hear the phonograph playing, though he did not recognize the music. *Frau* Bichler was sitting in one of the kitchen chairs with her bare feet propped up in another, looking at a copy of *Stars & Stripes*. She had small feet; almost delicate if not for the rough calluses. At Petersen's entrance, she bolted to her feet, tossing the newspaper aside. '*Guten abend, Herr Leuntnant!*' she smiled happily.

'Good evening, *Frau* Bichler,' he replied unenthusiastically.

Frau Bichler, cocked her head to the side and raised her eye brows. 'You bad day?' she asked haltingly.

Petersen offered a tired smile. 'Yes. Long day. Very long.'

'Lisbeth make good,' she smiled, her blues sparkling. She quickly brought Petersen a cold beer from under the back porch and some black bread with sliced cheese. Setting the food on the table in front of him, she smiled again and said, 'Good, *ja?*'

'Good, *ja!*' Petersen smiled taking a bite. '*Danke.*'

Chapter 20

Tom Petersen lingered in a coma for three days before he died. The Wood County coroner listed the cause of death as a skull fracture. The district attorney labeled it homicide. Young John was taken into custody over the heartbroken cries of his mother, her right arm in a white plaster cast. John was driven the two miles into Quitman in the back of a Ford pick-up truck. A deputy in a uniform like the one his father had worn, rode with him, leaning against the back of the cab. The cold wind on his face stung, but all he could do was try to shift one way and then another, his manacled hands prevented him from turning up the collar on his denim jacket.

The courthouse in the center of Quitman was the largest building in the county. Three floors were above ground, one below. The red brick building was fronted by four white columns, beneath which a pair of double doors led to the sheriff's office. John was photographed and fingerprinted. His belt was taken from him along with his pocket knife. Owing to his age, John was placed in a cell by himself. At just a little past his 13th birthday, John was the youngest county prisoner most folks could remember. The jail was cold, but the jailer gave John an extra wool blanket and if he pulled one over his head, he could stay warm.

On his second day in jail, he received three visitors: his mother, Reverend Smith from the church and Kane Anderson, one of Quitman's two lawyers. His mother and Reverend Smith had just come from the funeral, his mother's white cast a grotesque contrast to her black mourning dress.

'Are you alright son?' May asked.

'Yes ma'am. I'm awful sorry,' he said and he began to cry.

'Shhh now, it's alright,' she replied her red-rimmed eyes overflowing with tears. John looked at his mother, tears running down through the deep bruises under her eyes, her broken arm propped on the divided table in the interview room. He felt sorry for her. He knew he had evolved from her chief source of joy, to her chief source of sorrow.

Reverend Smith led the quartet in a prayer seeking God's forgiveness. He told John that he and his congregation would continue to pray for him and that Jesus' love would assure his eternal destiny. His duty done, the reverend left May and lawyer Anderson to tend to John's earthly destiny.

'Now John, as I understand what happened,' Anderson began, 'you were attacked by your father. Is that correct?' he asked in a flat, east Texas drawl.

'Well, no sir, he attacked Mother. You can see what happened yourself,' John said nodding toward May.

'John, it's important that you listen very closely to me,' Anderson leaned forward, peering at John through his round-lensed glasses. May nodded at John as the lawyer spoke. 'Now, you were attacked by your father, isn't that right?'

John hesitated and then slowly understood. 'Yes sir, that's right. Daddy charged at me and threw me on the ground. He busted my lip,' John pointed with his cuffed hands to his still swollen lip.

'And he scared you didn't he John?' Anderson continued.

'He did. I thought he was going to beat me. He'd already beat up mother.'

'So when you hit him, you were just trying to protect yourself, to defend yourself, weren't you John?'

'Yes sir. I was. I was defending mother and me.'

Anderson looked at May and smiled.

Chapter 21

As ordered, there were now sentinels on every door, every minute of the day. As a result, guards were now standing watch more frequently and with less rest during their 24 hours of duty. The hours on their feet and the added pressure the guards now felt weakened morale. Returning home was the one thought foremost on the men's minds. Their boredom and fatigue caused shorter tempers, particularly with the prisoners. It was a commonplace occurrence to hear the GI guards shouting and even cursing at the highest ranking surviving military and civilian officials of the Third Reich. The prisoners too were growing impatient. The prison routine was wearisome as was their continued separation from their families, unchanged by the ending of the war.

With the indictments delivered, the prisoners were now formally defendants in criminal proceedings of an unprecedented nature. As such, they had the right to competent legal counsel. The week after the indictments were delivered by Major Neave, the defendants began meeting with lawyers and struggling to mount a defense against damning evidence. On the last Friday in October, Goering's attorney, Dr. Otto Stahmer and his associate *Herr* Greinke, arrived to meet with their client. Petersen and PFC Seleck escorted Goering to the interview room which had been set aside for the prisoners and their counselors.

'Good day to you LT Petersen!' Goering boomed as his cell door was pulled open. Seleck shrank back a step when Goering made eye contact with him. 'I am off to see my barrister, yes?' Goering asked.

'Yes *Reichsmarschall*,' Petersen replied with a smile, 'except that we Americans call them lawyers among other names I will not repeat.'

Goering laughed loudly. 'Excellent! I love to joke and laugh. There is not enough of that around this dreadful place. You see,' he said looking at Petersen as they walked down the steps to the basement, 'too many of my colleagues here have already given up,' Goering lapsed into a sorrowful, mocking voice. 'They have decided what they did was wrong. But I tell you in fifty years the

German people will revere us for the way we rebuilt Germany from nothing!' He pounded his right fist into his left hand.

Petersen thought about how Goering had helped reduce Germany back to nothing, but fortunately they arrived at the interview room before he could give voice to his thoughts.

Stahmer and Greinke had already arrived. Goering greeted them like long lost friends and quickly introduced Petersen. 'This is my friend LT Petersen, from Texas.' Petersen shook hands with the German lawyers, and quickly briefed them on the interview room rules. There would be no direct contact between the prisoner and his attorneys. If something needed to be handed to one from the other, a guard would inspect the item and hand it to the recipient. The guard would stand at a discreet distance; far enough away so as not to eavesdrop, close enough to respond quickly to any breach of procedures. Petersen asked Goering if he understood the rules. 'Quite clear, lieutenant,' he smiled. Petersen directed him to be seated on one side of the interview table. Seleck took up a position several feet behind the *Reichsmarschall*. 'Gentlemen,' Petersen turned to the attorneys, 'do you have any questions about the regulations we have discussed?'

'I do not,' replied Stahmer in heavily accented English. Stahmer was in his 70's, sturdily built with a florid complexion and white hair. He wore a well-tailored three piece suit and carried an expensive looking briefcase.

Greinke turned to Petersen and asked, 'To clarify a point lieutenant: if I need to hand the *Reichsmarschall* a piece of paper, must you still inspect it?' Greinke's English was polished, with very little accent. He was slightly taller than his elderly colleague and appeared to be around 30 years of age. Petersen wondered what he had been doing for the last six years.

'Yes *Herr* Greinke. We must inspect anything passed between you and the *Reichsmarschall*. Neither PFC Seleck or I read German, so we won't divulge any information which might be written on the paper.'

'Thank you lieutenant. That is quite thorough.'

With that, Petersen withdrew to the area behind the attorneys and watched as they conversed with Goering. The two sides of the table were separated by a large glass window framed by wooden sides extending up perpendicularly from the center of the table surface. The frame had wire mesh built into it so the parties on either side of the table could communicate. Twice during the session, Greinke asked Petersen to inspect and then pass to Goering a sheet of paper. Although he could understand nothing of what was passing between the attorneys and their client, Petersen could see that Goering was alternately confident and uncertain, arrogant and receptive. His blue eyes danced from Stahmer to Greinke and back. He was quick to smile and equally quick to bluster. At times, he gestured dramatically, raising his voice to almost a shout. At times, he spoke quietly and without emotion. Finally, after a monotonous 90 minutes of doing mostly nothing, Petersen was relieved to see the session draw to a close.

'Thank you LT Petersen,' said Greinke standing and latching his leather briefcase. Petersen shook hands with the two lawyers, then he and Seleck, keeping a safe distance back, escorted Goering back to the steps leading up to the cell block.

'Did things go well *Reichsmarschall*?' Petersen asked as they climbed the stairs.

Goering looked at Petersen and then back at the steps. '*Ja*, as well as can be expected. The Russians, the English, the French, they have already made up their minds you know. Only the Americans would give me a fair trial. But even a country so great as yours cannot stand against its united allies. You must be careful of the Russians. They are barbarians. They fought without decency. Soldiers, civilians, women, even children,' Goering waved his hand side-to-side, 'all the same to them. They will wait until you go home and then they intend to rule Europe.' Goering paused as they reached his cell. 'I must ask you something. Your comrades, they treat us like criminals, but you do not. Why is this?'

Petersen hesitated, his hand ready to push the heavy door closed. 'Being a prisoner is tough enough without the chickenshit.'

Goering stared at Petersen as the heavy door was closed and bolted.

Chapter 22

John Petersen's case had been the talk of Quitman, and indeed most of Wood County, for several weeks. The story of what had happened at the Petersen home that night had spread around the county like weeds, fertilized with exaggeration and embellishment. The case had been page one news and most folks knew someone who knew someone with inside knowledge about it. That Tom Petersen had been a deputy sheriff heightened the fascination for many people who were tired of reading about the county's 13% unemployment rate or the growing tensions in Europe.

In Wood County, juvenile court was heard by the district court judge, Matthew Crawford, who normally presided over these cases in his chambers. Juvenile proceedings were less formal than in open court, though a stenographer transcribed the sessions. Judge Crawford was in his late 60's. He had a stooped posture and thinning white hair. He had two suits. One, made of navy died wool, he wore in the winter. In the summer, he wore a blue-striped seersucker with frayed cuffs. With both suits, he wore a string tie. His heavy-lidded eyes suggested that he was in a constant state of drowsiness, but his quick mind and quicker temper had disabused many lawyers of that notion. The district attorney was Theodore Werner, an ambitious young man of 35, who had his sights set on higher office. He was cunning, aggressive and publicity conscious. He had recently assured his reelection by securing the death penalty in the case of a Mexican migrant worker who had robbed and killed the farmer for whom he'd been working.

John, May and lawyer Anderson stood as Judge Crawford entered, wearing his navy blue suit. They had been seated together on a leather sofa to the front right of the judge's large wooden desk. Across from them, to the front left of the desk, stood Theodore Werner and an assistant from his office.

'Please everyone have a seat,' said the judge, sucking on a peppermint and settling into his large leather chair behind the desk. The top of his desk had been cleared of everything except his

fountain pen, telephone, a legal pad and the case file.   Judge Crawford cleared his throat and nodded at the stenographer. 'This is Wood County versus John Petersen.   Let the record show those in attendance,' the judge directed the stenographer.   'Now, lady and gentlemen, this court, in a juvenile matter such as is before us today, has great leeway in determining how formal we need to be.   I want these proceedings to be understood by all present, especially young Mr. Petersen, as what we do here will decide his immediate future.   The objective of this court is to serve the county and to do what is in the best interest in the long term for Mr. Petersen.'   The judge paused and popped another peppermint into his mouth.   'The district attorney, Mr. Werner,' explained the judge looking at John, 'will present the charges and give us a summary of the case.'

Werner stood and buttoned his suit coat.   His hair was black, combed back with a part on the left side.   He had dark eyes and full lips, which some of the local ladies found appealing, if rumor was to be believed.   He also had a keen mind.   'If it please the court,' Werner began, 'the county will show that the juvenile defendant, John Adam Petersen, willfully struck in the head and caused the death of Thomas Houston Petersen, a serving law enforcement officer of this county.'

'Thank you Mr. Werner,' the judge responded.   Then, turning to Anderson he said, 'And now, Mr. Anderson, please present your opening remarks.'

'Thank you your honor,' Anderson said rising to his feet.   'We will demonstrate using the testimony of the only witnesses to this tragedy that John Petersen acted in self-defense.'   Anderson nodded to the judge and sat back down.

'Very well Mr. Werner, please present your case,' instructed Judge Crawford.

'Your honor, the file before you contains the coroner's report listing the cause of death as one or more blows to the head of the victim with a blunt object.   This blow or blows caused multiple skull fractures and significant...'

'We get the picture Mr. Werner,' interrupted Judge Crawford. 'Let's move along.'

'Yes sir. At the scene, Sheriff Cochrane and Detective Wells interviewed the defendant and Mrs. Petersen. Both admitted that the boy,' Werner pointed to John, causing him to sit back slightly on the sofa, 'beat his father to death with the butt end of a .22 caliber rifle. Both also admitted that the rifle, in fact, belonged to the boy. Your honor, the district attorney concedes that there were mitigating circumstances in this case. The victim was abusive, particularly to his wife. For that reason, we have charged Mr. Petersen with manslaughter and not murder. But your honor, that in no way justifies the taking of the victim's life. In keeping with the informal nature of this hearing your honor, the county will rest subject to your questions and discretion.'

'Thank you Mr. Werner,' the judge nodded. 'Mr. Anderson.'

Kane Anderson nodded to John. 'Your honor,' he said, 'I would like to place John under oath so that we may hear firsthand how this dreadful event took place.'

'John,' Judge Crawford said, motioning him to come forward. 'Do you swear before God that you will tell the truth, the whole truth and nothing but the truth?'

'Yes sir.'

'Good. Now come and sit here in this chair by my desk,' the judge said waving John to a straight-backed wooden chair sitting to his right. Once the boy was seated, Judge Crawford explained, 'John, Mr. Anderson is going to ask you some questions, which you have promised to answer truthfully. Once he's done, Mr. Werner has the right to ask you questions as well. Shoot,' the judge said smiling, 'I may even ask one or two questions myself. Just answer the questions as best as you can, son.' The judge nodded at Anderson.

'John, tell us what happened the night your father was killed.'

John recounted how he had gone to bed and then been awakened; how he had retrieved his rifle from under the bed and confronted his father. He recalled that his mother's arm had been broken and that her face was red and swollen from having been punched. He told about the fight and the fatal blows. The recollections were painful to both John and his mother. May sat quietly, listening, tears streaking what little makeup she wore.

John had to stop several times to blink back tears and regain his composure. Finally, Anderson finished his questions. 'That's all your honor,' he said.

Theodore Werner stood again and tugging at his cuffed sleeves, walked over to John. 'Now John,' he started, 'I want to ask you for a few details about what happened. You said you heard noises and that you immediately thought your father was beating up your mother. Is that correct?'

'Yes sir.'

'Had this ever happened before?'

'Yes sir.'

'When?'

'About two or three years ago. Daddy beat up mother pretty good and he threw me across the kitchen and broke my collar bone.'

'Was your Mom hurt badly that time?' Werner asked.

'Yes sir. She couldn't go to church for two or three Sundays because she was embarrassed about her black eyes,' John said, walking right into Werner's trap.

'She was embarrassed?' Werner probed.

'Yes sir.'

'How did that make you feel?'

'Well,' John began, 'I felt bad because of my collar bone, but I felt worse 'cause of the way he'd made Mother feel.'

'Did you do anything about it?' Werner asked casually.

'I promised I wouldn't let it happen again,' John admitted.

'Your honor!' interrupted Anderson, springing up from the sofa.

'No, Mr. Anderson,' the judge intervened, waving him back to his seat, 'this is a fair line of questions.'

'John,' resumed Werner, 'when you heard the ruckus in the kitchen, you said you came out of your bedroom with your rifle. Was it loaded?'

'Yes sir.'

'What were you planning to do with a loaded gun?'

'I planned to stop him.' John answered as Anderson looked on helplessly. 'I just wanted to protect Mother, that's all.'

'And you were going to shoot your Daddy if that's what it took?'

John looked down at his hands. He looked at his Mother's streaked face. 'If that's what it took,' he said quietly.

'So, you came out of that bedroom armed and ready to shoot didn't you John? The only reason your Daddy didn't die of a gunshot is that his training as a deputy sheriff kicked in and he was quicker than you expected.'

John sat still, his ears burning. He couldn't look at his Mother.

After a short recess, Judge Crawford turned to his court reporter and said, 'Back on the record. John, you and your Mama and Mr. Anderson please stand and face me.' The judge looked down at the file in front of him and then at his hands folded in his lap. He looked up and fixed John with a firm, though not unkind stare. 'In the State of Texas, adjudication of delinquent conduct is not the same as conviction of a crime. My responsibility here, as I said earlier, is to act in the best interests of the juvenile and to serve this county. As Mr. Werner has ably pointed out, there are unusual circumstances in this situation which argue for leniency. I concur with this view. I also agree that the infliction of bruises and broken bones, though reprehensible, is not fairly balanced by the taking of a man's life.' Judge Crawford paused and again looked down at his folded hands, a weariness weighing on the features of his craggy face. 'John, I am sending you to Gatesville State School for Boys down in Coryell County. You will remain there until you reach the age of 18 years, at which time you may, depending on your record there, be released.' May was sobbing loudly now. Anderson was pale, a stunned look on his face. John simply nodded.

Chapter 23

Al Jolson greeted Petersen as he stepped inside the little house on *Gartenstrasse*. Jolson was warbling about his 'mammy,' Robert stretched out on the sofa, reading a book. A half empty beer bottle stood just below his right hand. *Frau* Bichler, as usual, was busy in the kitchen.

'Hello Robert! *Frau* Bichler!' John called out. Both turned to greet him, Robert with a wave, *Frau* Bichler flashing a smile.

This evening's fare was sausage and potatoes, with peas on the side. John ate everything on his plate, which *Frau* Bichler appreciated. 'You like? Was *gut?*' she asked placing her hand on John's shoulder as he sat at the table.

'*Ja, es schmeckt gut!*' John laughed, enjoying her blue eyes and her attention. *Frau* Bichler's English had nearly caught up with John's German, making it possible for them to make themselves understood to each other most of the time. Of course, Robert was still there to help with any involved conversations.

'So Robert, how's business?' John asked.

'Business is good,' he replied glancing up from his own plate as *Frau* Bichler cleared away John's. Stuffing another fat chunk of sausage in his mouth, Robert said, 'We've developed quite a network. I have a couple of limeys and a couple of frogs working with me now, as well as a couple of Russians. The Brits and the French are pretty resourceful. The Russians are pretty stupid, but they've got a lot more disposable income and they make very willing customers.'

'What are the hot items?' John was curious.

'Booze is always good. And of course cigarettes are nearly the currency of the realm. We are beginning to move some medicines. The Germans are good customers for that and they pay in farm fresh food, which is otherwise pretty hard to come by,' Robert reported.

'It sounds like you are developing quite the commercial empire. Watch your back, buddy. If the CID gets hold of you, you may never see the States again.'

'You worry too much,' Robert said.

'I'd just hate to see you living next door to Goering.'

'Hey, I almost forgot,' Robert stood up from the table and stepped over to the phonograph. 'I got a new album for you today. You like Glenn Miller, right?' he asked.

'Yep,' John said.

Within in a minute, Jolson had been replaced with 'Pennsylvania 6-5000.' Robert started dancing, crossing to the kitchen and pulling *Frau* Bichler out into the middle of the room. She giggled, then laughed as Robert spun her around the floor, fairly lifting her at times to avoid mashing her feet into the floor. John stood watching, tapping time with his foot. Robert and *Frau* Bichler continued around the imaginary dance floor. As the song ended, Robert spun *Frau* Bichler right into John. Startled, John looked down at her. She smiled and held up her hands, '*Tanzen?*'

John grinned and took her hands in his, trying not to step on her tiny feet. They worked their way through 'Little Brown Jug' and partway through 'Moonlight Serenade' before they got hopelessly entangled. Laughing, John let go and facing Lisbeth, bowed lowly. She blew a strand of damp hair out of her eyes and curtsied, smiling. Lisbeth blushed and turned away, grabbing Robert's plate from the table and hurrying back to the sink. John's gaze followed her.

'Careful, boy,' Robert said softly from over his shoulder. 'Good help is so hard to find.'

Chapter 24

On November 1, Captain Stevens called Petersen into his office. 'Special assignment for you today LT Petersen.'

'Yes sir,' Petersen answered, suddenly on edge.

'You have been requested to give a VIP tour of your cell block.'

Great, just what I need, Petersen thought. 'Who's the VIP, sir?'

'General Donovan. Know him?' Stevens asked.

'I know of him sir.' Bill Donovan had been a highly decorated soldier in the first war when he commanded a battalion of the famous 'Fighting 69th' of the New York National Guard in France. A wealthy attorney, he had served as a successful prosecutor after the war. Even though he was a prominent Republican--he had stood as his party's candidate for governor attempting to succeed Franklin Roosevelt in 1932--Donovan had been tapped by President Roosevelt to form the Office of Strategic Services once war broke out. After President Truman dissolved the OSS following the surrender of the Japanese, Donovan had come to Nuremberg to assist Justice Jackson's prosecution team in preparing the case against the remaining Nazi bigwigs.

Petersen scrutinized his uniform. He wanted everything to be right, from his tie to his boots and all the way through the cell block. General officers made him nervous. Encounters with them were fraught with peril. There was no upside to a general's visit. He never came to tell you what a good job you were doing. The best you could hope for was to be no worse off after he left.

General Donovan arrived alone and on schedule at 1000 hours. He was tall, with strong features and piercing blue eyes. He was powerfully built, like an aging athlete. He had a winning smile and an easy manner.

'LT Petersen,' he said extending his right hand and catching John off guard, 'I'm Bill Donovan.' Petersen snapped to attention and saluted. Donovan stood with his hand outstretched. Confused, Petersen dropped his salute and shook Donovan's hand. Only then did Donovan return the salute. Off to a great start John, Petersen thought to himself.

He guided the general through the cell block, describing standing procedures and answering questions. The general asked about his men and about the prisoners. He asked Petersen about his training and particularly about his service in the 84th Division.

'Which cell is *Reichsmarschall* Goering's,' Donovan asked.

'Just here on the right sir,' Petersen answered pointing two doors ahead and noting that Donovan had referred to his old adversary by his rank. Donovan peered into the cell. Goering, who had been seated at the writing table, looked up. He stood up and faced the door, hands on his hips, feet spread apart: a defiant pose. Donovan held eye contact for a moment then turned away. Petersen led him downstairs where he toured the infirmary, mess hall and interview rooms. Back up on the ground floor, Donovan thanked Petersen for the tour.

'I know you have plenty to do to stay busy and VIP tours can be a pain in the ass,' the general grinned. 'Thank you for your time. If I can ever be of help to you, please let me know.' Donovan again extended his hand. This time, Petersen shook it first and then offered a crisp salute, which the general returned in kind. 'Good luck to you lieutenant!' Donovan called as he headed out the door and across the yard, back toward the palace.

Chapter 25

After months of preparation, the International Military Tribunal scheduled the trial to begin on Tuesday, November 20. That morning, the defendants were awakened as usual and marched to breakfast. Following their meal, they were allowed to put on their best clothes, then each defendant was handcuffed to a guard. The prisoners filed out of C Wing through a covered walk way, their guards walking beside them on the right. They descended a flight of steps into the basement of the Palace of Justice. In the basement, handcuffs were removed and the defendants were escorted, three at a time, up to Courtroom 600 using a small elevator.

Colonel Gaffner had mandated a new courtroom uniform for his guard force. White helmet liners and white web belts made the guards both conspicuous and authoritative. Boots were bloused and white gloves were worn. In addition, a white nightstick hung from each guard's belt, just in case there was a problem.

The defendants were seated in the dock, separated from the rest of the courtroom by a low wooden knee wall. They sat in two rows of wooden chairs facing the judges' bench, with the prosecuting attorneys sitting at tables to their right and their own defense attorneys seated at tables in front of the dock. The interpreters, using technology developed for the Tribunal by IBM, sat just behind and to the left of the dock. A witness stand, to the left of the dock, about halfway between the defendants and the judges' bench, completed the arrangements in the courtroom.

Goering sat in the end chair on the front row of the dock, from which he had the best view of the courtroom—and the courtroom had the best view of him. As he looked around, he kept a self-satisfied smile in place.

The judges, two from each of the four conquering powers filed in as everyone in the courtroom stood. The four flags of the victorious nations stood as silent sentinels behind the judges. The French, British and American judges wore robes, the Russians uniforms. The judges sat behind their high bench and the president of the court, Lord Justice Sir Geoffrey Lawrence of Great Britain, picked up his ordinary gavel to call this most extraordinary court into session. 'The Trial which is now about to begin is unique in the history of the jurisprudence of the world and it is of supreme importance to millions of people all over the globe,' Sir Geoffrey began. 'For these reasons, there is laid upon everybody who takes any part in this Trial a solemn responsibility to discharge their duties without fear or favor, in accordance with the sacred principles of law and justice.' He then directed the prosecuting attorneys to read the indictments. Each nation's prosecutors took one portion of the charges, entering them in to the record of the trial. The pace was tedious, as the speakers had been advised to speak no faster than 60 words per minute in order for the interpreters to keep up. Simultaneous translation was provided in three languages, transmitted around the courtroom through more than 500 pairs of headsets connected to the IBM system.

When Sir Geoffrey adjourned the court for lunch, Gaffner realized he had made no plans for the defendants to eat. Already on edge by the slow pace of the proceedings and the warmth in the courtroom, Gaffner grabbed Stevens by the arm and motioning for Petersen to follow, guided them outside the courtroom into the corridor. 'The prisoners must be fed,' he said to them. 'What arrangements have you made?' He looked from one to the other.

Stevens spoke first, 'Sir, we can move them back to their mess below C Wing.'

'No captain, we cannot move them back to their mess below C Wing,' Gaffner responded in a mocking voice. 'We don't have time to take them down in that little elevator. It would require too many trips and I'm not about to march this bunch through the hallways with all these reporters and strap hangers around.'

'Sir,' Petersen offered. 'What if we get some sandwiches brought up here? We could just feed them in place and we wouldn't have to move them at all.'

Gaffner rubbed his jaw as he considered the idea. 'Right,' he decided. 'Get to it. Make haste lieutenant, the clock is already ticking.'

By the time Sergeant Goodman delivered sandwiches and coffee to the courtroom, the defendants were already making the most of their predicament. They had left the dock and were lounging in the chairs at the defense tables, visiting and talking with each other as they were never allowed to do in the prison. Goering was ever the leader, moving among the defendants, telling jokes, slapping backs and offering encouragement.

The refuse from the improvised lunch had been cleared away and the prisoners were once again seated in the dock by the time the court reconvened for its afternoon session. Petersen felt he had again rescued Gaffner, just as he had done by ad libbing a physical fitness program that day for the reporters. Still, he felt a deep animosity for the way Gaffner sometimes treated him, particularly when the colonel had been drinking.

Robert was waiting when John returned that evening to *Gartenstrasse*. He had a bottle of French champagne and three glasses. 'What's all this for?' John asked.

'This? Why this is to mark the historic occasion of the opening day of the International Military Tribunal!' Robert said, pouring champagne into each glass. He handed the first glass to *Frau* Bichler, who took it, seeming uncertain as to the cause of the celebration. He handed a glass to John and took the last for himself. 'This ah is not the end, ah,' Robert raised his glass, doing his best imitation of Winston Churchill, 'it is not even the beginning of the end ah. But it is the end of the beginning! Cheers!' This, even *Frau* Bichler understood. She drained her glass as John and Robert watched, then held it out for a refill.

'My heavens,' Robert said, grabbing the bottle and pouring. With a wink to John he said, 'Dynamite in a small package.'

Roasted hare with peas and potatoes *au gratin* was the dinner menu. By the time dinner was ready, *Frau* Bichler was on her fifth glass of champagne. Once she served the two lieutenants, she pulled up a chair and sat down at the table with them. John and Robert looked at each other quizzically, then back at *Frau* Bichler. Her blue eyes flashed and she reached for the bottle, tipping it up and watching the last trickle of champagne flow into her glass. She raised the glass solemnly. '*Deutschland!*' she said. She downed the drink and brought the glass back down to the table with a loud 'smack,' whereupon she promptly slid out of the chair and onto the floor.

Robert immediately started to laugh, and doing so choked on a bite of rabbit. John had started from his chair to assist *Frau* Bichler, but now turned to Robert who was starting to turn red. John thumped Robert on the back and the bite was dislodged. Robert coughed and cursed and laughed and coughed. John leaned down over *Frau* Bichler. She appeared to be sleeping, but with a slight grin stuck on her face. She looked completely contented. John had never seen her when she wasn't busy, in constant motion, cooking or cleaning. Now, asleep, she seemed much smaller. John knelt down and carefully picked her up. He carried her across to the sofa and laid her on it. Next, he strode across the room and disappeared into his bedroom, returning a moment later with a blanket. He covered her up and went back to his supper.

'I'm afraid you've been bitten, my friend,' Robert said eyebrows arched.

'Eat your peas.'

Chapter 26

The reading of the indictments dragged on through Wednesday morning until finally, the Russian prosecutor finished reading the last of the charges. At this point, Sir Geoffrey Lawrence called upon the defendants to enter their pleas. Goering was called first. A sentinel, holding a microphone attached to a pole approached Goering who stood and began, 'Before I answer the question of the Tribunal whether or not I am guilty . . .'

Lawrence rapped on the microphone before him with his pencil, his gavel having been liberated by a souvenir seeker after the opening day's session. 'Defendants are not entitled to make a statement. You must plead guilty or not guilty.'

Goering, glowered, pouting, then said, 'I declare myself in the sense of the Indictment not guilty.'

Lawrence proceeded down the dock, calling on defendant after defendant. Hans Fritzsche, a relatively minor official from Goebbel's Propaganda Ministry who seemed out of place among the high ranking Nazis in the dock, was the last to enter his plea: not guilty.

At this point, Goering stood again. 'I do not recognize the jurisdiction of...'

Lawrence was quick to interrupt. 'You are not entitled to address the Tribunal except through your counsel.'

Petersen, from his post by the elevator door, marveled at Goering's brashness. Even though he had been hastily rebuked by the president of the court, Petersen felt the defendants straighten up and sit taller in their seats after Goering's attempt to deflect the proceedings.

The privilege of opening the case against the accused had fallen to the lead American prosecutor, Supreme Court Associate Justice Robert Jackson. Recognized by Sir Geoffrey, Jackson stood, pulled down on the hem of his formal morning coat and stepped to the podium. He arranged his notes and began, 'The wrongs which we seek to condemn and punish have been so calculated, so malignant, and so devastating, that civilization cannot tolerate their being ignored, because it cannot survive their being repeated. That four great nations, flushed with victory and stung with injury stay the hand of vengeance and voluntarily submit their captive enemies to the judgment of the law is one of the most significant tributes that power has ever paid to reason.' Petersen glanced at the press gallery where more than 200 correspondents, literally from around the world, headsets on heads, were bent over scratching notes on their pads. Jackson was a dignified presence compared to the men in the dock. He was at once solemn and articulate, projecting an aura of fairness and justice. So great was his belief in the cause of the Tribunal, that he had taken leave from his seat on the Supreme Court to lead the United States' prosecution effort.

'Either the victors must judge the vanquished or we must leave the defeated to judge themselves. After the first World War, we learned the futility of the latter course,' Jackson continued, rarely glancing at his notes.

Petersen, like the rest of the courtroom, even the defendants, was enthralled by the measured cadence of Jackson's voice, his high ideals and his eloquence. Petersen listened, absorbed, as Jackson distinguished between the accused in the dock and their countrymen. Jackson laid out with precision how the national leaders of the Third Reich would be held accountable for their misdeeds; how in this war, the leaders would not escape the hand of justice.

On the ride down in the elevator following the day's session, Goering was silent.

'Did you hear the news?' Robert asked over their supper.

'Hear it? I saw it!' John replied. 'Jackson was terrific. He had the attention of everybody in the courtroom, even crazy Hess.'

'Yes, yes,' Robert muttered, his mouth full of potatoes and waving his fork in front of him. 'But that's not the news to which I refer.'

'Okay, what news?' John decided to go along, realizing whatever the news was, it would come out sooner and with less embellishment if he just asked.

'Jackson fired Donovan.'

'You're kidding?' John stopped eating and placed his fork on his plate. This prompted a glance from Lisbeth who was already washing dishes.

'I am not,' Robert said as he continued to chew.

'What happened?'

Robert swallowed and looked at John, leaning in a little closer. 'Did you ever wonder what the chief of the OSS was doing here? I mean this isn't exactly spy stuff. It's a trial! The scuttlebutt I'm picking up is that Donovan was here to cut a deal with one of the defendants, you know, try and get one of these guys to testify against the others and blow a hole in the defense strategy.'

'What kind of deal?' John asked.

'Well, that was the interesting thing,' Robert smiled and John could see he enjoyed dishing the inside scoop. 'Usually you think about a lighter sentence: you cooperate with me and you won't do hard time—or maybe you won't do as much. But, my sources tell me that it wasn't about that. It was about the means of execution. The military defendants in particular are afraid they are going to be hanged. They'd prefer a firing squad, if you can believe that. I don't see how it makes any difference. The end result is pretty much the same.'

'Yeh, I guess so,' John nodded, remembering the strong impression Donovan made on him. 'How'd that get him fired?' John asked.

'You've seen how Jackson is: The Law as a lofty ideal. What my guys tell me is that Jackson refused to deal with any of the Nazis. He told Donovan that cutting deals was all right for the kind of criminal prosecutions Donovan was used to but that higher principles were in play here. Next day, Jackson sends him a note saying their philosophies are too far apart for him to be useful here.'

'I'll bet a major general's not used to getting brushed off like that,' John replied. 'Who are these sources of yours anyway?'

'Ah, ah, ah,' Robert smiled, wagging a finger at John. 'Confidential, my friend, confidential. Knowledge is power.'

'I thought cigarettes were power,' John teased.

'No, no,' Robert laughed, 'cigarettes are gold!'

Chapter 27

The eloquence of Jackson's opening statement quickly faded away as the prosecutors introduced reams of documents seeking to prove that Hitler and the Nazi Party had conspired between 1933 and 1939 to plan for, prepare for and then wage 'aggressive war.' Following presentation of documentary evidence concerning the annexation of Austria, during which prosecutors had read transcripts of Goering's telephone calls to Ribbentrop in Vienna, the prosecution abruptly switched tactics.

From his post near the elevator, Petersen watched as technicians set up a motion picture projector and screen. Thomas Dodd of the prosecution staff requested the court's permission to present a documentary film on the Nazi concentration camps. 'This film represents in a brief and unforgettable form an explanation of what the words "concentration camp" imply,' explained Dodd. 'We intend to prove that each of these defendants knew of the existence of these concentration camps; that fear and terror and nameless horror of the concentration camps were instruments by which the defendants retained power and suppressed opposition to their policies, including their plans for aggressive war.'

With Sir Geoffrey's permission, the lights in the courtroom were dimmed and the whirring projector shot a beam of light onto the screen. A macabre dance of images reflected off of the screen and seared the minds of spectators. Skin-covered skeletons heaped in great piles; lifeless eyes searching the heavens. Gas chambers. Crematoria. Staggering, emaciated prisoners, leaning on one another in a desperate effort to remain upright. A small mountain of naked corpses shoved by a bulldozer into a mass grave.

Some gasped; others hurriedly left the room. When the screen finally went black after close to an hour of the most hideous photographic evidence of the Nazi's bestiality, the mood in the dock ranged from anger to outrage to shame. Frank, Funk and Fritszche wept. Schacht and Doenitz turned their backs to the court, indignant that they were accused of such inhumanity. Ribbentrop appeared shaken. Even Goering, who had quite enjoyed the earlier recounting of his role in the Anschluss, was disturbed. 'That film spoiled everything,' he muttered in the elevator after the day's session concluded. Petersen was silent. He had experienced the chaos of combat. He had witnessed cruelty by both friend and foe. Yet in the death and destruction of war, he never encountered such ruthless, institutionalized horror. Petersen had been stunned by this monstrous side of the Germans and of Goering. The ride to the basement seemed much longer than normal. Petersen could not comprehend how the man beside him, who seemed to so enjoy life, could have been so callous, so evil, to have perpetrated such cruelty and misery. When the elevator door finally slid open, Goering stepped silently off, his eyes cast downward.

Chapter 28

John was silent. He did not speak from Quitman all the way to Gatesville, except in response to the deputy's instructions. Deputy Woodring was not a talkative person. He was quiet, considered less than bright by the sheriff and most of his colleagues. That's why he was frequently dispatched with one of the county's patrol cars to deliver or pick up prisoners. It was judged to be a simple task and simple seemed right up Woodring's alley.

Leaving his Mother was the most painful event John had experienced. It was even worse than the death of his father or the hearing with Judge Crawford. Sheriff Cochrane stepped out of the small interview room on the ground floor of the courthouse to let John say goodbye in private. The sheriff waited just outside the door with Woodring.

John meant to look her in the eye, but he couldn't. Her eyes were already full of tears and he knew in a moment he would start to cry. 'Mother,' he started, 'I'm sorry. I didn't mean to...' His body was racked with sobs, tears rolled down making tracks through the light fuzz on his cheeks. May pulled him close with her left arm, making shushing sounds. The lump in her throat kept her from speaking above a whisper.

'I know son, I know,' she said stroking the back of his head with her left hand. 'It's gonna be alright,' she said, sounding less than certain. He hugged her back, careful not to squeeze too hard. Then Cochrane rapped on the door with his knuckles.

The trip to Gatesville covered more than 170 miles on two lane asphalt roads. The sun was nearly down by the time Woodring wheeled the Ford past the fence and into the grounds of the Gatesville State School for Boys. They got out of the car and walked across the dusty parking lot to the office, a cold wind blowing from the west, carrying dirt and leaves toward Waco.

Once inside, Woodring pushed John down onto a hard wooden bench sitting in the corridor. 'Now sit and don't wander,' the deputy said entering the office.

Within a few minutes, Woodring returned with another man. 'That's him,' Woodring said, nodding at John and handing a clipboard to the other man.

'All right, then,' the man said, quickly signing a form and handing the clipboard back to Woodring. The deputy pulled a carbon copy of the form off the clipboard and handed it to the man.

'Merry Christmas Petersen,' he called as he left the building.

Chapter 29

The trial lumbered along with little break in the prisoners' routine. Daily, they were marched, handcuffed to guards, to the basement of the Palace. Up in the little elevator they went three-by-three to the courtroom. There they sat as tens of thousands of words were uttered into the official record, each translated into three other languages. Day after day, the prosecutors presented their cases, against Hitler's cabinet, the Nazi Party, the SS, *Gestapo*, General Staff and High Command of the German Armed Forces. At last, at the end of the day on Thursday, December 20, Sir Geoffrey Lawrence adjourned the tribunal until after the New Year.

That evening, Colonel Gaffner hosted a Christmas party at his quarters, a comfortable house about 2 miles east of the prison. Gaffner and his housemate, Colonel Thomas, who worked in the Nuremberg headquarters as one of General Watson's department chiefs, laid out an impressive spread of food and beverages. Officers and civilians from the Tribunal, supporting Army units and Colonel Thomas' colleagues from Watson's headquarters were in attendance. The civilians included a number of pretty, young women who had come to Nuremberg in support of the work of the Tribunal. The clerical work of a trial prosecuting more than 20 defendants for crimes committed over a period of a dozen years and conducted in four languages was overwhelming and would have been a hopeless task if not for the capable and dedicated assistance of the secretaries, most of whom lived together in a housing complex known as 'Girls' Town.' A blue haze of cigarette smoke hung below the ceiling, but didn't dampen the moods within the house. Months of hard work had been required to get the trial started. The long hours had continued once the court sessions had begun. Finally, the revelers had a chance to relax, if only for a couple of weeks. Gaffner was in an expansive, jovial mood, feeling the reduction of some of the pressures of his command, now that the day-to-day stress of the trial was on hiatus. He moved almost gracefully through the crowd, a drink in one hand, a cigar in the other. 'Hello Wally!' he shouted across the buzzing room to an acquaintance. He grinned and waved to a pretty woman with bright red lipstick standing by an empty bookcase. She smiled back and winked. LT Petersen was standing in a corner, holding his drink, listening to a handsome young captain relate his exploits during the Battle of the Bulge to three lovely ladies, each captivated by the tale of his bravery and the flash of his blue eyes. Petersen's attention wandered from the captain and his ladies to Gaffner, looking now more like a politician on campaign than the dour commander Petersen knew. As if he felt Petersen's stare, Gaffner turned in his direction, smiled and nodded. Petersen offered a nod and raised his glass in salute. He was disappointed when Gaffner headed toward him.

'Good evening LT Petersen,' the colonel said with his smile still in place. 'Glad you could make it. Are you having a good time?'

'Yes sir!' Petersen answered, then added 'Thank you very much for the invitation, sir.'

'Of course. You need a break from the stress of responsibility every now and then, eh,' Gaffner said leaning close to be heard over the hum in the room. 'A little holiday cheer is just the thing,' he said with a wink, clinking his glass to Petersen's. 'Just you watch out for the ladies now young man. They go nuts for real combat soldiers,' he jerked his head toward the loquacious captain, 'like you and me!' He slapped Petersen on the back and leaned in again, his breath tinged with the scent of drink, 'Have some fun and Merry Christmas!'

'Thank you sir. Merry Christmas!' Petersen replied. With that, Gaffner resumed his circuit, shaking hands, slapping backs and flirting with the girls. Petersen excused himself from the captain's small group, but no one noticed. He moved around the outside of the room, eager to leave now that his attendance had been duly noted by his host. He was moving to his left, looking to his right when he bumped into a man in a cheaply cut blue serge suit. The contact sloshed Petersen's drink over the back of his hand and onto his tunic. 'Damn it,' Petersen muttered, looking up to see with whom he had collided. 'Sorry, sir,' he said to the man.

'Hey, don't sweat it, lieutenant,' the man said. 'I'm Dan Nealy, CID,' he said extending his hand. 'I work out of the Provost Marshall's office in General Watson's headquarters.' The CID, or Criminal Investigation Division, was the Army's detective agency. CID agents, they never identified themselves by rank, were authorized to investigate crimes committed under Army jurisdiction.

'Nice to meet you sir,' Petersen said. He introduced himself, wished Nealy a Merry Christmas and resumed his search for a back door, the front being too conspicuous for such an early exit. Gaffner's house was much larger than the one he shared with Simmons, with plenty of doors off a long hallway. Disoriented by the noise, the smoke and the jostling bodies, Petersen decided to take a chance on the last door on the right. He cracked it open and stepped inside. Immediately, he realized he had made a mistake. Ten feet away he saw the silhouette of a man's back and heard the sound of heavy breathing and the rustle of clothing. He stood still, silently figuring a way out without interrupting the amorous scene upon which he'd blundered. The man's arms were around a woman, her skirt pushed up around her hips.

'Stop!' For a split second, he thought he had been discovered, then realized the woman had spoken, but not to him.

'Let's just have a little fun,' the woman said.

'Oh c'mon doll,' Petersen heard Gaffner's voice pleading, 'this will be fun.'

'I said "Stop!"' the voice said again, louder this time and more emphatic.

'Give in, will you. It's Christmas for chrissakes!' Gaffner said, frustration in his voice. Petersen was frozen, afraid to stay, afraid to go, afraid to breathe.

'Ouch,' the woman cried, bringing up her hand and slapping Gaffner hard on his face.

Petersen felt this was his chance. He grabbed the door handle and cracked the door slightly opened.

'Ow! You little bitch!' Gaffner growled. Petersen slipped through the cracked door and into the hallway. He quickly retreated toward the living area and the crowd. He reached the front door, knowing Gaffner was in no position to notice, or even care about his departure. Looking back, he saw the pretty young woman with the bright red lipstick emerge from the hallway, straightening her skirt and looking to see if anyone noticed.

Chapter 30

Colonel Gaffner had determined that Christmas would be a typical day at the prison. There would be no special meals and no gifts. The only concessions he made to the holiday were for religious services, both Protestant and Catholic.

So it was that Petersen accompanied thirteen of the Protestant defendants to a Christmas Eve service in the basement mess hall of the prison. Chaplain Gerrity, in his basic German, read the Christmas story from the Gospel of Luke. The prisoners, sitting around four tables, listened attentively, occasionally nodding. Following the reading, Gerrity prayed. 'Almighty God, creator and sustainer of the universe, we beseech Thee to look upon us, to move us in this time and at this place toward a fuller reconciliation with Thee and with our fellow men. Grant that the spirit of Bethlehem be felt here in Nuremberg, indeed across this shattered continent and to the far corners of Your Earth. Grant that the spirit incarnate in our Lord and Savior Jesus Christ be felt in the hearts of all men and that this Christmastime herald a new age of peace on Earth and goodwill to men. For it is in the name of that Babe in the manger that we pray, Amen.'

Petersen noticed tears in the eyes of several of the defendants and even a couple of the guards. Next, Gerrity led his small congregation in a hymn. Most of the men sang along, albeit reservedly. Except for Goering. The *Reichsmarschall*, who sat on the front bench of the front table, belted out the hymn with the gusto with which he once sang the '*Horst Wessel Lied*.'

After Chaplain Gerrity's benediction and dismissal, the prisoners began their march back up the stairs, the spirit of the holiday diminishing with each step toward their cells. These men would not enjoy the home fires, nor would they receive family visits. For them, Christmas, the first peaceful one since 1938, would be a long day of reflection.

Goering drew even with Petersen as they reached the cell block. 'Merry Christmas to you LT Petersen,' he said with the familiar twinkle in his blue eyes and a contented smile on his lips.

'Merry Christmas to you *Reichsmarschall*,' Petersen responded as they reached Goering's cell.

'Here,' Goering said, holding out his closed fist. He opened it to reveal a small gold pocket watch. 'A small Christmas present from an old soldier.'

Petersen took the watch and turned it over in his hands. On the back was inscribed 'HWG.' 'Thank you *Reichsmarschall*. This is very nice. I am afraid wishing you a Merry Christmas may sound a little hollow.' Petersen hesitated, searching for the right words. 'I wish circumstances were different.'

Goering thrust out his hand and Petersen took it. 'As do I lieutenant; as do I.' Goering dropped his gaze, turned and entered his cell. The door was closed and the bolt slid home.

For the Christmas Eve meal at 22 *Gartenstrasse*, Simmons had acquired a goose. It was too large for the small stove, but *Frau* Bichler was nothing if not resourceful. She had trimmed the bird to make it fit and its delicious aroma, combined with the heat of the stove, created a wonderful Christmas atmosphere in the little house. Simmons had also provisioned the house with a supply of egg nog, which he and *Frau* Bichler were already well into by the time Petersen arrived home.

'Ho, Ho, Ho!' John called as he entered. 'Boy, it smells good in here!' he said making eye contact with *Frau* Bichler.

The three of them sat down to dinner together, a habit they had gradually fallen into since the night of the champagne. *Frau* Bichler continued to function as their paid servant, but the lieutenants had come to enjoy the company of this pretty, diminutive woman, never more so than during the holiday season.

Over the excellent goose and its trimmings, John described the worship service. Robert offered brief translations, so that Lisbeth could participate in the conversation. John told of the scripture reading and Gerrity's heartfelt prayer. When he described Goering's singing, the others laughed. When he pulled out the watch, they gasped. With wide eyes, Robert and then Lisbeth held the watch, turning it over in their hands, tracing the inscription with their fingers. Lisbeth's eyes moistened as she held the watch. She was uncharacteristically quiet and still. When she sensed the others watching her, she attempted a smile and handed the watch back to John. She spoke and Robert translated.

'She says that her husband thought of Goering as a hero and a great man,' Robert relayed. 'Now look at what has happened to him. Look at what has happened to all of us.'

With that, she stood up from the table and began to clear away the dishes. The two lieutenants sat silently for a moment, the difference between the victors and the vanquished as stark, if only for a moment, as on the field of battle. Then they stood and began to help Lisbeth clean up.

'Tell her we'll finish, Robert. Tell her to go home now before it gets any later,' John said. Robert dutifully translated and within a few minutes Lisbeth was bundled up at the door ready to walk home.

'Before you go,' Robert said and reached under the table. He pulled out a breadbox-sized package wrapped in plain brown paper and handed it to Lisbeth. Robert and John had put together a package of canned ham, a couple of cartons of cigarettes and some Scotch Whiskey, along with some chewing gum and Hershey bars. And one pair of nylons. 'Merry Christmas.'

For the second time, Lisbeth's eyes filled with tears. '*Fröhliches Weihnachten*,' she said. Stretching up on her tiptoes, she kissed Robert on his cheek. She placed her hand on John's forearm and kissed him on the cheek as well. She stepped out the door and disappeared into the cold night.

John and Robert sat at the kitchen table munching on the remains of their dinner, each nursing a cold beer. 'I almost forgot,' John said, standing. He went into his bedroom and Robert heard him opening drawers. He reappeared in a minute with a small bundle in his hand. 'I didn't wrap it,' John said, 'but I thought you'd like it.' He handed over an object wrapped in an old shirt.

The object was heavy. Robert unwound the shirt to find himself holding a Luger pistol. He turned it over carefully in his hands, rubbing his fingers along its smooth barrel and breathing in its oily scent. 'Wow, John,' he stammered. 'This is ...' for once, Robert Bentley Simmons was at a loss for words.

'Merry Christmas, roomie,' John said giving his friend a squeeze on the shoulder. 'Not many Yalies will have a Luger in their dorm room,' he smiled, satisfied that his gift was both unexpected and prized.

'Thanks John,' Robert replied weighing the pistol's heft in his right hand. 'This is the most fantastic present I've ever gotten. Wow!' he repeated to himself. 'Hey, you wait right here,' Robert said excitedly. 'I didn't wrap your present either, so close your eyes.' Robert crossed the room, glancing back to ensure John's eyes were closed. 'No peeking, now,' he warned. He entered his bedroom. 'Keep 'em closed,' he called coming back toward the kitchen.

John heard a 'thunk' and opened his eyes to find Robert standing with one hand resting on the top of a handsome mantel clock. It was about 2 feet long and 10 inches high with a round, champagne colored face defined by black hands and black Roman numerals.

'Robert, it's beautiful,' John said when he opened his eyes. He moved around his chair and ran his hand along the curved wooden sides of the clock. He gently lifted it, feeling the weight of its movement.

'It's Swiss,' Robert beamed, proud that his present seemed so pleasing to his friend.

'It's really nice,' John said with a devilish twinkle in his eye. Then turning back toward Robert added, 'but I've already got a watch.'

Robert's eyes widened and his mouth started to form words, but John couldn't keep a straight face and burst out laughing.

'I should have known better than to get you something nice,' Robert feigned disgust. 'Now you'll forever be asking me to tell you what time it is when the big hand is on the XII and the little hand is on the V!'

John wound his new clock and he and Robert carefully lifted it to the mantel over the small fireplace. Even with their bedroom doors closed, John and Robert could hear its steady tick-tock, tick-tock.

119

Chapter 31

The routine at Gatesville didn't change much over the holidays. The boys did not work on Christmas Day, which was traditionally set aside for family visits. Some of the boys, non-violent offenders with track records of good behavior, were granted furloughs for the holidays and were actually able to hitch hike home for three days. Boys exhibiting behavior problems or deviancies spent the holidays just like every other day, on closely supervised work details or in class. It was the same with new boys.

The boys were separated by age group. Boys up to the age of 13 were housed together in one two-story, open-bay barracks. They slept on bunk beds, a footlocker on either end containing each boy's coveralls, underwear, socks, school books and a Bible issued by the State of Texas. Their day began at 6 a. m. when the trustees moved through the barracks shouting, blowing their whistles and banging on trash cans and bunks with their sticks. The boys were marched to breakfast in their coveralls and school issue boots where they were served eggs, grits, biscuits, molasses and milk, much of which was produced on the school's farm. Maintenance period followed breakfast. During this hour, the boys mopped, cleaned, painted and repaired their barracks under the supervision of the trustees. Next, they marched to chapel, where the superintendent, Mr. Wallace, led them in the pledge of allegiance and the Lord's Prayer, before he presented a daily devotional. Chapel was also the time for administrative announcements, like the infrequent changes to the schedule or the anticipated arrival of a visiting politician. After chapel, the boys separated into their work groups. Here, the boys were mixed with all ages working together, the idea being that a work group of only younger boys would not be as capable as one which contained at least a cadre of older boys. The boys were marched to lunch at noon and then spent the next three hours in class. Academics were basic, focusing on reading, writing and arithmetic. An athletic period spanned the time between the end of classes and the start of the evening meal. Supper was served at 6 p. m. The boys studied until 9:30, then the doors were closed, the gates locked and the lights turned out until the whole cycle started again the next morning. This was the routine six days a week. Only on Sunday did the boys get a break from the routine, and then only after church service and lunch. Sunday afternoons they could visit the small library, play ball on the athletic field or in the gym and, on special occasions, listen to the radio over the loudspeakers in the auditorium.

By Christmas Day, John had been a ward of the State of Texas for only nine days--the longest nine days of his young life. He was used to life on the farm, to the open air, the sky above and the freedom of working on his own. He had spent most days outside, exploring or hunting. He had his chores to be sure, but had plenty of time after they were completed to venture out. Now, his every movement was watched, supervised, regulated. The food was dismal. The work was endless, the academics unchallenging. But the nights were the worst. Instead of the warm kitchen and his mother's home cooking, instead of Fibber McGee *or* Gangbusters *on the radio, he dined on the school's starchy institutional diet and fell asleep in a long open bay listening to the sounds of snoring and sobbing boys.*

Christmas Day wasn't too bad, falling on a Sunday. The boys were allowed to sleep until 7. Church service was Protestant and started at 9, after a typical breakfast. Church consisted of Bible study, singing, praying and a sermon, presented by one of several visiting preachers. On Christmas, the preacher was a special guest minister brought in from the Baptist college in Waco, some 35 miles away. He delivered a message filled with the love of God for wayward mankind, a love so great He had sent His only Son to deliver us from ourselves. Halfway through the sermon, Burrel Earle leaned over to John and whispered, 'I bet not even Jesus Christ himself loves Peavey.' John reckoned that Burrel, a 13-year-old from Galveston, was wiser than he had previously realized.

Shadrach Peavey was about the vilest human being with whom John had ever come in contact. Peavey was one of the trustees, at the moment the closest trustee, sitting on the end of the

*row, just five boys distant from where John sat. As the preacher
droned on and John's butt numbed, he stole an occasional glance
at Peavey, who seemed to be completely under the minister's spell.
Peavey had a beak of a nose, stringy, greasy hair and a face pock-
marked with pink scars. His eyes were watery and blood-shot. But
his most defining features were his teeth: crooked and brown from
the ever present wad of tobacco he kept in his bulging jaw. Even
in church, Peavey carried his spit can, making surreptitious
deposits at frequent intervals.*

*Peavey's physical repulsiveness, which included a pungent
personal scent, was complemented by his sarcastic personality.
He was uniformly loathed by the boys over whom he flaunted his
authority. He was quick to embarrass, humiliate and even beat
them, as John had already observed. That he was humorless and
ignorant, a sycophant and a bully only added to their disdain.*

*Monday, December 26, was a work day at Gatesville. Boys
who had been granted furloughs had until 6 p. m. to sign in at the
superintendent's office, thinning the ranks of the work groups that
went out that morning. Peavey and Masters, a particularly dim-
witted trustee, supervised a group of ten boys, which included both
John and Burrell. It was a gray, cold day in central Texas and the
boys were wearing their blue jackets and caps over the coveralls.
Their task this particular morning was to repair a livestock pen on
the school's farm.*

*They marched the half mile to the farm, carrying a set of post-
hole diggers, wire cutters, heavy staples, hammers and a roll of
barbed wire. Every few steps, Peavey let fly a stream of thick,
brown spit, leaving a trail of liquid tobacco in the wake of the
small procession. 'Come on me lads,' he drawled between spits,
'pick up the pace. You ain't got all day' which was technically
true. But, since classes had been suspended until after New Year's
they certainly had most of it. 'Earle,' Peavey barked, 'put your hat
on your head straight-like, like you s'posed to!' Burrell quickly
righted his cap and said, 'Yes sir, boss.'*

*The pen was located just outside a small barn and was used to
collect the school's milk cows before they were ushered in for their*

twice daily milkings. This morning's task was to replace the wire along the western side of the pen. It was badly rusted with one of the strands broken. 'Awright, you boys,' Peavey pointed to John and Burrell, 'get about taking off the old wire. The rest of you start laying out the new wire.' As he watched his crew begin its job, Peavey reached into his mouth and pulled out what looked like a small turd, absently hurling it off to his left.

'Hey!' shouted Timmy Moore, the back of whose head stopped the brown lump in mid-flight. Timmy whirled around, 'What the hell do you...' he stopped in mid-sentence when he realized it was Peavey who had launched the missile.

'What's a matter with you boy?' Peavey snapped, stepping toward Timmy aggressively, his hand already reaching for the switch at his belt. 'You got somethin' to say?' Peavey's rheumy eyes gleamed with malevolence, his lips pulling back to reveal his evil, brown grin.

'No sir, boss,' Timmy said timidly, turning back toward his task. But, it was too late. Peavey swung his switch, catching Timmy across his right shoulder. 'Don't you give me no damn lip, boy. You just do your work. Yo' mama ain't here to cuddle you up and I ain't either. Now get to work!'

Timmy choked back his sobs and began rolling out the barbed wire, holding the roll on a small dowel and stepping backwards as another boy held the wire's end.

'Mr. Peavey, sir,' John spoke up attempting to deflect Peavey's attention away from Timmy.

'What is it boy?' Peavey turned, his face a red mask of anger.

'Sir, a couple of these posts are rotted and need to be replaced.'

Peavey looked at the posts in question and, agreeing, sent two of the boys to the wood shop to fetch new ones. On alert now, the other boys worked diligently, pulling out the old staples and laying the new wire along the fence line. John and Burrell began rocking the rotted posts back and forth to loosen them. In the process, one of the posts snapped in two. John lost his balance and fell backwards, prompting peals of laughter from Peavey and Masters.

John got up, dusted himself off and removed his jacket. He picked up a shovel to dig around the base of the stubborn post.

'Now wait a minute me lad,' Peavey chuckled. 'I don't recall giving permission to ground your jacket,' he snarled.

'Mr. Peavey, sir,' John stammered hoping to get away with his mistake, 'if you please sir, may I remove my jacket?'

'Why that's real sweet of you to ask Mr. Petersen,' Peavey began with mock tenderness. 'Now you put that damn jacket right back on and don't presume no liberties with me again, lest you want to take it up with this here switch o' mine,' Peavey replied belligerently, shaking the switch in John's face.

'Yes sir, boss,' John said, pulling his jacket back on.

'I dee-clare,' Peavey ruminated to Masters running a dirty hand through his stringy hair, 'I don't know what's come over these lads. You'd think it was Christmas or the like.' This brought another brown toothed grin from Peavey, pleased by his own wit, and another loud laugh from Masters, who was just happy to be part of the fun.

By the time the two boys returned with the new posts, the entire work crew was on edge, eager to be done with their task and be on their way back to the barracks.

The posts were seated in the newly dug holes and the dirt packed back tightly around them. The wire was stapled into place and the boys set about cleaning up their work site, picking up their tools, the old rusted wire and the remnants of the replaced posts.

'Now just a minute here lads,' Peavey began, with a wink toward Masters. 'Seems to me that wire ain't very tight.' The boys all looked back at the wire, which did sag a bit, but which still looked more than equal to the task of containing placid milk cows. 'I think you all had better try again, only this time, stretch that wire before you nail it in place.'

'Mr. Peavey, sir,' Burrell replied before John could stop him, 'stretch it with what? We ain't got no come along and we ain't got no work gloves.'

'Well my lad,' Peavey leered, 'guess you'll just have to use your hands now won't ye?'

The boys looked at each other. Burrell turned to John with wide eyes and a worried expression. 'Go on,' John whispered from the side of his mouth opposite Peavey. 'You get one end and I'll take the other. And good luck.' John directed two of the boys to remove the new staples and divided the rest of the crew in half. 'Now be careful of the barbs,' he warned. 'Get a good grip.'

The boys, arrayed on either side of the strand of wire, pulled against each other like competitors in a cruel tug of war. 'Jerry,' John called out to the boy with the hammer, 'nail it up! Quick.' Before Jerry could nail the wire in place, the inevitable happened. One of the younger boys lost his footing, falling into the boy behind him. The result resembled a row of dominos, except that this row was still clutching a wire adorned with razor-like barbs. As the barbs tore through the boys' unprotected hands, a collective wail went up. John, the anchor at his end of the line, escaped with minor scratches. The boys in between him and Burrell had nastier wounds, ranging from deep scratches to wide slashes across their palms and fingers.

'Shit!' John cried, once again pulling off his jacket. He quickly wound it around Timmy Moore's ripped, bleeding hands as an improvised bandage.

'Stop boy!' Peavey shouted, charging forward. 'I done tol' you once: now put your damn coat back on!'

John's anger overcame his better judgment and he whipped his head toward Peavey, keeping the jacket firmly wrapped around the bawling Timmy's hands. 'You idiot,' John cried, 'how could you be so stupid that you didn't see this coming. Shut up and go get help!'

Peavey stared at John dumbfounded, a thin trickle of tobacco juice leaking from the corner of his mouth. He stood still as a statue for a moment, the color deserting his face, his eyes staring as if in a trance. Then in a flash, he raised the switch in his left hand and brought it crashing down across John's neck and shoulders. A second blow caught John on the side of his head, making his ears ring and his eyes water. Peavey reared back a third time as John fell, writhing in the dirt. As Peavey swung,

Masters stepped in front of him and arrested the downward arc of the switch.

'Enough,' Masters said as Peavey's wild eyes came back into focus.

Chapter 32

Three days after Christmas it snowed. Roads, upon which there had been little traffic before, except for the endless stream of refugees and displaced persons, were impassible while the snow continued to fall. *Frau* Bichler nevertheless trudged daily through the snow to attend to the cooking, cleaning and laundry at 22 *Gartenstrasse*. She usually arrived around 0800 and began cleaning and washing. In the early afternoon, she walked to the market district, buying for herself a simple lunch and procuring the food and other supplies that would be needed for the lieutenants' supper and her duties for the following day. Upon returning to the house, *Frau* Bichler would get to work preparing the main evening meal, the only one which she prepared every day, both lieutenants having breakfasted before her morning arrival.

Things had been slow both at the prison and in the palace. Much of the Tribunal staff had taken a few days off to travel to Paris, Rome or other cities better supplied than Nuremberg. Still others had managed to finagle a trip back to the States. Lieutenants generally did not have access to such luxuries as travel to exotic capitals, so Petersen and Simmons simply enjoyed *Frau* Bichler's cooking, not exotic, but far better than either of them would have been able to produce on his own. The three of them had fallen into the habit of eating together in the evening, although except for the night of the champagne, *Frau* Bichler did not linger at the table for the after supper drinks. On this night, the menu was hard rolls, sausages, potatoes and mustard.

Frau Bichler was not her normal, vivacious self. She was quiet, responding only when addressed and then seemingly without giving it her full attention. John thought she was withdrawn. Robert too noticed a difference.

'*Ist alles* OK?' Robert asked after she had put the meal on the table and assumed her seat.

She looked up and focused on Robert, 'Oh, *doch, ja.*'

The two lieutenants exchanged brief glances and then began to eat. *Frau* Bichler sat quietly, taking an occasional, if tiny bite of food. Her face was blotched and flushed. She was detached, the usual twinkle missing from her blue eyes.

She put the back of her hand to her forehead and, for a moment seemed to lose balance. John started and reached out to steady her. 'No, no,' she mumbled. John took her hand. He looked at Robert. 'She's on fire,' he said, a note of worry in his voice. Robert stood up and laid the palm of his hand on her forehead. He looked at John and nodded in agreement. Speaking gently to *Frau* Bichler, Robert led her to the sofa. John brought a wool blanket from his bedroom. *Frau* Bichler kicked off her shoes and stretched out, pulling the blanket up to her chin as she gave a little shiver.

John found some aspirin and poured some water into a glass. She took the pills and washed them down, nodded her thanks and closed her eyes.

By the next evening, Lisbeth was no better. She was still feverish and had developed dark circles under her eyes. She could not, or would not sit up and she had no appetite, even when John brewed some tea borrowed from Major Neave.

'I'm a little worried about her,' John said as he and Robert sat across the room at the table. They were munching on sandwiches. Neither had the will to cook while Lisbeth lay sick. 'Can you get her some medicine through your contacts?'

'I can, as you know, get anything we might need, short of Doris Day's phone number,' Robert answered. 'But, truthfully John, getting medicine would take a couple of days, even if I knew the right medicine to acquire.'

John rubbed his temples with the fingertips of each hand. 'I've got an idea,' he said.

'Good evening, sir,' Sergeant Hottle greeted LT Petersen when he walked back into C Wing. 'What brings you back to the Waldorf on such a cold and snowy evening?'

'Actually,' Petersen began, 'I'm looking for the doctor.'

Hottle checked his wrist watch. 'Let's see, yes sir, he should be done with his evening rounds. He's probably back in the infirmary by now.'

Dr. Schuster checked each prisoner nightly, administering sleeping pills to those who needed them. As Sergeant Hottle had guessed, he was already back in his infirmary by the time Petersen reached the basement.

'Ah, a pleasant surprise,' the old doctor said with a smile as Petersen knocked on his open door. The doctor had taken off his coat and was seated at his desk putting away the supplies left over from his day's activities.

'*Herr* Doctor,' Petersen began plaintively, seizing Schuster's attention, 'I need to ask a favor; a favor of some discretion.' Schuster smiled benignly. His mind pictured several scenarios in which a young officer might need discreet medical attention, each of which might provide a delightful distraction from his current routine. The doctor turned in his chair to face the young lieutenant.

'How can I assist you?' he asked in his most dignified, professional manner.

Robert was still seated at the table when John arrived back at the house with Dr. Schuster in tow. He had been keeping watch over Lisbeth, who had been sleeping fitfully. John introduced Robert and the doctor, then led Schuster over to the sofa. The doctor quickly shed his scarf and overcoat, handing them to Robert who laid them across the back of a chair. John pulled another chair over for the doctor to sit on.

'Please get me a glass of water,' Schuster said. He opened his black bag and took out a thermometer, which he gave three quick and vigorous shakes. He gently woke Lisbeth and spoke to her in their shared tongue.

He glanced back over his shoulder and said, 'Gentlemen, if you will excuse us, please.' The two lieutenants recognized immediately that this was not a request. They removed themselves to Robert's bedroom and closed the door.

Schuster read the thermometer. He pulled his stethoscope out of the bag and unbuttoned the top buttons of Lisbeth's blouse. She looked into his lined face as he listened to the sounds of her breathing and her heart. He gave her the glass of water and commanded that she drink it. He used a small penlight to check her eyes, ears and throat. He asked her questions to which her inflamed throat croaked out answers.

Dr. Schuster rummaged around in his bag looking for the right medicine. He pulled out a small bottle of clear liquid and from it filled a syringe. He helped Lisbeth remove her blouse and gave her an injection in her upper arm. He patted her on the shoulder, pulled the blanket up to her chin and told her to go back to sleep.

'*Danke Herr Doktor,*' she whispered.

'Once again, LT Petersen, you have summoned my help at the right moment,' the doctor reported as Petersen walked him back through the frigid darkness to the prison. They crunched along on the frozen snow, their steps crackling, their breath billowing as white fog. 'I believe your friend has strep throat. Careful that you do not contract it yourself as it is contagious, especially,' he raised an eyebrow, looking sideways at Petersen, 'among people living in close contact.'

'She's our *haus frau, Herr Doktor,*' Petersen corrected.

'Of course. At any rate, within a few days she should be much better. I have given her a new drug that your Army uses to treat infections. It is a real life saver I am told. It should be more than enough to help your frie... *haus frau* back to health.'

'I cannot thank you enough for helping us, Dr. Schuster,' Petersen said. 'She takes very good care of LT Simmons and me. I'm not sure how we would get by without her. She has no family around here and she has no one to look after her.'

The old doctor stopped in the snow and turned toward Petersen. He smiled his gentle smile and said, 'Of course she does, LT Petersen. She has you.'

Chapter 33

Slowly but steadily Lisbeth's health improved. Within a couple of days of Dr. Schuster's nocturnal visit, she was back on her feet, the dark crescents beneath her eyes fading away. As she felt better, her happy personality returned and her energy level improved noticeably.

Daily, Petersen would stop by the doctor's prison infirmary and give a brief report on her progress. The old doctor would nod and, satisfied that she was recovering, would advise Petersen to ensure she continued to rest and drink water.

As an added bonus, electricity was restored to the block during the last week of the year. No longer did the household have to function by lamp light.

At night, John and Robert would take turns serving Lisbeth who would do her best to eat whatever they had overcooked. By the end of the week following Schuster's visit, Lisbeth was back to normal, cleaning, shopping and cooking.

John arrived at the house at 1900 hours on Thursday. The New Year had started, and with it the familiar routine of the prison and the trial were back. The weather was still very cold, but had been clear for two days. The warmth of the sun was melting snow, only to have it refreeze overnight. The results were slick roads and walkways and a civilian population even more miserable and at risk of disease for lack of adequate housing and heating.

John hung up his overcoat and went into his bedroom where he unlaced his boots. He slipped a pair of old sandals on over his wool socks, giving his feet a chance to breathe. Lisbeth stopped her work in the kitchen and knocked on the frame of John's open door.

'Hello Lisbeth,' John said, looking up with a smile.

'*Guten Abend Herr* John,' she said. She stood leaning against the door frame. She was slimmer than the last time John had noticed her figure. Probably due to not eating for a week, he told himself. Her blue eyes looked away for a moment, as if she was trying to decide something. Having apparently made her decision, she looked John in the eyes and said, 'I thank you for to call the doctor for my sick.'

'You are welcome,' John said, suppressing a smile. He was amused by her English and touched by her thanks. 'I am glad you feel *besser, ja*?' he smiled.

'*Ja, besser*,' Lisbeth beamed.

The front door crashed open, startling them both. Robert staggered in, struggling under the weight of a large brown package. 'Hello John! Hello Lisbeth!' he called out, wrestling his load over to the table. 'Come and look at this!' He looked up and saw John standing in his bedroom, just beyond Lisbeth. Lisbeth, who still had one hand resting on the door frame, had turned to watch Robert. 'Oh,' Robert stammered, 'I'm sorry! Jeez, I'll just...'

'Robert it's OK,' John said blushing. 'Lisbeth was just thanking us for getting Dr. Schuster to come.'

'Oh, of course, of course. Look, look at this beauty,' Robert returned his attention to the oversized package. He gently began to peel away the brown paper wrapping to reveal a Blaupunkt radio.

'Whoa!' whistled John. 'Very nice! Where did you...' he stopped.

Robert's eyes were glowing with pride. 'One of my better deals John, one of my better deals. Watches John. You have no idea how these tiny time pieces appeal to the Slavic races!'

John and Lisbeth had both come over to the table and were inspecting the dials and cabinet of the radio set.

'What's the big deal about a watch?' John asked, peering at the tuning dial.

'It's not a watch,' said Robert.

'You just said you got this for a watch,' John reminded his friend, glancing at Robert.

'It's not a watch,' Robert repeated. 'It's a status symbol! These Russians are all peasants. Peasants don't wear watches; they tell time from the position of the sun. They don't need watches. Hell, half of them have never even seen a clock, much less one they can wear on their wrist!' Robert was on a roll. 'They have no middle class, only the rulers and the workers. They have this huge army over here and they're all getting paid with the occupation currency the Russians print. They've got more money than they know what to do with and they have to spend it here. They aren't allowed to take it home. So these poor slobs see watches and feel the cash in their pockets and presto: a bull market in chronological apparatuses.' He paused for breath, eyes twinkling, a wide smile splitting his moon-shaped face. 'If I just had a Mickey Mouse watch,' he dreamed aloud, 'I could trade it for a life time's supply of beluga caviar!'

'A supply of what?'

'Fish eggs, John, fish eggs.'

'But why would you want…'

'Never mind, my friend,' Robert waved the question away. 'Grab that end.' Together, John and Robert lifted the radio off the table and set it down gently on a small chest of drawers pushed against the wall. Robert plugged the set in and turned it on, waiting impatiently for it to warm up. Lisbeth seemed as interested as the two lieutenants. She stood beside John, her hand resting casually on his shoulder, as he leaned over and adjusted the tuning. After a couple of minutes, the trio began to hear static, an occasional whistle and pop. Then, John detected a signal. It was the AFN station broadcasting big band music from the Grand Hotel.

'Ah,' Lisbeth smiled, clapping her hands. She grabbed Robert's hands, pulling him to the middle of the room and they began to dance to a polka. When the music paused, she switched partners, coaxing a protesting John out onto their private dance floor. The music resumed and Doris Day began to sing 'Sentimental Journey.' As the tempo slowed, John pulled Lisbeth closer, until their bodies brushed against each other. She looked up to discover he was looking at her. She tried to smile, but found herself looking down, and then resting her head against his shoulder.

Chapter 34

The trial droned on with a cadre of prosecutors continuing the cases against the various organizations of the Nazi machinery. Daily, the defendants were handcuffed to a guard, marched to the Palace, uncuffed, stuffed into the elevator and hoisted to Courtroom 600. There they sat day-after-day as American, British, French and Russian prosecutors submitted document-after-document into the trial's record. The documents, which had been translated from German into French, Russian and English, painted a damning picture of the organizations, and their many members, the more prominent of whom now sat in the dock.

As they marched the prisoners back to the jail, generally around 1730 hours each day, Petersen could see the slumping shoulders, anxious expressions and shuffling gaits that betrayed the defendants' collective dismay.

On Saturday, with the trial in recess for the weekend, the prisoners' routine once again included exercise in the yard between C Wing and the gymnasium. A gray, cold day with low clouds reflected the attitudes of the prisoners. Petersen was in the yard watching the prisoners along with a squad of guards. Another group, led by Sergeant Hottle, was searching the cells for contraband.

'Hello Lieutenant,' Goering called as he strolled by in the course of his circuit about the grounds.

'Good afternoon, *Reichsmarschall*,' Petersen said falling into step with Goering, but maintaining a noticeable distance between them. 'I hope you are well.'

'Well? As well as can be any man on trial by his conquerors in a court of convenience,' Goering laughed darkly. 'But, yes, I am well.' They walked on a short distance, the cool air bringing color to their cheeks. 'I am different than the rest of my colleagues,' Goering said.

'Yes sir, I've noticed,' Petersen replied, bringing a smile and small chuckle from the *Reichsmarschall*.

'I have no illusions about the outcome here,' Goering continued, thrusting his hands in his pockets. 'I am the last of the leaders of the Third Reich. The British, the French, especially the Russians and even you Americans must have what you call a scapegoat. You must have someone to point to and say 'he is responsible and so he must pay.' I am to be your scapegoat. My colleagues here,' he gestured toward the other prisoners trudging around the perimeter of the bare yard, 'did not share my position of authority in the Third Reich and therefore do not share my notoriety in the courtroom. They still cling to some faint hope that they will emerge from this trial with their lives spared. I do not believe in such fantasy.'

Petersen looked over at Goering to see the *Reichsmarschall* staring at the ground, his face void of expression.

'LT Petersen,' he resumed, 'I have a small favor to ask of you.' Petersen met Goering's eyes. 'I have a young daughter. She is eight, a delightful child. I fear that I will never see her again.' He paused. 'Would you mail a letter to her from me?'

'*Reichsmarschall,* can't you send letters?' Petersen asked, eager to avoid the potential pitfalls of granting Goering's request.

'Yes, but our letters are all read and censored. Some thoughts a man wishes to keep private, to share only with those for whom they are intended. You understand this?'

'Yes sir,' Petersen said. 'Wouldn't it be easier to give the letter to *Herr* Stahmer or *Herr* Greinke?'

'This I am not allowed to do,' Goering replied, maintaining his measured pace. 'I cannot pass any items to my barristers. What I think I can do is to give the letter to Dr. Schuster when he makes his evening rounds to dispense our sleeping pills. You could obtain the letter from the doctor and no one would be any wiser, as they say.'

'All right,' Petersen relented, figuring the risk was minimal and understanding at least in part the loneliness of his prisoner. 'I'll get the letter from the doctor once he gets it from you.'

'Thank you LT Petersen,' Goering said. 'You have a soldier's strength, and his compassion.'

Three days later, Dr. Schuster asked LT Petersen to stop by his infirmary. Over a cup of coffee, the doctor informed Petersen that Goering had given him a letter. 'He instructed me to give this letter to you,' Schuster said, handing Petersen a thick white envelope addressed to Edda Goering. 'He said you would know what to do with it.'

'Mail it I guess,' said Petersen.

Chapter 35

The format of the International Military Tribunal was different than an American criminal court, yet many aspects were retained.   In Nuremberg, the prosecution occupied weeks presenting the cases against each of the defendants, one after the other.   Only after these accusations were laid before the court, largely in the form of translated documents, would the defendants' counsels begin their defenses.

On February 7, the case against Goering was scheduled to begin.   As usual, the prisoners were awakened and escorted to breakfast.   Following their meal, they returned to clean their cells, which had just been searched.   Except for Goering, of course, whose cell was cleaned for him.   At 0930, the prisoners were lined up, handcuffed to a guard and escorted to the Palace basement for the ride up to Room 600 in the elevator.

LT Petersen rode up with Goering.   Goering was tense, but determined not to let it show.   He had maintained his usual steady banter with both his fellow defendants and his guards.   He kept a jovial smile in place.   As the elevator rose, Goering glanced at Petersen, 'Wish me luck, lieutenant,' he grinned.

'Good luck sir,' Petersen automatically responded.

After the defendants were seated, Petersen took up his station along the rear wall of the courtroom, near the elevator door. Everyone stood as the president of the Tribunal, Sir Geoffrey Lawrence and his fellow judges filed into the court.   Sir Geoffrey called the court to order and M. Mounier of France began the prosecution of Goering.   Mounier painstakingly reviewed the indictment against Goering, illustrating with documentary evidence the *Reichsmarschall*'s actions in preparing for war, utilizing slave labor, pillaging art and industry, and his culpability in the infamous 'Commando Order' which directed the execution of Allied soldiers involved on commando-type missions behind German lines.   All of the documents were contained in large books, copies of which were presented to each of the judges and defense counsels.   Mounier read certain passages, but generally used a narrative style in which he referred the court's attention to a specific document in order to make his point. Goering sat impassively in his customary chair in the dock, arms crossed, listening. His lawyer, Dr. Stahmer was less patient with the proceedings. 'I must contradict what M. Mounier has said,' he interrupted the prosecutor's discussion of the Commando Order, directing his remarks to Sir Geoffrey Lawrence. 'There is no proof that these things took place or that the Defendant Goering is responsible. The Defendant Goering was quite unaware of these events and had nothing to do with matters of that kind.'

'You will have the opportunity to present arguments that this evidence has really no reference to him at the appropriate stage in your defense,' Sir Geoffrey ruled. 'Do you understand what I mean?' Stahmer resumed his seat and whispered to his associate Greinke, who nodded and scratched some notes on the pad before him.

Mounier droned on for hours, but finally, in the late afternoon, he completed the case against Goering. Remarking upon the lateness of the hour, Sir Geoffrey adjourned the court. After the eight judges filed out, everyone else in the courtroom began to move, collecting their papers, notes, attaches and moving toward the doors as a low buzz replaced the quiet cadences of the translators. The defendants stood and stretched and began their short journey back to the prison. Petersen chose to ride down on the small elevator with the *Reichsmarschall*. Goering's eyes darted quickly to Petersen as the door slid closed. 'Well,' he began with bravado, 'if that is the best they can do, I shall not long be your guest here LT Petersen,' he laughed. 'At no time did the Frenchman connect me to any so-called crimes. Every charge he made was circumstantial. They will see that I was a soldier and that although I hated war, I did my duty.' Goering's face glowed, as if he had just won the first round.

Chapter 36

John, Burrell, Timmy and the other boys of their age group sat on the first two rows of the auditorium's wooden seats, hands in their laps and eyes straight ahead. Dusty sunlight seeped through the windows to their left. The weather had turned warmer with the beginning of spring and with the war in its second year, the boys' schedules had been modified to allow more time to work in the school's expanded vegetable gardens. Superintendent Wallace had determined that the school should be self-sufficient in the production of vegetables in order to help the war effort. It wouldn't hurt with his budget either, given he could work the gardens with free labor. So it was that the 17 year-olds had been excused from their work detail on this May morning for what they had been told was a special lecture. The boys waited with a mixture of gratitude and curiosity, happy to be out of the sun, but doubtful that the lecture would maintain their attention for long.

'On your feet!' Masters cried out from the rear of the auditorium. The boys jumped up and stood silently and motionless, eyes still straight ahead.

'Sit down boys,' called the familiar, friendly voice of Superintendent Wallace from behind. As they sat, the boys heard the tread of two pairs of feet. Wallace came into their field of view, a short, stout uniformed man trailing just behind.

'We have called you in this morning to consider a message from Major Thompson,' Wallace gestured toward the stout man. 'He is from the recruiting office at Camp Hood and he has a proposition that I would like each one of you to weigh carefully. Major,' Wallace said turning to Thompson, 'the floor is yours.'

'Thank you superintendent,' Thompson started. He was wearing a khaki tunic, shirt and trousers with a matching tie. A light sheen of perspiration beaded his forehead. 'As you men know, our country is battling the forces of fascism all over the world. As you know, this requires a great deal of equipment, weapons, supplies, food and men.'

Burrell whispered out of the side of his mouth to John, 'I think he's going to increase the butter beans quota from the garden.' John stifled a grin. The major continued.

'Men, men. That's what my visit is all about today. Our country needs smart, highly motivated, well-trained men to fight the Germans and the Japanese...'

'...and since we can't find any, we've come to you,' Burrell whispered causing Timmy to snicker out loud. The major looked quickly toward his end of the row, then continued. 'Uncle Sam is willing to make you men a deal. You enlist in the Army and we will work with the State of Texas to expunge your records. It's like getting a fresh start, a second chance, if you will.' The boys exchanged furtive glances all along both rows of seats. 'If you enlist for the duration of the war,' Major Thompson reiterated, 'you will enter the Army with a clean record and clear future...'

'...if you live,' Burrell muttered.

'Superintendent Wallace has given me permission to set up a recruiting station in the hallway. I hope you will give this offer serious and prayerful consideration and that you will decide to join in the defense of your country. Thank you.' Once the major finished, Wallace told the boys they could have 15 minutes to think about his proposal. After that, they either joined the Army or went back to Gatesville's gardens.

'What do you think?' Burrell asked John. Timmy stood with them in a small knot of boys at the foot of the auditorium's stage.

'Well, as much as I've come to love it here,' John said, as the others chuckled, 'I think I've made about all the contributions to agricultural science that I care to make. I'm going to sign up,' John stated with a finality that belied the few minutes he had expended in reaching his decision.

'Okay, then,' Timmy nodded, 'if you go, I go.'

'Me three,' said Burrell.

The three boys shook hands and marched out of the auditorium and into the Army.

Chapter 37

'Munich, John. Just think of it!' Robert enthused. 'Three days in the cradle of Nazism, drinking beer, eating *Wursts* and fraternizing with *frauleins*!' Robert was going to assist with the interrogations of several potential prosecution witnesses who had been located in the Bavarian capital. 'It is said to be the most picturesque of cities.'

'Good for you. Don't worry about little old me,' John said with phony self-pity. 'I'm sure I'll be alright. I'll just focus on guarding the most dangerous assembly of criminal masterminds the world has ever known; men responsible for the deaths of tens of millions and the destruction of a dozen nations and countless cities.'

'I weep for you,' Robert responded happily.

'I take you care,' Lisbeth said, coming up behind John and laying her hand on his shoulder. This caused both lieutenants to laugh out loud, with Lisbeth joining in.

She looked at Robert with her bright blue eyes and dimpled smile and pointed at him saying, 'You come soon back!' This brought a second round of laughter.

Petersen found the routine of the Tribunal nearly as tedious as that of the prison. Every weekday after breakfast, the prisoners were escorted back to the Palace courtroom. There they sat through a two to three hour morning session followed by a lunch recess. Following the first day's session, in which Gaffner had failed to provide a plan for lunch, a makeshift mess had been created for the prisoners in an attic room. When court was in session, the defendants ate their midday meal there, avoiding the press and other spectators and negating the need to make an additional trip back and forth to the prison. Following lunch, the afternoon session began, usually running until 1700 hours.

February passed slowly, like a long, cold winter's night, each day bringing more prosecution presentations concerning the crimes of the accused. Following the prosecution's case against Goering came the cases against Hess, Ribbentrop, Keitel, Speer, Doenitz and the others. Based on the current pace of the proceedings, it appeared as though the defendants would not begin their defenses until early March.

Simmons left for Munich on Tuesday, February 12. It had turned cold again, with a light snow carried on an icy north wind. The grey sky hastened the arrival of darkness, which already needed little assistance. Petersen left the prison bundled against the weather. He wore his overcoat, with a wool scarf tucked around his neck and black leather gloves protecting his hands. He walked briskly with his head down, but the wind lashed at his exposed cheeks, turning them a bright red.

He opened the door to #22 *Gartenstrasse* and had to tug it hard behind him lest the wind fling it fully open. He stood for a moment just inside the door, shivering, his shoulders aching, Jack Benny cracking jokes on the radio. Lisbeth left her cooking and came to help him with his coat. 'Oh, you cold!' she said noticing his cheeks and his clenched fists. It was as if the cold was reluctant to let him go even though he had escaped to the warmth of the house. John peeled off his overcoat and tugged at his gloves and scarf. Lisbeth hung them up and then returned to where he stood shivering. '*Hier*,' she said, wrapping her arms around him. 'Warm, *ja*?'

'Ja,' John replied through his still chattering teeth. 'Much better.' John felt Lisbeth's warmth against him. She had pinned his arms to his side. Now, he pulled them out gently and wrapped them around her small body. She looked up at his red face and laid her head on his chest, pressing herself against him. John hesitated, then he brushed his lips against the top of her head. She once more turned her face toward his. John kissed her lips and pulled her tighter. He smelled her scent and felt her tongue brush against his. He let his hands slide down her back and onto her hips. Lisbeth felt John growing against her abdomen. She broke off the kiss and fixing him with an intense, penetrating gaze, pulled his hands from her hips, holding them in her own. She smiled at him and tugged gently, leading him toward his bedroom.

By the time they got to it, supper was burnt and hardly edible. Lisbeth giggled as she sliced off some bread and cheese to go along with their very cold beer. She was wrapped in a warm glow and John's robe. John had thrown on a pair of trousers, a t-shirt and his old sweater. John, for his part, could not look away from her dancing blue eyes. 'What are we going to tell Robert?' John wondered out loud, causing Lisbeth to giggle again. Under the table, her bare foot rubbed against John's. After their snack, they made love again and afterward lay holding each other, Lisbeth rubbing her fingers across the thick pink scar on John's upper left arm. The warm bed was in sharp contrast to the cold outside.

Chapter 38

John awoke confused, uncertain of his surroundings. He felt Lisbeth's warm, smooth body next to him and remembered the previous evening. In the darkness, he heard the loud tick-tock from the main room. It was cold in his bedroom, the heat from the stove having subsided in the night. John moved carefully to avoid waking Lisbeth. He found his wrist watch and stared at its luminous dial. It was still very early, but he felt an energy he'd never known. Quietly, he collected his uniform in the dark and crept into the kitchen to dress. He donned his overcoat and slipped back out into the freezing air.

Petersen shaved at the prison, taking advantage of the plentiful supply of hot water there. He dropped in on the basement mess hall to grab a cup of strong coffee and check in with Sergeant Goodman. 'At it early this morning, sir,' Goodman said by way of greeting.

'Fine morning Sergeant Goodman!' Petersen replied. With mug in hand, he climbed the steps and strolled through the cell block, stopping to chat with the sentinels standing watch over their mostly sleeping prisoners.

'Ah, good morning lieutenant!' Goering's voice boomed through the block as Petersen drew adjacent to his cell. PFC Rogers stepped aside to allow Petersen to see Goering through the inspection port.

'Good morning *Reichsmarschall*,' Petersen said with a smile. 'You are the early bird this morning, aren't you?' A puzzled expression covered Goering's large face. 'Sorry, sir,' Petersen said. 'It's an expression: the early bird gets the worm.'

Goering laughed heartily. 'Yes, I like this! The early bird! And what about you my friend. You too are the early bird!'

'Yes sir. I was anxious to get moving this morning. It is very cold outside. Almost as bad as last winter.' Petersen regretted his remark even as it escaped his lips. Goering's smile faded away.

'Yes,' he remembered, 'last winter was the coldest in 40 years. Where were you this time last year LT Petersen?'

'Someplace much colder *Reichsmarschall*. Much colder, much dirtier and not nearly as safe.'

'Ha, yes. Last year, I was much warmer, much cleaner and much safer!' Goering responded with an ironic chuckle. 'But here we are now. I have been meaning to ask you a riddle lieutenant. What is the difference between a German and a Frenchman?'

'I don't know sir.'

'A German has hard hands and a soft heart; a Frenchman a hard heart and soft hands!' Goering laughed at his own joke and Petersen couldn't help but chuckle. 'You seem in good humor this morning, lieutenant. If I did not know better, I would say a woman is involved.'

Petersen checked himself, then winked at Goering, 'You never know sir.'

'Ah! A good German girl I hope!'

'Good morning to you *Reichsmarschall*,' Petersen nodded.

As PFC Rogers resumed his post, Goering turned away from the door and smiled to himself.

The day in court seemed interminable to Petersen. The Russian prosecutors presented reams of evidence of German brutality toward Soviet prisoners of war. Standing his normal post near the elevator, from where he could observe his guards neatly arrayed behind the defendants' dock, Petersen had no access to, nor need for headphones. He could, therefore, rarely follow the Russians' case, unless one of the English or American judges interjected a question. The day dragged on, his vision filled with uniformed soldiers, the officers of the court and the defendants, his mind filled with the scent of Lisbeth's body, the sparkle of her eyes and the pleasing sound of her laugh. He wondered what she was doing as the morning session droned on; what she was buying in the market as he escorted his prisoners to their attic lunchroom; and what kind of welcome she would give him when he returned home in the evening.

Petersen was eager for his day to be over as he trailed the defendants back to the prison. The air was brisk outside as the parade of prisoners and guards made its way along the covered walkway connecting the Palace to C Wing. Petersen followed the line into the cell block and saw Captain Stevens standing outside the office talking with Colonel Gaffner. 'Lieutenant Petersen,' Stevens called him over with a wave of the hand.

'Yes sir.'

'Unannounced body search, lieutenant,' Stevens said. Gaffner stood off to the side, eyes on his prisoners, fidgeting.

'Is there a problem I should know about sir?' Petersen asked, a more appealing body waiting for him elsewhere.

'Damn it lieutenant!' Gaffner roared, turning on Petersen, his face red, his eyes wide with anger. 'Why is it you think I owe you an explanation with every order?' Gaffner moved in on Petersen, causing the lieutenant to take an involuntary step back. By now, all eyes in the cell block were watching the confrontation. 'When a superior officer gives you an order, you will carry it out! Do you understand me son?' Gaffner fumed.

'Sir, if there is a specific…'

'I asked you a question, lieutenant! Did you hear me? Do you need me to repeat myself?' Gaffner's jaw jutted out, his hands on his hips. From across the cell block Goering was reminded of the Duce in high form.

'No sir!' Petersen gave up. He was, once again totally embarrassed in front of the men he was supposed to lead. Once again, he failed to understand what had caused the colonel to blow up. 'I'll see to it right away sir,' he said, attempting to reestablish control of the situation.

'That's more like it,' Gaffner snapped, a frown covering his face. 'Now get to it.'

By the time the prisoners had stripped and been searched by Dr. Schuster, redressed, fed and escorted back to their freshly searched cells, it was already 2000 hours. Sergeant Goodman was angry because no one had notified him in advance that the serving of supper would be delayed. The prisoners were annoyed by the indignity of the search and the mind-numbing, seemingly endless routine of their days. The guards were annoyed because nine months after the end of the war they were still in the Army and still in Germany. Petersen was perhaps the angriest of all. His

146

bewilderment at the colonel's tirade was as great a concern as his humiliation in front of his men—not to mention his prisoners.

He made his final rounds of the cell block, checking on the sentinels, reviewing their standing orders and peering into the cells. Each guard had a small light fixture with a metal shade which was shined into the cells during the hours of darkness. After Ley's suicide, Gaffner had ordered that prisoners remain under surveillance at all times, even while they slept. As he passed from guard to guard, Petersen looked each man in the eye, searching for a clue as to how that man viewed him after the colonel's outburst. Most of the men seemed to have forgotten it already. Petersen had a reputation among his men as easy going but professional. He wasn't much given to displays of rank, but tended to recognize men based on how well they performed their assigned missions. To most of his sentinels, Petersen was highly favored over Gaffner, Stevens and even the other lieutenants.

Goering was waiting as Petersen approached his cell. Petersen spoke to the guard, Corporal Bartles, while the *Reichsmarschall* listened. In no mood for any further delay, especially after having been so publicly reamed by Gaffner, Petersen did not intend to engage Goering.

'Lieutenant Petersen,' Goering spoke just loud enough for Petersen to know that Goering knew he could hear.

'Yes sir,' Petersen replied sharply.

'That should not have happened. Your colonel was unprofessional.'

Petersen stared through the grated window, his jaw set, his eyes locked on Goering's. 'Good evening, *Reichsmarschall*.' He turned and walked away. Goering watched him go, nodding his head slowly.

As Petersen reached the door, Captain Stevens called to him. 'John, you need to talk?'

'No sir!'

'Might help.'

'Thank you sir. If that is all sir,' Petersen snapped a salute which Stevens casually returned. Petersen grabbed his coat and scarf and shoved open the door.

The short walk home usually allowed him time to put the day's events into perspective and by the time he reached *Gartenstrasse*, he had burned off some of his anger. It was still cold, but the wind had died down and the stars looked down on him with a benign beauty.

Lisbeth had been waiting, fussing over the evening meal, trying to keep it edible until he arrived, looking every few minutes at the clock on the mantel. When at last he stepped through the door, she fairly flew into his arms. They embraced and kissed and John felt his cares melt away like old snow caught in the afternoon sun. As they kissed, Lisbeth's fingers worked quickly unknotting his tie and unbuttoning his shirt. He quickly caught on and began to undress her, backing her toward the bedroom. He tugged her cotton slip over her head, exposing her small white breasts. He flashed back to the sight of the prisoners, 20 of them, white and naked, bent over and awaiting Dr. Schuster's examination. He chuckled. '*Was?*' Lisbeth eyed him tilting her head. 'Nothing,' he said, laying her gently on the bed.

Chapter 39

During the next day's lunch recess, Petersen sought out Captain Stevens. Petersen found him at the small canteen on the ground floor of the Palace, sitting alone, drinking a Coke and eating a sandwich. 'Sir, I wanted to apologize for snapping at you last night when I left.'

'Don't worry about it John,' Stevens said, taking a swallow from the bottle.

'Sir, why is it that the colonel has it in for me? What have I done?'

'Well there are a couple of possibilities as I see it lieutenant,' Stevens explained. 'One: you have something in your background that concerns him and he is testing you to see if you can perform under pressure.'

'And two, sir?'

'He's just an egomaniacal shit head. Take your pick,' Stevens said shoving the last bite of his sandwich into his mouth and licking his fingers. 'If I get a chance, I'll see what I can find out. In the meantime, just give him a wide leeway. You're doing a fine job, John. And this won't last forever—it just seems like it will.'

Court had adjourned early for the weekend to give the judges time to consider motions from both the prosecution and the defense. Petersen arrived home to find Lisbeth busily cooking and Robert back from his visit to Munich.

'Ho, the prodigal returns!' John greeted his housemate as Robert stood up from the table. He advanced across the floor, shaking his friend's hand and slapping him on the shoulder. 'A good trip I hope?'

'Most excellent my friend! And here I return to our humble home, a warm fire by the hearth, good food a-cooking and cold beer awaiting! Lisbeth has filled me in on what's happened since I've been gone,' Robert continued returning to the table and resuming his seat. John hesitated, glancing to Lisbeth, who winked at him, and then back to Robert, who carried on as if nothing had changed.

'Tell us about your trip Robert,' John steered the conversation. Over their meal, Robert entertained John and Lisbeth, describing his trip scene-by-scene and episode-by-episode, first in English for John and then in German for Lisbeth. He told of the trip itself, the people he met, the food he ate and the beer he drank. He carefully avoided any discussion of his interrogations out of sensitivity to Lisbeth. As they ate, and Robert talked, John stole glances at Lisbeth. The corners of her eyes crinkled when she smiled at Robert's tales. When she caught John looking at her, she would smile, then nudge his foot under the table.

Once Robert finished his third beer, his narration began to slow. Lisbeth stood and cleared the table, carrying the dishes to the sink. As she busied herself cleaning up from the meal, John leaned over to Robert.

'I need to tell you something pal,' he felt himself flushing. 'While you were gone, I... well, we...'

'You began an illicit affair with our *hausfrau*,' Robert interjected.

John was stunned, speechless, his mouth hanging open, his face red. 'I ... how did you know?' he finally managed, embarrassed.

'Well hell you Texas stud,' Robert laughed, 'The two of you have been circling each other like dogs in heat for two months! What took you so long?' He glanced at Lisbeth's back as she bent over the sink. 'She's a good woman, John, strong, self-reliant. She has to be to survive what she's been through, what this war has cost her. I know she likes you. Just be careful how you play this thing, if you know what I mean.'

'I'll be careful,' John nodded, not sure at all what Robert meant, but relieved that he had responded as he had.

'Well, friend,' Robert resumed, 'I shall be sleeping in tomorrow, so the two of you keep things to a low moan and be quiet in the morning.' With that, he set his bottle on the table and stood. He squeezed John on the shoulder as he made his way past and called out to Lisbeth in the kitchen, '*Gute nacht!*' John went to Lisbeth and put his arm around her waist. He bent and kissed her on the cheek and helped her finish. He was eager that she should be freed for other activities.

Chapter 40

Goering's lawyers, Dr. Stahmer and *Herr* Greinke, were increasingly frequent visitors to the prison. They met with their client in the visitation room to review the strategy of the defense they would shortly be called upon to present. Stahmer and Greinke were a study in contrasts. Stahmer had a head of thick white hair and wore thick glasses. He was slightly stooped and had the gait of a septuagenarian. He carried a small leather attaché case and wore a three piece suit of a conservative cut. He was formal in his manner and his speech, and seemed to weigh carefully both his words and actions.

Greinke was far younger than his mentor. Nearly six feet tall, he had dark hair, which he kept oiled and combed back, a part high on the right side of his head. He was well muscled and moved with the grace of an athlete. He carried most of the team's legal documents in a heavy, black brief case and seemed to speak only when Stahmer, or their famous client, spoke to him. As Petersen stood silently watching the three men converse, he wondered again where Greinke had spent the last six years. Petersen guessed Greinke was about 30, making him, except for Petersen and the guards, the youngest man in the courtroom at any time, and certainly the youngest of the Germans.

In early March, the multi-national prosecution team finally rested its case against the so-called criminal organizations of the Nazi regime and the twenty-one individual defendants. On Friday, March 8, Sir Geoffrey called the tribunal to order. After dispensing with administrative announcements, he rapped his gavel and recognized Dr. Stahmer for the beginning of Goering's defense. Petersen, at his customary post near the elevator, stood silently, aware that history was playing out before him.

Stahmer initially followed the pattern established by the court, which encouraged the introduction of documentary evidence. The elderly lawyer immediately attacked the prosecution's contention that Goering had planned aggressive war. He quoted Marshall Foch, French hero of the Great War, who attested in 1927 that Germany had disarmed according to the Versailles Treaty.

Stahmer further expounded that since none of Germany's foes in the first war had completed the disarmament called for by the Treaty, Germany was technically released from her obligation to disarm.

Stahmer next called his first witness, Air Force general Karl Bodenschatz. Bodenschatz had been the adjutant to the famous Red Baron during the first war and had come to know Goering when the latter had assumed command of von Richthofen's squadron following the ace's death in combat. During the most recent war, Bodenschatz had been Goering's representative at the Fuehrer's headquarters.

Dr. Stahmer asked the witness to recall Goering's response to the infamous 'Kristall Nacht,' the wild nights of rioting targeting German Jews in November 1938. Bodenschatz relayed Goering's dismay at the event, remembering that he had personally called in Joseph Goebbels, the Gauleiter of Berlin, to explain that this was contrary to Germany's best interests. The general also testified that Goering had worked to prevent the outbreak of the war, meeting secretly with British business leaders to ease tensions between the two countries arising from Germany's aggressive moves towards Poland. Under questioning from Dr. Stahmer, Bodenschatz told the court that Goering had also opposed the 1941 attack on Russia, arguing with Hitler that a war on two fronts would be too dangerous to contemplate. Following a break for lunch, Stahmer asked Bodenschatz if he was aware of the atrocities reported from the concentration camps. Predictably, Bodenschatz said he was not and that he was of the opinion that Goering was not either.

Once Stahmer finished questioning his witness, the prosecution, in the person of Justice Robert Jackson, rose for its cross examination. Jackson was a respected jurist. His appearance was distinguished, his manner toward Bodenschatz icy. 'Witness, you would like us to believe that Goering was shocked, even offended by what happened to the Jews on Kristall Nacht.'

'He said it was a great wrong and that it was economically foolish. He said it would harm Germany's prestige abroad,' Bodenschatz recalled.

'Did you not know,' Jackson bored in on the witness, 'that just two days after these riots, Goering ordered that German Jews, the very victims of these hateful crimes, pay one billion Reichsmarks as a fine? Did you know that he ordered the confiscation by the state of insurance proceeds that should have compensated the Jewish victims for their losses? Did you know that he then issued a new decree excluding Jews from the economic life of Germany? Did you, witness, know these things?

'Well,' stammered Bodenschatz, 'I heard this, but I personally had nothing to do with it. I was just his military adjutant at the time.'

'Of course,' Jackson nodded at the witness. 'You were just a soldier; a soldier following orders.' Jackson paused, then, shaking his head with contempt, he addressed the court, 'I have no further questions for this witness.'

Petersen switched his gaze from Jackson, standing, facts at his command, controlling the tempo in the courtroom, to Goering, seated in the dock, jaw tight, eyes glaring, helpless and beyond redemption.

Chapter 41

John, Burrell, Timmy and four of the other Gatesville boys were driven to Camp Howe, some 60 miles north of Dallas. There they were examined, measured, poked, prodded, inoculated, clothed, equipped and, finally, assigned to the 333rd Infantry Regiment of the 84th Infantry Division, the Railsplitters. The division, which had served in the Great War, had been reactivated the previous October, and was filling its ranks to full strength in anticipation of overseas deployment. John and Burrell were assigned to Baker Company. Timmy, because he spoke some German, a skill completely hidden from friend and foe alike at Gatesville, was assigned to the regimental headquarters company.

As the newest members of the company, John and Burrell were assigned as riflemen in 2LT Allgood's platoon. Their platoon sergeant, Will Martin, had sinewy, muscled arms, strengthened from picking oranges in his native central Florida. He seemed competent and efficient and by any measure was a damn sight better than Shadrach Peavey. 'Where you boys from?' Martin asked as he assigned them as tent mates.

'Quitman, Texas,' John said.

'Galveston, Texas,' Burrell replied.

Martin arched an eyebrow and made a note in their personnel files which he had spread before him on a folding field table in the platoon headquarters tent. 'Guess you joined the Army to see the rest of the state, huh?'

'No Sergeant,' Burrell responded, 'Just to see less of Gatesville.'

'Well, welcome to the Railsplitters, boys. The scuttlebutt is that we are training to fight the Germans, but you never know with the Army. They may be teaching us about German tactics just to throw off all the Jap spies that are watching us.'

'Jap spies?' John asked.

'Yeah, there're hundreds of them around here, all disguised as prairie dogs.' Martin chuckled. 'Third tent down on the left,' Martin pointed the way. 'Get your gear squared away and make sure everything fits. The mess tent is all the way at the end of the

row in the other direction. Meet me there in 30 minutes and I'll introduce you to Lieutenant Allgood.'

Accustomed as they both were to a structured, disciplined environment, the two Gatesville alumni adapted quickly to Army life. The early morning calisthenics, endless inspections, weapons and small unit tactics training that they experienced daily were not unlike the regimented schedule they had kept at Gatesville. The food was adequate and their tent offered relatively private accommodations compared to their housing arrangements at school. The Army training was rigorous and not always well organized, but there were no Peaveys around and the adventure of going off to war was more appealing to the 17 year-olds than the excitement of tending gardens.

Chapter 42

On Monday, March 11, the tribunal reconvened after its weekend recess. Dr Stahmer continued the defense of Goering by attempting to rebut the prosecution's accusations that Goering had been an accomplice in the promulgation of the 'Commando Order,' which Hitler had later extended to Allied airmen engaged in 'terror bombing.' Stahmer first called General Erhard Milch, the former inspector general of the *Luftwaffe*.

'What were *Reichsmarschall* Goering's orders to the troops under his command concerning captured enemy terror fliers?' Stahmer asked Milch.

'I do not know his precise orders,' Milch began, 'but I believe his general attitude was that...'

'Your Honor, if it please the court,' Justice Jackson was on his feet, 'we have been very liberal in permitting all kinds of statements to be heard, but this,' he gestured towards Milch, 'surely cannot be considered valid evidence. The witness has stated he has no direct knowledge of the subject.'

'I should like, Your Honor, to rephrase my question,' Stahmer intervened. Sir Geoffrey Lawrence nodded his consent. 'Did *Reichsmarschall* Goering ever tell you he was against cruelty in the treatment of the enemy?'

'Yes,' Milch nodded. 'He said that once they had been shot down, they became our comrades.'

Next, Stahmer called Bernd von Brauchitsch to the witness stand. Von Brauchitsch had served as Goering's chief adjutant, responsible for making the *Reichsmarschall*'s daily arrangements.

'Colonel von Brauchitsch, in the course of your responsibilities, did you learn that 75 Royal Air Force officers escaped from the Sagan, Stalag Luft III, in late March 1944?' Stahmer asked.

'Yes, I heard this at the time.'

'Were you informed that 50 of these officers were shot while trying to escape?'

'I heard this much later,' the witness replied.

'And what role did *Reichsmarschall* Goering play in these shootings?' Stahmer continued.

'None,' von Brauchitsch replied.

'And what about the so called terror-fliers? *Herr* Hitler had ordered that enemy fliers who were captured should be shot. What was the *Reichsmarschall*'s attitude toward this order?'

'The *Reichsmarschall* disagreed with this order and took steps to see that such measures were not carried out by the *Luftwaffe*,' von Brauchitsch explained. 'The idea was to appear to follow this order, but in fact it was not carried out.'

'Thank you Colonel von Brauchitsch,' Stahmer concluded. 'Your Honor, I have no additional questions for this witness.' As the day was growing late, Sir Geoffrey adjourned the tribunal before beginning Justice Jackson's cross examination.

Following the tribunal's Tuesday session and the return of the defendants to their cells, Captain Stevens approached Petersen to let him know he was to report to Colonel Gaffner at 0800 the following morning.

'Any idea sir what I should be prepared for?' Petersen asked, dreading the encounter.

'He either wants to compliment your fashion sense or offer career guidance,' Stevens said with a wink.

At 0800 hours on Wednesday morning, Petersen, under the watchful eyes of Corporal Wilson, rapped smartly on the colonel's office door.

Petersen heard a muffled 'Enter' from inside. He took a deep breath and plunged ahead, closing the door behind him, stopping in front of the colonel's desk and saluting. 'LT Petersen reports, sir.'

Gaffner looked up from the papers covering his desk and offered a crisp salute in return. 'At ease lieutenant.' Gaffner pushed back slightly from his desk and leaned back in his chair, his hands behind his gray head, his eyes puffy and red. 'I thought you and I ought to have a little talk.'

'Yes sir,' Petersen responded, wondering what in the hell Gaffner had to say that he would find of interest.

Gaffner dropped his hands to the arms of his chair, leaning to the left. He smiled. 'You may have noticed that I have been a bit harsh on you John. May I call you John?'

'Of course, sir,' Petersen answered. May I call you Doug, he thought.

'You see John,' Gaffner looked around the room, then snapped his eyes back on Petersen, 'I know what it takes to make a good officer, a leader of men, someone who puts his mission first and gets the job done. I know what it's like to lead men in combat. It takes nerve, John, the ability to make tough decisions quickly and to carry on when bone tired and weary. That's the ultimate responsibility on an officer. I need to know if you have what it takes. The Army is already shrinking. Every day, thousands of men revert to their civilian roots. The politicians are so anxious to get the Mamas and the wives off their backs, they are willing to gut the finest fighting force that's ever existed. And they are doing it in the face of a new menace that may be worse than the Nazis ever dreamed of being. Are you following me here, son?' Gaffner paused.

'Sir,' Petersen responded, not following Gaffner at all but determined not to admit it.

'The Russians are like the Nazis' evil twin. All the atrocities the Huns committed on the eastern front, the Russians repaid with interest. Now these bastards want to take over Europe and make it their own territory.'

What the hell has this got to do with me, Petersen wondered.

'You're probably wondering what the hell this has to do with you. See, the Army is going to need a cadre of experienced and capable officers to rebuild around when the shit hits the fan with these Soviet pricks. Now I know you didn't get here by the most conventional path, so it's my job to evaluate whether you're cut out to be one of those officers. That's why I'm laying it on you pretty thick John, to see whether you've got what it takes.'

'Sir, I'd like to think my record in combat is worth something in your evaluation,' Petersen braved a reply. 'Maybe you don't consider me a gentleman, sir?'

'Careful the motives you attribute to me, lieutenant,' Gaffner dropped the first name familiarity, wagging a thick finger at Petersen. 'Your work here has been good. Your soldiers perform their duties and they don't cause disciplinary problems. You have also shown an interesting ability to think on your feet.'

'But, sir?'

'But, I have to know that you will do your duty out of loyalty to your country, not simply out of loyalty to me,' Gaffner said. Petersen was stunned. He felt more loyalty to Dr. Schuster than he felt to Gaffner; more loyalty to his guards, to the prisoners, more loyalty even to Goering. The idea that this strutting, alcoholic son of a bitch assumed he had earned Petersen's loyalty struck the lieutenant as ludicrous.

'What about it lieutenant?'

'You can count on me, sir,' Petersen replied, hoping his answer would curtail the conversation and hasten his exit from Gaffner's presence.

'Right!' Gaffner barked, slapping his right hand on the desk. 'I knew I could count on you. Now you get back to work and do your duty son and make me and your country proud.'

Petersen popped back to attention and saluted. Gaffner, never leaving his seat, saluted and said, 'Dismissed!'

Chapter 43

Reichsmarschall Hermann Goering was called to the stand in his own defense on Wednesday, March 13. Petersen, from his customary vantage point, thought Dr. Stahmer looked more tired than usual, his ruddy face deeply lined. The lawyer, wearing a conservative grey suit with a white shirt and blue tie, coached Goering through an account of his early life. Goering recounted his youth and his service in the Great War, when he had risen from an infantry lieutenant to the commander of the famous Richthofen Squadron. Goering recalled his first impressions of young Adolph Hitler, with whom he shared political views. He described the rise of the Nazi Party and Hitler, sharing the role he had played in helping broker the agreement that finally led to Hitler's appointment as Chancellor of Germany. Throughout the day, Goering held forth, displaying an impressive memory for facts and an almost theatrical delivery. The press gallery seemed to hang on every word, relishing this insider's view of the most heinous regime the world had known. Finally, with Goering showing no signs of fatigue, Sir Geoffrey gaveled the session to a close at 1700 hours.

Goering continued on the stand the following day, again giving lengthy answers to Dr. Stahmer's mostly general questions. Despite an occasional interruption caused by technical difficulties with the IBM simultaneous translation system, Goering continued to talk, the court continued to listen, the correspondents continued to scribble. Finally, on Friday morning, Justice Jackson could stand it no more. Following a question Stahmer posed concerning the character of the war against France, Jackson intervened.

'I must ask the Tribunal how this question is relevant to the charges which have been filed against the defendant. We have been treated already to two days of very vague and general questions which seem designed simply to give the defendant a forum for talking. If we are to move through the defense cases of all 21 defendants within the balance of the 20th century, we must move forward with issues of greater relevancy,' Jackson complained with ill-disguised irritation.

Sir Geoffrey, surprised by Jackson's veiled rebuke of his control of the proceedings, nonetheless agreed with the chief prosecutor and ordered Stahmer to confine his questions to issues raised in the prosecution's case against Goering.

Stahmer turned his focus toward the charge that Goering had conspired to make aggressive war, questioning his client on Hitler's decision to go to war with Russia in 1941. 'I warned the Fuehrer that we were fighting the great power of the world, the British Empire, and that it was likely that America would soon come into the war and we should be confronted with the second great power,' Goering remembered. 'I told him that attacking Russia, the third great power would pit us against the rest of the world, the other nations being of little consequence. I even reminded him of the dangers of the two front war which he himself had written of in _Mein Kampf_. Unfortunately, as history has shown, he did not agree with me.'

Chapter 44

John, Robert and Lisbeth enjoyed their Friday supper together. Despite their intensifying romance, Robert had exhibited no feelings of awkwardness in the presence of his friends. Things seemed very much as before. John was pleased, because while he and Lisbeth could communicate quite effectively on a physical level, the language barrier still existed, and Robert could help break it down. They sat after dinner, each drinking a cold beer from under the back steps, discussing Goering's days on the stand. Lisbeth had been listening to the radio, trying to improve her limited English, and she was determined to participate in the conversation.

'From what I've heard,' Robert observed, 'Goering rambles through an oral history of the Third Reich. My correspondent friends tell me that the Tribunal has given him great latitude in answering Dr. Stahmer's questions.'

'He does go on… and on… and on,' John deadpanned, drawing a snort of laughter from Robert, who translated his comment for Lisbeth. She smiled at John and reached for his hand.

'How long do you think this is going to last?' John asked.

'Well, assume for a moment that Goering is the most important of the defendants in the eyes of the prosecution. This would be true for political and public relations reasons as well as because of his high rank within the Nazi regime. So figure that his defense will be the longest. Figure that he has already gone what, two and a half days? Say he goes another two days. Then, you've got cross examination and you know every single one of those prosecutors is going to want a piece of his fat ass.' Lisbeth giggled. 'It could last for two weeks,' Robert surmised. 'Then you get Hess, von Ribbentrop and 17 more defendants. I tell you my friend, we could be here the rest of the year.'

John glanced at Lisbeth. 'I can think of worse places to be,' he said.

Chapter 45

Simmons was right: Goering's defense lasted two more days. Goering's testimony continued in the same manner as before with open-ended questions and long, unchecked answers. The prosecutors grew increasingly restless and impatient with the court's tolerance of what seemed irrelevant journeys into immaterial matters. Finally, on Wednesday, March 16, the prosecution's chance to cross exam Hitler's number 2 man arrived. Justice Jackson, in his formal black suit, took the lead.

'Defendant,' Jackson began coolly, 'please explain the concept of the Leadership Principle.'

The *Reichsmarschall* shifted his weight in the witness chair. 'Yes, I should like to explain this idea. It is a reversal of the concept of authority which one would normally encounter in a democracy. In the west, and in Germany before the war, responsibility is held by the highest officials, but their authority comes from the majority of the people who elect them. The Leadership Principle reverses this so that authority comes from the top, in our case, the Fuehrer, and is passed downward. Responsibility, on the other hand, begins at the bottom and passes upward.'

'In other words,' Jackson paraphrased, 'you did not govern by the consent of the people?'

'Nonsense,' Goering scoffed. 'We repeatedly called on the people to express their consent for the programs we undertook. We did this through the plebiscite. The Fuehrer knew that to govern in this manner required the confidence of the people.'

'But defendant, you did not permit the election of those who opposed you.'

'Correct. The people acknowledged the authority of the Fuehrer. As he had their confidence, it was not their concern to question the direction of his leadership. You see, the Leadership Principle reposed the authority in the...'

'If you will simply answer my question, we can move ahead and save a great deal of time,' Jackson brusquely interrupted.

'A fuller explanation is necessary Mr. Jackson, so that the court may understand…' again Goering was cut off.

'Your counsel may bring this back up…' Jackson responded until he too was interrupted by Sir Geoffrey.

'Mr. Justice Jackson, the Tribunal desires to hear the defendant on this point and thinks we should listen to his explanation.'

Jackson was annoyed at the court's continued appeasement of Goering and his endless answers, but he maintained his composure. 'Thank you Mr. President,' he said to Sir Geoffrey. Turning back to Goering he said, 'Please resume your explanation.'

Goering smiled, a twinkle in his eye, and renewed his soliloquy, while his fellow defendants in the dock nodded their approval. Perhaps, they thought, the tide of the Tribunal would turn their way.

During the normal midday break in their attic lunchroom, the other defendants treated Goering as a champion prize fighter or Olympic medalist. He received slaps on the back, handshakes and words of encouragement. Lunch that day was more lighthearted than usual for the defendants. Even the half-crazy Hess laughed with his old colleagues.

Following the lunch recess, Goering was back on the stand, facing off again with Jackson.

'In light of your explanation, your very detailed explanation, of the Leadership Principle,' Jackson prefaced his first question, 'did you or any of your fellow defendants attempt to obstruct Hitler's plans?'

'It should be quite clear from history that none of us had any desire to interfere with the Fuehrer's plans from the very beginning. You must keep in mind that we are dealing with events that happened over the course of 25 years,' Goering lectured to Jackson as though he was a mere law student. 'Your question is very vague.'

'And you have completely avoided answering it,' Jackson retorted. 'Let me be more precise for you. Did you object to the military necessity of an attack on Soviet Russia in 1941?'

'Yes, of course, as I have previously testified, I told the Fuehrer that...'

'A simple, short answer is preferable, defendant,' Jackson cut in.

'Yes, as I have said repeatedly,' Goering replied, feeling control of the debate ebbing away from him.

'And yet, in June of that year, you executed an unprovoked attack on the Soviet Union.'

'Yes.'

'Well defendant,' Jackson moved closer to the witness box and swept his hand toward the dock, 'it seems as if you were all Hitler's yes men.'

'All of the no men were six feet under Mr. Jackson,' Goering quipped. Laughter broke out in the visitors' and press galleries prompting Sir Geoffrey to rap his gavel. Jackson's face was red, his advantage erased by Goering's easy manner and offhand joke. Smiles and the occasional smirk split the faces in the dock.

Jackson buried his irritation and plunged ahead with his cross examination. 'Despite your influence with Hitler, you eventually found yourself disassociated from him, did you not?'

'Yes. The distance between us continued to grow after the invasion of Russia.'

'Why?' Jackson was back on the offensive.

'The inability of the *Luftwaffe* to protect our cities from 1944 on embarrassed the Fuehrer. As I was commander-in-chief of the *Luftwaffe*, he distanced himself from me and I no longer held the position of influence with the Fuehrer.'

'In fact defendant, there came a time in early 1945 that Hitler made a new will, appointing Admiral Doenitz as his successor in the event of his death. I quote from this statement,' Jackson looked down at his notes. 'Goering and Himmler, quite apart from their disloyalty to my person, have done immeasurable harm to the country by secret negotiations with the enemy which they conducted without my knowledge and against my wishes, and by illegally attempting to seize power for themselves.'

'I never betrayed the Fuehrer, never at that time negotiated with a soldier of any enemy power. I believe this will was the result of the scheming of those around the Fuehrer to usurp my position of influence and assume it for themselves. I am deeply grieved that the Fuehrer would ever have believed I could betray him.' Goering looked down at his hands, a crestfallen expression on his face, the jolly champion banished by the facts.

Chapter 46

'He got his ass kicked, it is as simple as that,' Robert expounded, as he and John strolled through the shadowy blocks between the Palace and *Gartenstrasse*. The March weather had turned warmer and the days were growing noticeably longer. The two friends headed home, crossing *Hansa Allee* through shafts of early evening sunshine beaming between the houses and shops. 'A Supreme Court Justice for Pete's sake! You would think he could handle a straight forward cross examination.'

'I'm no lawyer,' John replied stepping around a cat looking for a handout, 'but I didn't think it was too bad. I thought Jackson scored some points.'

'Not according to Smith and some of the other reporters.'

'Who?' John asked.

'Smith from CBS.'

'Well he ain't on the court now is he, Robert,' John stated.

'You miss the point, as you so often do,' Robert shook his head in mock dismay. 'You are technically correct, my literal friend. The press does not sit on the court. But their observations of the court inform millions of our fellow citizens of the good ole USA, not to mention several dozen other countries. Do not underestimate the importance of public opinion, both on our side and the German side. If good old Hermann can recapture his status as a folk hero, it could bode ill for the forces of righteousness.'

Chapter 47

The cross examination of Hermann Goering continued through March 22. Occasionally, the attorneys clashed over the admissibility of documents or the relevancy of testimony, but gradually the massive amount and crushing weight of the evidence overcame the loquacious *Reichsmarschall*. The prosecutors ground him down, day-after-fatiguing-day. The final statement of the prosecution was left to the French chief prosecutor M. Champetier De Ribes. 'We have heard this defendant's answers, or rather we have heard his propaganda speeches. It is the opinion of the prosecution that the defense shall not be able to complain that it has not been given every fair and equitable opportunity. It has squandered these past days without any weakening of the prosecution's overwhelming accusations. That being the case, Mr. President, the prosecution has no further questions for this defendant.'

The trial broke for the weekend. Although Petersen's duties never allowed an official day off, he and Lisbeth slept late on Sunday. Petersen coaxed himself from her warm embrace to attend chapel. If truth be told, he was seeking the Almighty's understanding more than His forgiveness. He had long considered himself a sinner and figured God already knew him well enough to know his will was weak where Lisbeth was concerned. The Protestant prisoners, including Goering, attended Chaplain Gerrity's Sunday services without fail. Petersen wasn't sure if it was out of a need to commune with God, to cleanse their souls of their hideous deeds or simply to break the routine of another day in captivity. On this Sunday, after the most intense week of the trial, the good chaplain was preaching on forgiveness. He read scripture from the *Luther Bibel*. '*Petrus sprach zu ihnen: Tut Buße und lasse sich ein jeglicher taufen auf den Namen Jesu Christi zur Vergebung der Sünden, so werdet ihr empfangen die Gabe des Heiligen Geistes.* Then Peter said unto them, Repent, and be baptized every one of you in the name of Jesus Christ for the remission of sins, and ye shall receive the gift of the Holy Ghost,' Gerrity repeated in English for the guards and other Americans present. 'We are all with sin,' he continued, resting his elbows on a wooden lectern which had been put in place for his service in the basement dining hall. As usual, the prisoners sat at three tables up front, the guards and other worshipers at back tables or along the rear wall. Gerrity peered over the tops of his reading glasses, his head tilted forward, an earnest expression accompanying his words. 'Sin is part of our human nature. Just as surely as Adam and Eve ate from the tree of the knowledge of good and evil, we, as their descendants, are a mixture of these characteristics. As much as God would like us to be without sin, we cannot be. As much as we would like to be without sin, we cannot be. And yet as Peter preached, if we will repent, if we will accept Jesus Christ as the savior of our hearts and souls, our slate of worldly misdeeds is wiped clean. This is the message of hope that has endured for two thousand years. A message that has outlasted dark times, times of pestilence, famine, fear and war. It is a message that survives even unto this moment as we dwell here together in this unusual church, in this unusual place and time. It is a message as vibrant and meaningful for those of us here as to those who first heard Peter utter these words in ancient Jerusalem.' Goering, sitting at the front table, nodded in agreement as the chaplain spoke. At the conclusion of the service, Gerrity led the worshippers in the Lord's Prayer. The mixture of the two languages, as each recited the prayer in his own tongue, created a different cadence to the prayer, causing Petersen to lose his place, although he had recovered by 'amen.'

As the prisoners lined up to march back up the stairs to their cells, Chaplain Gerrity tugged at Petersen's elbow. 'Good morning, John,' he said with a smile. 'I am so pleased to see you here. I think it is greatly beneficial to our German congregants to see Americans worshipping with them.' Gerrity paused, watching the last of the prisoners disappearing up the stairs. 'He really is the same God, you know.'

'The same, sir?' Petersen asked, meeting the chaplain's eye.

'Yes. Our God, the Germans' God. The one they prayed to during the war is the same God we prayed to during the war. *Gott mit Uns.* God with us. He is the God of all peoples and nations.

We would do well to remember that even though we sit in judgment of their earthly deeds, the final judgment belongs to Him alone.'

Chapter 48

Hess, 'the crazy one' according to Goering, was the next defendant to present his defense. At times Petersen, from his post beside the elevator, was convinced that Simmons was right: this bloody trial would last until the end of the year. When Justice Jackson or Sir David Maxwell-Fyffe, one of the English prosecutors, was speaking, Petersen would follow along with the arguments and counter arguments. When the French or Russian prosecutors or the German defense lawyers spoke, he was generally at a loss to comprehend the issues under discussion.

The trial lumbered through the end of March and into April. The days grew longer and warmer, trees and flowers began to bloom. The German people welcomed their first peaceful spring in half a dozen years with their usual industry. Nuremberg, like cities all over the country, began its painfully slow return to normal. It was a trip that would take a decade, but it began in earnest that spring as crews rebuilt bridges, reopened roads and restored buildings. Commerce, slow during the winter, began to grow and spread. Whereas materials were still in short supply and many food items were still rationed, the start of a new growing season filled the populace with a renewed optimism. Life, as tough as it had been, was finally, inexorably getting better. For Petersen too.

'LT Petersen, stop by my office when you get a minute,' Captain Stevens said on a mid-April stroll through the cell block. Petersen wondered what he had done now. Had he incurred Gaffner's wrath without realizing it? Had he done something notably well? Had his relationship with Lisbeth leaked beyond the four walls of *Gartenstrasse*? There was only one way to find out. So, at 1600 hours, Petersen stood in the doorway of the captain's office and gave a short knock on the door frame.

Stevens glanced up from a copy of the *Saturday Evening Post*, 'Come in lieutenant. Take a load off,' he said waving Petersen into a wooden, straight backed chair. 'Good news, John,' Stevens began.

'The trial's over, sir?' Petersen asked facetiously.

'Not that good,' Stevens responded with a smile. 'But, you are getting a short break from it. I am authorizing a pass for you. Easter is coming up and you are to take a few days off and un-ass the area.'

'Great, sir! Thank you!' Petersen smiled. He was genuinely excited about the opportunity to go somewhere, anywhere, as long as it was outside the grey confines of Nuremburg. A few days in the countryside would be a heavenly distraction from the tedium of the past eight months.

'Here is your pass and a travel voucher. It will let you ride the train pretty much where and when you like. You are to stay in uniform of course and if you run into any trouble, call me here or check in at the closest Provost Marshall's office. Any questions?'

'No sir. Thanks a lot. I really appreciate this,' Petersen gushed. He already had a good idea of where and with whom he would spend his short vacation.

'You've earned it. Go and have some fun. See you back here on Monday.'

Chapter 49

Bright and early on Thursday morning, John and Lisbeth walked to Nuremburg's *Hauptbahnhof*, or main station, to catch a Munich-bound train. They traveled light, one small bag a piece. By 0830, they were moving south, toward Bavaria's other great city, where the Nazi party had been born. They sat together in the compartment of the gently rocking car. In the 11 months since the surrender, German and Allied engineers, working together, had repaired much of the damage done to the major rail lines. Of course, much remained undone and some repairs, particularly bridge reconstruction, were of a temporary nature. Still, the German trains, as was their legacy, ran mostly on schedule.

As the train approached Ingolstadt, the conductor slid open the compartment door. '*Fahrkarte, bitte*,' he said looking over his glasses at the American soldier and the German woman, ticket punch in hand. John handed over his ticket. The conductor examined it, punched it and handed it back with a smile and a pleasant '*Bitte schon.*' Lisbeth proffered her ticket which the conductor took without a word or a smile. He punched it perfunctorily and handed it back without making eye contact, then quietly slid the door closed. Lisbeth looked down at the ticket, her face impassive. John reached for her hand and held it. She looked at him and smiled. 'It is *nichts*,' she said, 'nothing.' John kissed her on the head and pulled her closer.

Munich's massive railroad station sat in the heart of the city and had been heavily damaged during the war. Rail and other transportation centers had been priority targets for Allied heavy bombers and although the bombers were not the most accurate weapons, they managed to inflict significant destruction through the sheer weight of their numbers and the tonnage of ordnance they could deliver. Hammering, sawing and other construction sounds mixed with the hiss of the trains and the coupling of cars to create a cacophony through which John and Lisbeth wandered in search of the connecting train to Berchtesgaden. Lisbeth pulled John by his free hand toward the posted train schedule. She ran her finger down the bright yellow poster until she found what she was looking for. 'Come,' she said with a smile on her face and a twinkle in her eye and John fell in love with her all over again. She led him to Track 8, where a shorter train of just five passenger cars sat waiting. Within minutes, they were aboard and the train began its slow exit from the yard. Again they turned south, leaving the city gradually, the large city blocks falling away alongside the train, giving way to industrial areas and warehouses, neighborhoods and then the rolling, green Bavarian countryside. The train stopped briefly in Rosenheim to take on and disgorge passengers, then resumed its rumbling way toward the Alps. The train slowed as it wound through mountain passes, climbing steep grades.

Shortly after noon, the train pulled into the Berchtesgaden *Hauptbahnhof*. The station sat at the bottom of a steep hill, just above the River Isar. John and Lisbeth walked up the hill using a set of steps cut into its side, to reach the village above. To avoid the appearance of impropriety, they booked separate rooms at *Gasthof Watzmann*, though they intended on using only one. The hotel was large by the standards of the village. It stood three stories tall, with yellow plaster walls and a red tiled roof. Window boxes, containing blooming red geraniums, hung below each window. A coat of arms was painted above the arched double doors that led into the small lobby. The Union Jack flew alongside the Soviet and American flags beside the hotel's entrance.

The day was bright, clear and warm. The air was crisp and fresh. The surroundings were dominated by the Obersalzberg, the mountain just south of the village. Snow-capped its peaks, its lower shoulders blanketed by lush green pastures and speckled with the darker green of fir trees. The contrast to Nuremberg, just a few short hours in the past, could not have been more dramatic, or more pleasant.

Soldiers wearing all kinds of uniforms strolled the streets of Berchtesgaden. John didn't recognize all of them, though he spotted the British, French and Russian easily enough. John and Lisbeth shopped at a grocer's, a small bakery and butcher shop, coming away with the makings for a picnic lunch. Next, the pair hiked north of town, through an upward sloping forest of tall, straight fir trees. John looked like a tourist in the big city, always looking up. The blue sky was only partially hidden by the tall green sentinels. Shafts of sunlight filtered through their boughs, causing steam to rise from the decaying floor of the forest. 'It's like a sanctuary,' John thought. The only sounds were the fall of his and Lisbeth's footsteps and the gentle whisper of the wind through the branches.

Following a well-worn footpath, they emerged from the forest into the bright April sunshine. Lisbeth led him by the hand as they continued to climb the side of the hill, wading through tall grass and wildflowers. Finally, she stopped. She turned completely around, looked at John and said '*Hier*,' pointing to the ground and smiling at John. The spot Lisbeth had picked was in the center of a green field, speckled with colorful wildflowers. Just below were the dark green trees of the forest through which they had hiked. Rising above them, two miles to the south, were the mountains. Like nothing he had ever seen in Texas, these jagged peaks jutted up to dramatic heights, their snowy tops vivid against the azure sky. Lisbeth spread out the blanket they had borrowed from the hotel and John set the picnic basket on one corner. He and Lisbeth sat down on the blanket. He took her in his strong arms and kissed her. 'We eat first,' Lisbeth smiled, opening the bags from the shops they had visited.

Never had so simple a meal been so delicious. Cheese, rolls, sausage, beer and apples seemed the perfect menu for the spectacular setting Lisbeth had chosen. 'You like the food?' Lisbeth asked, her eyes catching the sunlight.

'*Ja*,' laughed John, 'and the company.'

She smiled at him, but he was not sure she understood. 'I love you,' he said. At this she looked down at the apple in her hand. '*Ich liebe dich*,' he repeated in German. Lisbeth looked up at him, tears brimming in her eyes. She put her fingertips to his lips.

'Shhh,' was all she could say.

'Lisbeth, I love you. I want to know all about you,' John said rapidly.

'Oh, yes. You know me,' she answered, brushing away her tears and trying to smile.

John reached out to her and pulled her against his chest. 'Tell me. Tell me where you were born, where you grew up, where you went to school, how you got to Nuremberg.' He knew he was going too fast, but felt Lisbeth relaxing in his arms, as though she had reached a decision to confide in him.

'I am from Ramsau, a little town by here close,' she said haltingly.

'We should visit. I could meet your family,' John offered lightly.

'Oh no,' Lisbeth shook her head. 'They are gone all. The war makes them go away.'

'Where did they go?'

'They go to war. My brother go to sea. My father *und* mother go to Munich to war work.'

'Did they sur... have you heard from them since the end of the war?' John probed gently.

'No. No one. They are all dead,' she buried her face into John's shoulders and sobbed.

'What will happen to us?' John wondered aloud. He held her close and stroked her hair.

Their time in Berchtesgaden was idyllic. The weather cooperated, giving them three glorious spring days. They would hike in the foothills daily, carrying a picnic lunch. In the evenings, they would dine at small *gasthauses*, eating farm fresh food, so different from the fare generally available in Nuremberg. At night, after checking in at the hotel, they would rendezvous in one of their rooms and make love.

On Easter Sunday, their last day, Lisbeth led John to a Catholic church in the village. The parishioners remarked among themselves at the arrival of the young soldier and his German girl. Some felt toward Lisbeth what many French, Belgians and Dutch had felt toward their women who had consorted with the German occupiers. Despite these feelings the worshipers were generally hospitable toward John and Lisbeth. They were, after all, in church. John had never attended a Catholic service and found the rituals intriguing if not altogether comprehensible. Mainly, John watched Lisbeth and tried to do what she did.

The sky clouded over as they checked out of the hotel and walked down the steep hill toward the train station. A light rain began to fall as the Munich train headed southwest out of the station before turning to the north. The trip north took longer than their Thursday journey and they did not arrive back in Nuremberg until 2100 hours. They exited the *Hauptbahnhof* across from the Grand Hotel, turned west on *Frauentorgraben* and walked the mile back to *Gartenstrasse*.

Chapter 50

The four days of rest rejuvenated Petersen. He stepped back into the daily routine of the prison with an enthusiasm that was badly needed. Both the prison cadre and the prisoners had lived for months under high levels of stress. The guards continued to watch the calendar and count their points. The prisoners continued to listen to the Tribunal and say their prayers. Petersen's even-handed treatment of both his soldiers and his prisoners contrasted with some of the more temperamental officers. And none was more mercurial than the commander of the Internal Security Detachment, Colonel Douglas Gaffner.

On a late May afternoon, the colonel, accompanied by Captain Stevens, made an unannounced walk-through inspection of the cell blocks. He started on the third level, where some of the lesser known defendants were housed, and worked his way down. Petersen was on alert. He had already quickly reviewed his on duty guards, giving their uniforms and equipment a brief check and asking them questions he thought the colonel might ask. If he got a 'wrong' answer, he would explain to the soldier what the correct answer should be given the guards' standing orders.

'Good afternoon, LT Petersen,' Gaffner said with apparent good humor stepping off the bottom step of the spiral stairs and arriving in cell block 1.

'Good afternoon, sir!' Petersen snapped to attention. 'May I accompany you on your tour, sir?'

'Wouldn't have it any other way, son,' Gaffner said with a wink. Apparently thought Petersen, the 'good' Gaffner had come today. The thought passed quickly as they stepped off together toward the first cell, but not so quickly as to cause Petersen to drop his guard. He well knew how quickly Gaffner's mood could shift.

Down the row of cells they strode with Stevens a step behind. Gaffner was pleased with the attentiveness of the sentinels, who were, without exception, alert and focused on their assigned prisoner. He was pleased with the overall conditions in the cell block, observing through the inspection ports that the cells were being maintained in a proper state of police. Likewise, the cleanliness of the central corridor was satisfactory. But, there was always a 'but.'

'Very good LT Petersen, very good indeed,' said the colonel as they stopped adjacent to Goering's cell. The *Reichsmarschall*, who had been reading at his table, heard Gaffner's voice and approached his cell door, peering around his guard to get a glimpse at what was going on. 'But,' Gaffner continued. Here we go, thought Petersen. 'But, there is a lack of crispness to the uniforms of our soldiers here.'

Careful boy, Petersen warned himself. 'Sir, if I may offer a suggestion?'

Gaffner nodded, 'Go ahead, son.'

'Sir, we're standing guard watch in our winter uniforms: wool shirts, trousers, ties, tunics. Our sentinels are on 24 hours at a time and, well sir, they get hot, they sweat, their uniforms get wrinkled. What if we switch to a summer uniform, sir?'

'Khakis?' Gaffner asked, tilting his head and arching his eyebrows. 'Not a bad thought LT Petersen. Not bad at all. Captain Stevens: your thoughts?'

'Oh I concur sir. Excellent idea.'

'OK then,' Gaffner paused, rubbing his chin with the back of his hand. 'Khakis are the proscribed uniform of the day effective immediately. The same accoutrements will be worn as with the winter uniform. Any questions?'

'No sir,' Stevens and Petersen answered as one.

'Issue the appropriate orders Captain Stevens. Thanks for the good idea LT Petersen.'

'And so he says "Thanks for the good idea LT Petersen," and that's that,' laughed John recounting the details of Gaffner's visit to Robert and Lisbeth.

'You just never know with that old SOB, do you?' Robert asked, shaking his head.

'What is khakis?' Lisbeth asked. As Robert translated, John stepped into his bedroom and pulled a wrinkled pair out of a drawer.

'Here Lisbeth,' he said holding them up. 'These are khakis.'

'Okey-dokey,' she said, drawing a chuckle from the boys.

'I believe John, that Gaffner has a love-hate fixation with you,' Robert analyzed. 'He doesn't like you for some reason, but he recognizes your value to his mission.' Robert's brow wrinkled. He scraped at the label on his bottle of beer. The one drawback to the warmer weather had been the increasing difficulty of keeping the beer supply cold. 'Why does he not like you?' Before John could offer a guess, Robert plunged ahead, 'Is it because you are younger, stronger and better looking? Is your combat record more distinguished than his? Perhaps he considers you a threat because you enjoy great respect among your soldiers and your prisoners? I confess I don't know what it is,' Robert concluded.

'I have an idea,' John said, 'but just an idea.' The others looked at him with their full attention, leaning in just slightly. 'Maybe he knows that I know he's an alcoholic.'

'How do you know that?' Robert asked, interested, but not overly surprised.

'Well, one night when he chewed me out royally, he was stinking of alcohol. His eyes are bloodshot about half the time. And then, he has these wild swings in temper. Once minute he seems normal, the next he blows up like a volcano.'

'Have you ever thought about a career in psychology, doctor?' Robert asked in jest.

'Oh, he is good doctor!' Lisbeth interjected, causing them all to laugh.

'At any rate,' John continued, 'the important thing with Gaffner is to see the eruption coming and stay out of the way of the lava!'

Chapter 51

Training for the 84th Infantry Division intensified as summer turned to fall and the division moved into the Louisiana maneuver area. Beginning in September 1943, the elements of the division deployed to the swamps, working first on small unit tactics, then company-level operations. By February 1944, the maneuvers had progressed to regimental size, mixing the various combat and support arms into combined operations for the first time. With General Bolling in command, the entire division conducted combined arms exercises in April. Much of the work involved the coordination of different units in large operations: infantry working with armor, artillery and air support.

'I hate Louisiana,' Burrell complained after a six day field exercise, a trickle of sweat rolling down the side of his face. 'It smells bad, it's hotter than Texas and it's always wet! Look! Look at my feet!'

'Oh please!' John jerked away, 'what is that horrible smell?'

'Very funny, Bob Hope,' Burrell said in disgust. 'I never thought I'd miss Gatesville, but at least it's mostly dry there.'

'Well, you can have Gatesville, buddy. I'm never going back,' John retorted.

'I been thinking John,' Burrell said, changing the subject as he laid back on his cot and stared at the canvas roof of the tent.

'Did it hurt?' John teased.

'I'm serious now John,' Burrell said. 'See my face? I ain't laughin' here,' he said pointing to his mouth. 'Do you think the Army's training us in all these swamps so they can send us to the Pacific to fight the Japs?'

'What difference does it make? Japs or Germans?' John replied, laying out his cleaning kit next to his rifle.

'Well, those Japs, they aren't Christian, John.'

'Burrell you ain't gonna go to church with 'em, you're gonna kill 'em. What's religion got to do with it?' John asked.

'Well, I figure, if I kill a German, at least I know what happens to his soul, you know?' Burrell said, his brow wrinkled in thought. 'With one of those Japanese boys, I just don't know.'

'I wouldn't worry about it too much Burrell. The very fact that the Army has spent the best part of a year training us in these snake and alligator filled swamps probably means we won't be within 5000 miles of any jungle. We're probably training here because this is the biggest piece of land Uncle Sam could find that nobody else wanted. Besides, with the invasion last week, my guess is the Army is going to be throwing every division it's got into France.'

That's one of the things Burrell liked about John and one of the things that made him a good squad leader, despite his young age: he always had things well thought out.

To Burrell's immense relief, the division began moving to Camp Kilmer, NJ for staging to England in early September. By the first of October, the Railsplitters were in England, having made the Atlantic crossing without loss. A month later, the 84th Division rolled across Omaha Beach.

Immediately, this fresh, but green division was moved into the front lines near the Dutch-German border. Orders came quickly and the 84th attacked and captured Geilenkirchen, the second largest German city to be taken so far in the war. From there, the division pushed forward, toward Germany's vaunted Siegfried Line of defensive fortifications.

'Listen up!' LT Allgood shouted to his Baker Company officers and NCOs. Allgood was now the company commander, the captain and lieutenant formerly holding the job already wounded and out of action. 'Battalion has assigned us the task of holding these road junctions to protect the battalion flank.' Allgood unfolded a Michelin Guide map and pointed with a yellow pencil to Lindern and two north-south running roads that intersected with Highway 364, the main axis of advance for 1st Battalion. 'I want first platoon to take the lead, Sergeant Martin. You will have priority of mortar support. Utilize the railroad embankment for concealment and cover and establish your positions so you have the intersection with Highway 24 covered with intersecting fields of fire. Once you secure this intersection, LT Long and second platoon will leap frog to secure the

intersection, here,' he pointed to an unmarked road about 300 yards to the east. 'Third platoon, Sergeant Walden, you are in reserve. Mortar section, Sergeant Parks, set up in this area,' another stab at the map. 'Questions? OK, kick off in one hour. I make it 0548, now. Let's go. Good luck!'

Under cover of darkness, the platoon stepped off at 0648, making no noise save for the crunching of their boots on the frozen ground. Petersen's squad was in the lead, Sergeant Martin behind them and the other squads following in trail. By 0730, Petersen's squad was in position along the railroad embankment, facing to the southeast, where the sky was already turning a pale pink. Petersen moved along his line, positioning his men and weapons. 'Look alive now Burrell,' he said quietly. ' The Germans are going to come right at us with the sun behind them. Set up your BAR so you can cover from the intersection down to that stone wall where the road bends around to the right. See?' John pointed.

'OK John.'

Sergeant Martin walked forward bent low to inspect his squad leader's deployment. 'You know Will,' Petersen said, 'we're awfully exposed here, even if we do have this embankment to duck behind. I think we ought to pull back to those houses there,' he pointed to a row of three connected houses 50 yards away on the north side of the tracks. 'And that one behind you,' Petersen pointed to a 2-story house closest to the intersection, 'would make a real fine observation post and give us some overhead cover.'

Martin looked around and assessed the situation. 'I like the way you think John. Reposition your men, but make sure you specifically designate routes of advance. LT Allgood says to expect an attack and to be ready to chase the Germans down once they fall back.'

It was nearly 0830 before the sun was fully up, but only minutes later that Lincoln, one of the squad's sharper lookouts reported movement from the southeast. 'Go get Sergeant Martin and tell him to get up here with his radio man,' Petersen told Lincoln. Lincoln scampered down the stairs and out the front door of the house, racing toward Martin's command post. Peering out of an upstairs bedroom window, Petersen scanned the brown fields in front of them, slowly swinging his search into the sun. He held one hand above his binoculars' lenses to shade them from the sunlight and tried to hold them steady with the other. There. In a copse of trees, about half a mile away, he could see small dark figures moving in the shadows. He gave up shielding the binoculars and set both of his elbows on the sill of the window, being careful to stay behind the lace curtains. He could make out two armored half-tracks mounting machine guns. He reckoned he was watching a reconnaissance unit of some kind, which meant a larger force might be lurking not too far off.

Martin climbed the steps behind him, panting from his run across the open and now sunlit ground. 'Whatcha got?' he asked getting right to the point. Martin had developed a good opinion of Petersen upon his arrival at Camp Howe. He found Petersen to be resourceful and level-headed during the Louisiana maneuvers. Since their arrival at the front, Martin's opinion had been reinforced. Petersen was one of the valuable breed of men who could think clearly even during the confusion of combat.

Petersen pointed out the reconnaissance unit in the small woods.

'How about we flush them out,' Martin said pulling his radio operator forward and reaching for the radio's handset. 'Blue Dog 4-6, this is Blue Dog 1-6, fire mission, enemy troops under cover. Reference Able, add 300, left 1000, over.' Martin released the transmit button and waited. Within 30 seconds, he and Petersen heard a faint 'toonk' from behind them in the town. Four seconds later, a mortar round exploded 50 yards short of the trees, causing the German soldiers to dive for cover. Martin was back on the radio rapidly issuing adjustments to the mortar crew. From the trees, Martin and Petersen saw clouds of black smoke billow up as the half-tracks were rammed into gear, the sound of their engines reaching the house a few seconds later. Mortar rounds began exploding in the tree line in rapid succession. 'Right on the money!' Martin shouted into the radio. 'I'm going to stay with you for now John,' he said. 'If they come from there,' he pointed toward the smoking woods, 'I'll have a better vantage point from here.'

Second platoon was making its move toward the unmarked road junction when all hell broke loose. It started with artillery fire. The German forward observers walked their rounds from 100 yards south of the railroad tracks right across them and onto the ground where second platoon was attempting to establish its positions. LT Long's men were at a tactical disadvantage to begin with as there were no structures near enough to the junction to provide the kind of observation and cover first platoon had been able to take advantage of. Four German panzers, trailing infantry, proceeded slowly across the fields, just behind the advancing artillery barrage, heading directly toward second platoon's objective. From Petersen's window, the rumbling tanks looked like giant, smoke-spewing beetles, chewing up the frozen ground and throwing clods of dirt into the air behind them.

'I think we need to hit them in the flank and either call in fire support or relinquish our priority to second platoon,' Petersen shouted above the din to Martin. The pop of rifles and rip of machine gun fire carried across the tracks, signaling that the attack was intensifying. Martin, with the better vantage point chose the former option and began directing mortar fire against the tanks and infantry. He also called LT Allgood, apprising him of the situation and recommending he commit his reserve to strengthen second platoon.

'I got an idea,' Petersen told his platoon leader and quickly outlined a simple plan. He sent Lincoln to round up the platoon's bazooka and took his squad down the stairs and out the north facing front of the house. The squad raced along the north side of the railroad embankment, the rumble of the tanks' engines growing louder and deeper. Sulfur smoke floated over their heads. The ping and pop of rifle and BAR fire rang in their ears, interrupted by the throatier booms from the tanks' guns. When the squad was 15 yards short of the intersection, Petersen stopped. He put the bazooka in front, with Burrell and his BAR right behind them. 'Now listen,' Petersen shouted over the growing racket, 'when their tanks climb up the side of the railroad tracks, knock their treads off! Understand?' Lincoln and the others, eyes wide with the intensity of battle, nodded and took up positions from which they could see the tanks approaching. Fortunately, second platoon was attracting the enemy's full attention. Closer and closer the tanks crept, firing their main guns and machine guns at the outmanned second platoon. As the lead panzer eased up onto the railroad tracks, Lincoln fired his bazooka. The round hit the inside of the left tread just in front of the rear drive wheel. The giant machine slewed toward Petersen's squad as its left track unspooled onto the ground. A second bazooka round penetrated the exposed and more lightly armored underside of the tank, setting off a violent explosion inside it. None of its crew escaped.

The destruction of the lead panzer now drew unwelcome consequences. One of the three remaining tanks fired its main gun toward the squad, causing them to duck reflexively. The round sailed high, but machine gun fire from the tank tore into the railroad bed, sending splinters of rock and wood flying. Sergeant Martin's work with the mortars was fast thinning the ranks of the follow on infantry as were Burrell's accurate bursts from the BAR. Suddenly the second tank reared up, leaving the relative flat of the road and field in an attempt to scatter Petersen's men by running right through them. As the tank teetered in the moment before it toppled across the railroad tracks and regained its momentum, Lincoln placed a bazooka round through its belly. It rocked forward onto the tracks, sat motionless for a fraction of a second and then exploded, the turret hurtling 50 feet backwards, white flames shooting toward the sky. Petersen's men ducked again, the noise of the explosions numbing their ears and their senses, the heat from the blazing tank tanning their faces.

The remaining tanks and few surviving infantrymen began to withdraw, leaving the field and the road strewn with corpses and the blackened, burning hulks of two panzers. Scattered shots from the remnants of the badly mauled second platoon and from Petersen's squad harassed the retreating Germans. Petersen, confident that the enemy would need to time to recover before he could attack again, moved to reorganize his squad and strengthen its positions. He found Burrell 10 feet below the embankment, laying on his back, staring at the morning sky, a large hole in his chest. Blood was spreading from it like the petals of a blooming, *crimson flower. 'Burrell!' Petersen yelled. 'Medic! Medic! Hey buddy, look at me! Burrell, look at me, right here!' John shouted, ripping the bandage from his friend's first aid kit. 'Hang on Burrell!' he said, trying to keep the panic out of his voice. 'I got you covered,' he pressed the bandage into the hole, covering his fingers with warm, sticky blood. Burrell blinked, once, twice. He focused on John's face. 'I don't want to die,' he gasped. Then he did.*

Chapter 52

One-by-one the defendants presented their defenses. One-by-one the prosecution cross examined the defendants and their witnesses. The days of summer dragged slowly by. By the final week of July, the individual defendants completed their cases and the prosecutors were called on to present their closing remarks. Justice Jackson, acknowledged by all to be stronger in oratory than in cross examination, gave the court the Americans' final argument.

'May it please the Tribunal,' Jackson began, nodding to Lord Justice Sir Geoffrey Lawrence then swinging his gaze along the bench to the seven other judges. 'Over the past eight months, this Tribunal has done what no other court in history has ever attempted. It has provided a forum for criminal accountability of the leaders of an aggressive, war-making nation. Because of this Tribunal, history will never have to wonder what the leaders of Nazi Germany might have said. History will know that whatever could be said, they were allowed to say. They have been given the kind of a Trial which they, in the days of their pomp and power, never gave to any man.'

Petersen slowly scanned the row of guards standing behind the prisoners' dock in their khaki uniforms, helmet liners and white gloves. He looked to his right at the visitors' gallery, making eye contact with Simmons who was seated next to an attractive woman. Simmons winked and smiled.

Jackson continued, 'We are not trying these men for their obnoxious ideas. They have no monopoly on offensive thoughts and by the laws of free societies they are entitled to hold these thoughts. Rather it is their overt acts which we charge to be crimes. These men saw no evil, spoke none, and none was uttered in their presence. This claim might sound very plausible if made by one defendant. But when we put all their stories together, the impression which emerges of the Third Reich is ludicrous. If we combine only the stories of the front bench, this is the ridiculous composite picture of Hitler's Government that emerges. It was composed of,' Jackson turned and pointed to Goering, 'a Number 2 man who knew nothing of the excesses of the *Gestapo* which he created, and never suspected the Jewish extermination program although he signed over a score of decrees which instituted the persecutions of that race.' Jackson next singled out Hess, 'Hitler's Number 3 man was merely an innocent middleman transmitting Hitler's orders without even reading them, like a postman or delivery boy.' He turned his righteous indignation on von Ribbentrop. 'His foreign minister knew little of foreign affairs and nothing of foreign policy.' Jackson worked his way along the dock, damning each man with the bitter fruits of his own actions.

Jackson turned his attention back to the Tribunal. Rarely consulting his notes, he highlighted the case against Hitler's henchmen. He lifted up painful examples of their cavalier approach to making war and heartbreaking details of their results.

'These defendants now ask this Tribunal to say that they are not guilty of planning, executing, or conspiring to commit this long list of crimes and wrongs,' Jackson approached his eloquent conclusion. 'They stand before the record of this Trial as bloodstained Gloucester stood by the body of his slain king. He begged of the widow, as they beg of you: "Say I slew them not." And the Queen replied, "Then say they were not slain. But dead they are..." If you were to say of these men that they are not guilty, it would be as true to say that there has been no war, there are no slain, there has been no crime. I thank the Tribunal for its attention.' Jackson sat. Mr. Dodd, his associate, reached across the American prosecution table to shake his hand. Sir David Maxwell-Fyffe and Sir Hartley Shawcross nodded their congratulations from the British table.

Sir Geoffrey recessed the court.

'He was spectacular,' John said with undisguised admiration. 'I never heard a better speech, unless it was his opening. Of course that was so long ago that it has faded into a dim memory,' he laughed.

They were seated with Lisbeth at the table enjoying another fine supper.

'For once I agree with you John,' Robert said. 'An eloquent speech and a damning one. I would not offer any good odds for the defendants.'

'By the way, Robert, who was the girl?' John asked with a sly smile.

'Ah, an acquaintance from the Provost Marshal's office. A lovely young lady; very proper too.'

'Do I detect a romance?' John dug deeper.

'Don't be ridiculous,' Robert scoffed. 'It's strictly business. She is the personal secretary to the Provost Marshal and as such possesses, from time to time, certain information which I find useful in the conduct of my extracurricular affairs.'

'What happens to them?' Lisbeth asked. She had been listening quietly. She had been working on her English, listening to the American Forces Network on the radio and reading any American magazines the lieutenants could lay their hands on.

'To whom, my dear?' Robert asked.

'Goering and the others.'

'Most likely,' Robert spoke with an air of authority, 'they will be hanged as criminals.'

'They are not criminals!' she insisted. 'They are soldiers, like you!' she pointed her finger across the table at Robert's chest.

Robert raised his eyebrows and exchanged a quick glance with John. 'I believe Lisbeth that the court will find otherwise,' Robert said slowly.

'Then you should shoot them!' Lisbeth said, her wide eyes flashing with apparent anger.

'My dear,' Robert responded lightly, 'I won't shoot anybody.'

'Me neither,' John was quick to add, trying to lighten the suddenly serious tone of the conversation. He was uncertain what had prompted Lisbeth's outburst.

'They are soldiers, like you,' she said, her eyes darting back and forth between the two lieutenants. 'Do not hang soldiers. Shoot soldiers.'

John and Robert looked at each other, but thought better than to argue with Lisbeth.

In bed that night, John lay on his side, his arms around Lisbeth, his legs tucked up under hers. She was still and quiet, and tense. 'What's wrong?' he whispered into her ear. Lisbeth reached up with her right arm and ran her fingers across the scar on his upper arm.

'It is disgrace to hang soldiers and navy men,' she said. 'If they make wrong, you shoot.'

'It is not up to me. I don't decide,' John replied hoping she understood the meaning of his words.

'Hanging makes angry German people. Is bad thing,' she said. She fell silent. John felt a tear drop onto his hand.

Chapter 53

'LT Petersen!' called out Captain Stevens as Petersen walked by his office on the way to the basement mess hall. 'A moment of your time please.'

'Yes sir,' Petersen stepped into the small office. Stevens was rummaging through a file drawer in search of some critical piece of paper, without which the collapse of the entire Army of Occupation was imminent. 'Dammit!' Stevens swore, slamming the drawer shut with a loud crash. 'I'll never make it as a secretary,' he smiled at Petersen, who chuckled. 'I need a favor, LT Petersen,' he continued.

'Yes sir.'

'Your colleague, LT Rose, has gotten sick. I have sent him to his quarters. I need you to accompany the good doctor on his pill run tonight. He usually starts around 2030 hours and takes 45 minutes or so. Can do?'

'Can do easy, sir,' Petersen responded.

Dr. Schuster made nightly rounds, consulting with the prisoners on their health and generally listening to their concerns, real and imagined. In the course of his visits, the doctor was authorized to dispense sleeping pills to those prisoners who desired them. Most did. The prison was a large building with floor to ceiling open spaces between the multi-layered cell blocks. Even at night, when there was little activity, the building was loud, sound carrying through it like an echo chamber. Although lights were turned out at 2130, the lights in the corridors stayed illuminated at all hours. And, of course, there was the annoyance of the guards, peering constantly through the doors and shining their lamps into the cells to ensure their prisoners were not engaged in self destructive activity.

Schuster was usually escorted by LT Rose, who had drawn the night duty shift in the prison. Petersen walked down the stairs, past the mess hall and stepped into the infirmary. There he found the elderly Schuster neatly arranging rows of pills on a metal tray.

'Good evening LT Petersen,' the old doctor said with a weary smile. He was wearing a white lab frock, his thick glasses sliding down his long nose. 'How are you?'

'Very well doctor.'

'And how is your friend?'

'She is fine, sir. A picture of health in every way,' Petersen smiled.

'It pleases me to hear this,' the doctor replied. 'I am afraid the long term prospects for my patients here are not so promising as hers.' The doctor stood slowly and lifted his tray from the desk. 'Ready lieutenant?'

Dr. Schuster led the way back out of his office and up the stairs into the cell block. For each prisoner who wanted them, he passed out a red pill, which he and Petersen watched the prisoner swallow with a gulp of water. Next he gave them a blue pill and the routine was repeated. Petersen ordered each man to open his mouth for a quick inspection after taking the second pill. Colonel Gaffner had issued strict orders that all medication must be taken immediately. He did not want to risk a prisoner hoarding pills for a suicide attempt.

As they moved down the row of cells, Petersen asked, 'Why two pills doctor? Isn't one sufficient?'

'So it might seem and so it might be under ordinary circumstances, but,' he waved his hand at the drab white walls and wire mesh of the prison, 'here is not exactly ordinary. The first pill is Seconal. It helps one fall asleep rather quickly, but it does not create a very deep sleep. In a bright and noisy place like this,' he glanced toward the distant roof, 'it may not be enough to ensure a good night's rest.' They stopped at the next cell, repeated the same routine and then moved on. Dr. Schuster continued his pill explanation, 'The blue capsule is Amytal, which causes a rather deeper sleep. So, the two, taken together, offer good prospects for a restful sleep.'

Finally, the old doctor and the young lieutenant arrived at Goering's cell. 'Good evening sir, doctor,' Private Harris nodded, unbolting the door and swinging it open.

194

'Ah, gentlemen!' boomed Goering, 'do come in! A pleasant surprise, to have two friends call,' Goering's eyes twinkled above his broad smile. He was wearing a pair of blue silk pajamas and looked as though he was ready to crawl into bed.

'*Guten Abend, Reichsmarschall*,' Schuster said.

'Good evening, *Reichsmarschall*,' Petersen echoed.

'To what do I owe the pleasure of your company,' Goering turned to Petersen.

'LT Rose is ill.'

'Oh? I am sorry to hear this. He is not as hardy a man as you LT Petersen! Perhaps if he had a doctor as good as ours, he would be in better health!' Schuster smiled at the compliment. 'Well to business, then,' Goering said taking first the red and then the blue capsules. He washed them down and handed the small cup back to the doctor. They exchanged 'good nights' and left Goering to his slumber.

On the way back to the infirmary, Dr. Schuster stopped halfway down the stairs and turned to Petersen. 'Thank you for your assistance, LT Petersen,' he said. 'And thank you for your courtesy to *Reichsmarschall* Goering. I am afraid he does not receive favorable treatment here. None of them do really, but with Goering it is as though he is already condemned. The authorities here treat him with contempt. It is refreshing to see him treated with some measure of respect.'

'I was happy to help doctor. Even a prisoner deserves some dignity,' Petersen said, adding to himself, 'and don't I know it.'

'Perhaps you will be able to assist me again,' Schuster said, balancing the tray on his left hand as he shook Petersen's hand.

'Any time I can help, doctor, please let me know,' Petersen answered.

Chapter 54

The Tribunal spent August hearing the defense of the various organizations charged with criminal conduct. Counsel for the SS, *Gestapo*, Nazi Party, General Staff and other organizations presented materials and witnesses in the hopes of securing favorable verdicts for their collective clients. Finally, on August 30, Sir Geoffrey Lawrence notified the defense counsels and the prosecution that the Tribunal would hear the final statements of the individual defendants the following day.

Friday, August 31, was a warm, clear day with a blue sky and high, white wispy clouds. Petersen and his guards escorted the defendants through the covered walkway and into the basement of the Palace of Justice. There, they uncuffed the defendants from their escorts and began the time consuming process of transferring the accused up to the top floor courtroom. Three at a time, they rose in the small elevator.

As the elevator arrived back in the basement, Sergeant Lewis stuck his head out and summoned LT Petersen over. 'Sir, she's starting to clunk real badly toward the top.'

'Well,' Petersen glanced quickly around, 'we've only got to make a few more trips. Let's see if we can get them all upstairs.'

Lewis completed two more trips in the protesting elevator. 'OK, sir,' he said, ready to make the last lift with Petersen and Goering as his passengers. They stepped into the tight compartment, Petersen pressing his back against the rear wall, Goering and Lewis in front of him. 'Ready when you are Sergeant Lewis,' he said. Lewis closed the grate and the door and slid the control handle to the up position. The compact car began to rise slowly, giving a jerk every few feet. As they reached the top floor, the elevator came to a premature halt. Lewis toggled the handle back and forth, but the stubborn elevator refused to budge. 'Can you open the door?' Petersen asked calmly.

'Let's find out,' Lewis replied. He pulled the grate back to the right and then wedged the fingers of both hands into the tiny gap between the edge of the door and the side of the compartment. Goering looked on patiently, a light sheen of sweat appearing on his forehead in the warm, still air of the elevator. Lewis tugged and the door budged slightly. Fortunately, PFC Rogers, already in the courtroom and having already experienced an uncertain ride in the elevator, noticed that the door was stuck. From the courtroom side, Rogers also grasped the door and pulled. That was enough to free the door and the captives inside. The elevator had halted about a foot below its normal stop, causing Goering to climb up to get out. 'Well, *Reichsmarschall*,' Petersen said, 'at least we've given you the opportunity to make a dramatic entrance.' Goering grinned, grasped both sides of the opening and pulled himself up. He strode purposefully to his customary seat in the dock, all eyes in the courtroom following his path.

'Article 24, paragraph D of the Tribunal's charter,' Sir Geoffrey began after gaveling the crowded courtroom to order, 'allows any defendant who so desires to make a statement to the Tribunal. Counsel for the defendants have indicated that each of their clients wish to avail themselves of this opportunity. The Tribunal calls forth the defendant Hermann Wilhelm Goering.'

Goering, in his best loose-fitting, pale blue *Luftwaffe* uniform, rose from his position of prominence in the dock. Once again, a sentinel held up a microphone into which he could speak. Goering eyed the eight men whose judgment would decide his fate. He cleared his throat. 'The prosecution has steadfastly failed to prove its charges against me,' he began. 'They have presented no basis for their despicable allegations. They claim that as the second man behind the Fuehrer, I must have known everything that happened. This is a ridiculous assertion, unsupported by the evidence. We have heard repeatedly from the prosecution that the worst crimes were kept the most secret. This is true. They were kept even from me! These mass murders surprise me, sicken me and are incomprehensible to me. I was never involved, never involved in such despicable activities. I did not order the execution of Jews, nor did I condone the shooting of enemy fliers.' Goering spoke without notes, his large face intense, his gaze burning into the judges on the bench above him. 'There is no evidence presented where any unit under my command carried out any such action!

The prosecution has brought forth third and fourth hand documents, poorly translated and misinterpreted. They have entered into this court's record comments made by me over a span of 25 years and taken without context.'

Goering punctuated his statements by slapping his broad hands together and by stabbing a thick finger at the prosecutors' tables. 'The people of Germany placed their trust in the Fuehrer. Having placed this trust in him, they had no further influence on events. The German people are loyal, courageous and self-sacrificing. They fought like lions in a life or death struggle which began against their will and against their desires. They, like me, are free of guilt. I did not want this war, nor did I cause it. In fact, as has been testified here, I did all in power to prevent this war, on both fronts. I accept responsibility for the things I have done, but not for things which I did not. I never desired to enslave or make war on foreign peoples, nor did I conspire to commit the atrocities made known to me only here in this court. My only motive during the first war, during this last war and during the intervening years has been my love for the German people and my desire for the happiness, freedom and greatness of the German nation. For this, I call on the Almighty as my witness.' Goering sat, his chin high. The other defendants nodded their heads in approval, rallied by Goering's defiance.

Following Goering, each of the other defendants, from Hess through Fritzsche was allowed to make his statement.

As the clock headed inexorably toward 1700 hours, Sir Geoffrey finally brought the day to its conclusion. 'The Tribunal will consider the statements of the defendants in its deliberations. We now adjourn to consider judgment. Before we do so, the Tribunal expresses its appreciation for the high degree of professionalism and dedication exhibited by the counsel for the defense and the counsel for the prosecution in the pursuit of their duties in this unprecedented endeavor. Thank you gentlemen,' Sir Geoffrey nodded first toward the defense and then to the prosecution. 'We are adjourned.'

With the elevator out of service, Petersen held the defendants in the dock until the courtroom was cleared of all the press, spectators and lawyers. He sent Sergeant Lewis ahead to ensure the stairwell was clear. Then, with the defendants again manacled to their guards, Sergeant Hottle led the procession out of the courtroom. Petersen trailed behind Goering, the last prisoner in line.

It had been an emotional day for the defendants. For several, it was the first time they had spoken before the tribunal since it convened ten months earlier. For others, like Goering, it had been an opportunity to speak freely, to say what was on his mind, without the risk of interruption or challenge. Although the defendants now awaited the judgment of the Tribunal, and with it a glimpse of their fate, at least part of the weight seemed to have been lifted off their shoulders by the conclusion of the trial.

They descended the stairs, flight by flight, maintaining their column of twos, prisoners on the right and guards on the left. They reached the ground floor and headed toward the walkway between the Palace and the prison. They continued through the walkway and filed through the door into C Wing and their cell block. Petersen stood watching on the door step as the last few pairs stepped inside. He heard the sound of running steps pounding down the walkway behind him and turned to see Colonel Gaffner, red-faced, hurtling toward him. Unsure of what was compelling his commander, Petersen came to attention and saluted. The door swung shut behind him as Goering disappeared inside.

'What are you thinking?' Gaffner shouted, skidding to a stop in front of his lieutenant. 'Do you have any idea, any idea at all of what you are doing?' the colonel raged, veins on his neck popping out, his bloodshot eyes bulging.

'Sir, I...,' Petersen began, still holding his salute, uncertain and confused by Gaffner's fury.

'Why the hell did you march your prisoners through the entire building?' Gaffner demanded. 'Don't you understand the enormous risk you just took?' Gaffner continued to pepper Petersen with shouted questions. 'Are you trying to make me look like an idiot, boy? Like an incompetent? Are you trying to get people killed here, son?' Gaffner was swinging his large head back and forth, spitting the words out, nervously slapping his riding crop against his left thigh.

'Beg the colonel's pardon, sir,' Petersen attempted to regain control of the situation, 'the elevator broke and we had to ...'

'Dammit boy!' Gaffner spat, 'there's a whole bunch of Germans out there,' he waved his right arm generally toward the wall surrounding the prison, 'that would like nothing more than to free these Nazi sons-of-bitches and you just gave them a golden opportunity!'

Petersen had had enough. 'Well it doesn't look like anything happened, does it colonel?' he snapped. Gaffner sputtered once and then let fly with a right hook. Petersen saw it coming and ducked enough that the blow glanced off the left side of his forehead, knocking his helmet liner to the ground. Gaffner was apoplectic, and was drawing back his left arm for a punch to Petersen's gut when suddenly Captain Stevens was between them, grabbing the colonel around his shoulders and shouting at Petersen.

'Get inside now, lieutenant!' he shouted. 'Move!'

Petersen hesitated only a moment, glaring at Gaffner, who was still struggling to free himself from Stevens. Petersen reached down and snatched his head gear, turned and went inside.

He was breathing hard and trembling with anger and embarrassment when Stevens stepped into the cell block. Without a word, the captain grabbed Petersen by the arm and pulled him quickly into his office. Stevens closed the door behind him and paused, looking down at the floor. 'Are you OK John?' he asked, still somewhat winded himself.

'No sir. I'm not OK and I won't be OK until I get out from under the command of that stupid son of a bitch out there,' Petersen bit off his words. He was working hard to maintain his composure in front of Stevens whom he respected. Stevens crossed behind his desk and fell back into his chair. He motioned for Petersen to sit down.

'Tell me what happened out there, LT Petersen,' Stevens ordered in a voice that now conveyed a more official level of concern.

'Maybe you can tell me sir. What did our commanding officer say? We had just returned the prisoners to the cell block and he comes running up behind me and lays into me like I've just peed in General Eisenhower's corn flakes. Some bullshit about how I've just put everybody's life in danger. I still have no idea what I've done to deserve any kind of reprimand,' Petersen complained.

Stevens nodded. 'Lieutenant, if you choose to make a formal complaint, I will write a statement attesting to what I saw, which is you being struck by your commanding officer. I cannot state what provoked his action, but I would tell what I saw.'

Petersen was beginning to calm down. He had stopped shaking and knowing that Stevens seemed to see things the same way he did, reassured him. 'Look sir,' he said, eyes fixed on the captain's, 'I don't want to cause trouble and I don't want to be involved in trouble. I just want to do my damn job and get the hell out of Dodge. I just don't get what sets him off like that. What did I do?'

'Gaffner's a jerk. He wants to be Patton but the war's over. Plus, as you have previously observed, he drinks too much. I think that's why his emotional equilibrium is so out of whack,' Stevens offered.

'You're starting to sound like a shrink,' Petersen smiled.

'Gaffner's living in some fantasy world,' Stevens continued in a serious tone. 'He's convinced some band of Nazi werewolves is going to try to break these guys out and set up a new Reich somewhere south of here in the mountains. I think that notion is clouding his judgment. He sees this trial as so close to being over, but still sees the long shadows of the boogie man just beyond every corner.'

'Why doesn't General Watson relieve him?' Petersen asked. 'I can't be the only guy he treats this way. Surely someone else has noticed he's got a screw loose.'

'Nobody wants to take on a colonel, especially one with a good combat record,' Stevens explained. 'Just two minutes ago you yourself refused to take him on when you had every right to do so. People just want to get this done and go home.'

Chapter 55

Dusk had fallen by the time Petersen left the prison. He had made his customary tour of the mess hall, checking in with Sergeant Goodman. He had stopped by the infirmary for an update from Dr. Schuster and had inspected his guards at their posts. His last stop had been back at Stevens' office, where he found the captain pulling on his coat and preparing to leave. He thanked Stevens for stepping in and preventing a disaster with Gaffner.

As he turned the corner off *Hauptstrasse* and began to walk down *Gartenstrasse*, a jeep of military policemen raced by behind him, headlights ablaze. He was absorbed in his own thoughts of the day, still unsure what caused Gaffner's seemingly bitter animosity towards him.

The bright light was in his face before he realized what it was. Looking up, he saw two husky MPs, one directly in front of him and one immediately to his left, just off the sidewalk, standing in the street. A small spotlight from a jeep holding two other MPs was shining in his face, partially blinding him.

'Good evening, sir,' said the MP in front of him. 'I wonder if we might see some identification please.'

Petersen looked from one MP to the other, then at the jeep. 'Sure,' he said, his senses on alert. He reached into his pocket and the MP in the street flinched. Petersen moved slowly, extracting his ID card and deliberately handing it to the MP sergeant on the sidewalk. The sergeant clicked on a hand held flashlight and studied Petersen's identification card. He clicked the light off, handed the card back and saluted, 'Thank you LT Petersen,' he said. 'Have a nice evening sir.'

'OK, thanks,' Petersen said, but the MPs had already boarded their jeep. The driver slapped it into gear and the jeep sped up the street, the spotlight swinging back and forth, illuminating the alleys and the covered entrances to the buildings on either side of the street. Petersen shook his head in wonder. Maybe they're chasing werewolves too, he thought. They weren't.

Lisbeth was back to her cheerful self, her smile dazzling to John. She greeted him with a long kiss and pulled him by the arm to the table, where a plate of warm and tasty noodles and pork awaited. She retrieved a lukewarm beer for him, opened it and sat it on the table. She pulled up a chair and sat beside him.

'Shouldn't we wait on Robert?' he asked.

'No. Is hot. Eat,' she replied.

'How was your day?' John asked, repeating what had become a daily ritual. They had agreed that Lisbeth would work on improving her English and John's question gave her a chance to practice conversation. She related the events of her day, including her trip to the market and what she had listened to on the radio. She liked the radio, especially the music programs. Jack Benny and the other comedies were hard to understand, as were the hourly newscasts.

Lisbeth was singing a Dinah Shore song when the front door burst open and Robert jumped inside. He quickly closed the door behind him and stood quiet and still, peering through the front window. Lisbeth and John watched from the table, equally quiet and equally still. A light clicked on in John's head.

'I told the MPs you would be home about 2030 hours,' he said.

'You what?' Robert's eyes widened.

'Yes, I told them you were usually busy with commercial matters on Friday evenings and that I would turn off all the lights and then turn 'em right back on when you got here.' John stood and made his way toward the floor lamp by the sofa.

'Wait John!' Robert pleaded, almost breathless. John stopped and stared at his friend. Robert's mind was frantically trying to understand what was happening when, unable to sustain the charade, John broke out into boisterous laughter.

'You should have seen the look on your face!' he panted as another wave of delight rolled over him.

Robert was not amused, his lips drawn into a tight grimace. 'Very funny,' was all he could say as he disappeared into his bedroom. He came back out a few minutes later, dressed in an old sweater and a pair of well-worn corduroys. 'OK Costello,' Robert said, 'see how funny this strikes you!' He tossed a fist sized bundle of occupation script to John, who caught it in his left hand.

'Whoa! How much is this?'

'About 10,000 marks. Who's laughing now?' Robert asked with an air of satisfaction.

John plunked the roll of bills down on the table. Lisbeth picked it up and studied it. 'Robert, all kidding aside, I did have an unplanned meeting with the MPs tonight. They were patrolling the street and they stopped me to check my ID. Are you up to something that I need to know about?'

'I am always up to something, John. I think you know that by now. But no, most definitely no, you do not need to know about it.' Robert grabbed a plate and before Lisbeth could react, was scooping noodles and pork out of a pot on the stove.

'I don't want to see you get nabbed pal. The MPs are pretty serious and so is the CID. If you get caught with your hand in the cookie jar, they are going to slam you like a screen door,' John warned his friend.

'How quaint. I hope this is not the level of English you are teaching our beautiful friend here,' Robert said gesturing toward Lisbeth, who smiled. 'Don't worry about me John. I have an in with the CID. I know their next move before they do.'

Chapter 56

Family visits were scheduled during the month of September. With the Tribunal in recess for the eight judges to consider verdicts and sentences, Petersen and LT Langley had set up two interview rooms in which the defendants could host family members. LT Rose's illness had developed into a serious case of pneumonia and he had been evacuated to the large Army hospital in Frankfurt.

The reunions were often tearful events; the participants in many cases had not seen each other throughout the entire war. This was particularly true of the military men. Keitel, for instance, like so many Germans, had suffered great personal losses during the war. Two of his sons were missing in action, the third, confirmed dead. Of his two daughters, only one had survived. His reunions were sorrowful events. Some of the defendants had no family, or at least none who would claim them.

These visits, like the defendants' meetings with their lawyers, were strictly supervised. Physical contact was prohibited, although some of the guards looked the other way when younger children attempted to hug their fathers.

The defendants also passed time in a 'social' room set up on orders from Gaffner. In this room, each defendant was allowed to invite three other defendants for an hour long chat. Each was permitted to host two such evenings.

The visits and the socials helped pass the time, time that marched inexorably toward an appointment with the Tribunal's judgment.

When he adjourned the Tribunal on August 31, Sir Geoffrey Lawrence had intended that it reconvene to announce its judgments and sentences on September 23. As the judges deliberated, it soon became apparent that agreement on the verdicts and sentences for each of the individual defendants and the Nazi organizations would not be reached in time. Sir Geoffrey moved the final session of the Tribunal back a week, to the following Monday, September 30.

The Tribunal spent that Monday reading its judgments of the major organizations. As expected, the Nazi Party leadership corps was declared a criminal organization, as was the *Gestapo* and the SS. The Reich Cabinet, which the Tribunal found to be an organization in name only, with no real authority, was not declared criminal, nor was the German General Staff. Monday's adjournment set the stage for the final session of the Tribunal and the judgments on the individual defendants for their roles in plunging Europe into the catastrophe of total war.

Tuesday was a gray, overcast day in Nuremberg. An early autumn front was moving in from the west and rain was in the forecast. The leaves on the trees were already showing their fall colors and the cool air was thickening with humidity. The defendants were in a gray mood as well, the day of judgment upon them.

At 1000 hours, the president of the Tribunal, Lord Justice Sir Geoffrey Lawrence, rapped his gavel and the court chambers fell silent. Petersen, at his post in the rear of the courtroom near the repaired elevator, looked once more down his row of silent guards. Lined up behind the defendants' dock, their eyes were fixed straight ahead, their hands pressed together into the smalls of their backs. He looked into the dock, all of the defendants were present and all were unusually attentive. Petersen looked into the visitors' gallery, speckled with uniforms of green, brown, navy, blue, and khaki. He saw Robert's round face, uncharacteristically solemn, focused not on the lovely young lady beside him, but on the judges' bench. There, beneath the brightly colored flags of the conquering nations, Sir Geoffrey cleared his throat.

'Article 26 of the charter provides that this Tribunal state the basis of its judgment on the innocence or guilt of each defendant,' Sir Geoffrey said, adjusting his glasses and pulling a sheaf of papers toward him. 'The defendant Goering.' Petersen saw Goering lean forward slightly, placing his large hands on either knee, his face vacant of expression. Sir Geoffrey looked down at his notes. 'Goering is indicted on all four counts. He enjoyed the closest most influential of relations with Hitler, at least until 1943. He has testified that Hitler consulted him and kept him informed of all important decisions. He commanded the *Luftwaffe* in Germany's wars of aggression against Poland, Norway, France, the Low Countries and the U.S.S.R. He directed that slave labor be imported from conquered territories for use in war industries. He persecuted Jews, leveling massive fines on them. In 1941, he directed Himmler and Heydrich to bring about a 'complete solution' to the Jewish question in German occupied territory.'

Lifting his eyes from the pages before him, Sir Geoffrey focused a cold stare on Goering, who met the judge with steely eyes. 'There are no mitigating factors. His guilt is unique in its enormity. The record discloses no excuses for this man. The Tribunal finds this defendant guilty on all four counts of the indictment.'

A tremor of excitement shuddered the spectators. Reporters scribbled madly. Goering remained impassive. Sir Geoffrey moved on to Hess. Down through the dock the solemn roll call continued. Hess, guilty. Keitel, guilty. Jodl, guilty. Doenitz, Speer, Raeder, Rosenberg all guilty. In the end, only von Papen, Hitler's erstwhile vice chancellor, Fritzsche and Schacht were declared not guilty. The Tribunal recessed.

Petersen was uncertain what to do with the three former defendants whom the court had acquitted of criminal wrong-doing. He quickly directed the guards assigned to von Papen, Fritzsche and Schacht to escort them out of the courtroom and to hold them in the attic room used for the prisoners' luncheons. Those who had been judged guilty were escorted back into the small elevator for their descent into the Palace's basement. There they would wait until they were recalled, one-by-one, for the pronouncement of their sentences.

Gaffner had planned ahead for once. As a preliminary to the sentencing of the prisoners, he stationed an Army doctor with sedatives and two burly military policemen near the back of the court room just in case any prisoner lost his composure.

At 1450 hours that first day of October, Sir Geoffrey and his seven grim faced colleagues waited for the elevator door to slide open. The court room was full. No empty seats remained except those in the prisoners' dock. Petersen waited beside the door. He had given Sergeant Lewis a list of the order in which the prisoners were to be returned to the court room. Each would have his handcuffs removed in the elevator by his assigned guard. When the small car reached the court room, the guard and Sergeant Lewis would remain in it, the cuffs carefully concealed behind the guard's back. The defendant would be called forward to receive his sentence. The first name on Lewis' list was Goering.

Precisely on schedule, the elevator door slid open. All eyes in the chamber focused on the figure of Hermann Goering, his light blue tunic and trousers baggy on his reduced frame. He walked purposefully to the witness stand and came to attention behind it. Sir Geoffrey paused, looking at the man before him, a man who only six years earlier had stood on the eastern shore of the English Channel planning the invasion of Sir Geoffrey's homeland. 'Defendant Hermann Wilhelm Goering, on the Counts of the Indictment on which you have been convicted, the International Military Tribunal sentences you to death by hanging.' Goering paled, looked down at his feet, then turned and disappeared back into the elevator.

Chapter 57

The cell block was quiet, the prisoners alone with their thoughts. There would be no more social periods for the condemned. Petersen made a last check of his guards and then began his solemn walk home. He dreaded facing Lisbeth. She had made her views on the subject of the trials, and particularly the sentences, clearly known before the Tribunal's September recess. A misty rain was falling, muffling the sound of his footsteps as he walked home in the darkness. The musty smell of damp masonry added to Petersen's melancholy.

Lisbeth was outwardly calm as she kissed him at the door. She gave him a brief embrace and hung up his raincoat on the rack. She led him to the table and sat down beside him, keeping firm hold of his hand. 'I must to you something say,' she said, her English continuing to improve. John nodded. 'The court's decision is not good. These men did their jobs,' her eyes were intense, focused on his. 'They followed orders. Like you. Like Robert.' She looked away, now holding his hands in both of hers. 'They do not deserve to hang,' she said softly.

John reached out and placed his right hand under her chin, gently turning her face back toward his. 'Lisbeth,' he said slowly, 'please understand. I can't do anything about the court's judgment. These men were more than soldiers. They were politicians and policy makers,' John was not sure Lisbeth understood all his words. 'They have good lawyers and they can appeal...'

Lisbeth snorted and pulled her hands away. 'What good is appeal?' she asked. 'Appeal is to same countries that condemn them.'

John knew Lisbeth had followed the trials and assumed she had read of the appeals process in the German papers. Those found guilty by the Tribunal could indeed appeal, not to the Tribunal, but to the Allied Control Council in Berlin. Of course the Control Council was, as Lisbeth had noted, composed of representatives of the same four conquering powers which sat on the Tribunal. John supposed that to most Germans it looked so similar as to make no real difference. He further supposed that a people so used to the totalitarian abuses of power would not, or could not, imagine that the outcome of the Tribunal was anything other than the victors exacting revenge from the vanquished.

John left his chair and knelt beside Lisbeth. She sat still, looking at him, hands in her lap. He reached for her hands. 'You are the most important thing to me,' he said. 'Not the Army, not the court or the prisoners, you. If I could change this for you, I would. But this is far beyond my power to control,' he said. He knew this was not what she wanted to hear and so he was surprised when she leaned forward and hugged him.

'You are good man,' she said, but there was no joy in her words.

Later, they sat together in the darkened house, the only light from the glow of the radio's dials. They listened to Harry James' orchestra and a brief news summary. Lisbeth relaxed a bit. Maybe, John thought, she said what she needed to say and that will be the end of it. Of course it wasn't.

Chapter 58

On Wednesday, Colonel Gaffner directed that all prisoners once again be assigned new cells. In keeping with the structure of his military mind, he decreed that prisoners serving term sentences be confined on the third tier cell block. Those sentenced to life imprisonment were assigned to the second tier. The condemned men were to remain on the ground floor, but in different cells.

As the guards looked on, German workers from the neighboring wing of the prison were brought in to move Petersen's prisoners and their belongings. Security was tight. Each worker was carefully searched before being allowed into C Wing. A guard accompanied each worker the entire time that worker was inside C Wing. Sorting the seventeen remaining prisoners was a relatively simple job. The majority of them would not be moving upstairs. Eleven of them, including Goering, would merely transfer into a different cell, still on the ground floor.

As the last of the cell exchanges was completed, Captain Stevens motioned Petersen into his office. 'A new assignment for you LT Petersen,' Stevens said brandishing an official looking paper. 'You have been assigned the additional duty of Property Officer as LT Rose is no longer around to fulfill the many and varied obligations of the position. Here's the key,' he said, tossing a small brass key to Petersen. 'All you have to do is control access to the baggage room. If one of the prisoners needs anything from their luggage, use your best professional judgment. Any questions?'

'Who else has a key, sir?' Petersen asked, annoyed at LT Rose for coming down with pneumonia.

'I have one and there's one in the colonel's office safe.'

Goering was in a listless mood. His face was drawn and dour, its gray color matching the autumn weather. He sat in his wooden chair facing the blurry cello-glass window which the dying, late afternoon light was struggling to penetrate. Petersen, as was his daily custom, peered through the guard's opening into the *Reichsmarschall*'s cell, prompting Goering to look around.

'Ah, hello LT Petersen,' Goering said without his usual bravado. He stood and walked over to the door, hands thrust into the pockets of his trousers.

'Good afternoon, *Reichsmarschall.*'

'You see I have a new room and a new view for my last days on earth,' Goering swept his arm toward the window. 'It is not right, you know,' he said.

'What's that, sir?' Petersen replied.

'It is not right that I should be hanged like a criminal. I was a soldier, like you!' he said, pounding his chest with his fist, color rising in his cheeks. 'And here I sit, judged by a bunch of clerks, men who never fired a shot, who never lived in the mud or watched their friends die. Those fat, old bastards sat through the war in their warm dens with their hot food. What do they know of duty?' Goering swung his head back and forth as he talked. 'Except maybe for the Russian,' Goering added. 'He looks like a tough son of a bitch.'

'Yes sir,' Petersen agreed, having had the same thought about General Nikitchenko, one of the Russian judges.

'LT Petersen,' Goering drew closer to the door and lowered his voice to just above a whisper. 'I must ask you a favor. I refuse to die as a criminal, swinging from the end of the hangman's rope. You must help me.'

'Sir, I don't see how I can…'

'I have asked to be executed by firing squad. You would honor me, and our most unusual friendship, if you would command this detachment,' Goering's eyes were steady, focused on Petersen's face through the wire grate of the door.

'*Reichsmarschall,*' Petersen stammered, 'that would be up to the Tribunal. I am just a soldier here sir. I'd help you if I could, but I can't.'

Goering stared back through the opening. 'Of course,' he said, breaking eye contact and shaking his head. 'I am afraid I am going soft in the head in here,' he attempted a laugh, but it died in his chest. 'You are a good soldier LT Petersen. I would have been proud to serve with you. Orders must of course be obeyed and one must take care to abide in his place.'

Chapter 59

'He wanted me to shoot him.'

'You're kidding!' Robert responded in amazement. 'Right then?'

'No, Einstein! He wanted me to command his firing squad,' John explained.

'I thought he was going to be hanged!' Robert was a step behind the flow of the conversation. Lisbeth however was listening intently.

'That's right. He was sentenced to hang, but he's appealed to the Control Council to be shot,' John said, glancing at Lisbeth.

'He should be shot,' she said, her chin stuck out and her hands resting on her hips.

Robert dared a look at her and then turned back to John. 'Will the Council acquiesce?'

'You tell me, you're the man with the inside dope.'

Robert took another pull from his beer, which was mercifully growing colder with each passing day. 'My guess is that they won't mess with anything the Tribunal has decided. For one thing, they don't have good legal standing to do so since the Council is more of an administrative body. They're ready for all this to be over. Everybody is. This is the last chapter of the war. The whole world is ready to move on, especially the Germans,' Robert said looking to Lisbeth.

'Yes,' she said, 'especially the Germans.'

Chapter 60

'Especially the Germans,' Captain Allgood said. 'The battalion S2 says their morale remains very high despite the weather and they show no signs of giving in. Of course given the ass they've been kicking over the past few days, my morale would be pretty good too.' Allgood was leaning over a makeshift table in a barn in the snow covered Belgian countryside near the village of Verdenne. His Michelin Guide map was stretched out in front of him and his platoon leaders. The 84th Division, after its impressive successes spearheading the Allied attack into Germany, had been withdrawn from the front in early December. The division missed the initial German onslaught through the Ardennes forests, but was hastily shoved back into the lines on December 19th. Now, on Christmas Eve, with the temperatures hovering near zero and blowing snow obstructing vision and grounding Allied air support, the 84th, and Baker Company were preparing to take the offensive. 'Hey, check that blanket,' Allgood shouted at his clerk, pointing to a wool blanket draped over the barn's one window. He nudged the kerosene lantern closer to the map and resumed his mission briefing. 'Our job is to advance along this road,' he said pointing to a farm road running to the southeast out of the village. 'The Krauts are in defensive positions in these woods here,' he marked an 'X' on the map with his pencil.

'Lieutenant Dickens, 3rd platoon will advance on the left. Sergeant Petersen, you take 2nd platoon on the right. Sergeant Martin and 1st platoon in reserve. Mortars will be here,' he jabbed at the map again, 'priority to 3rd platoon.'

Petersen would like to have had priority, a little extra firepower could make a big difference in a frontal assault against an entrenched enemy. But, Dickens was new and needed all the help he could get. This was his first offensive after a week holding the line against countless German attacks. This would also be Petersen's first attack, at least as the platoon leader of the under strength 2nd platoon. Petersen had been assigned as platoon sergeant following the attack at Lindern where LT Long and half the platoon had been killed or wounded. Allgood knew the

214

mauling would have been worse if not for Petersen's quick attack into the German flank.

'Sir, one question,' Petersen spoke up.

'Shoot.'

'How far is it from here to here,' Petersen put one finger on the south end of the village and the other on the tree line suspected of harboring the enemy's positions.

'I make it at just over a mile of wide open, snow covered ground, with little or no cover and concealment,' Allgood said. 'We get no breaks on this one. Our only advantages are surprise and cover of darkness. If we're lucky, it will snow too. We go at 0100. Good luck and Merry Christmas.'

'Merry Christmas, sir!' the platoon leaders responded. With that, they gathered their gear, bundled up and stepped into the cold, harsh darkness.

Second platoon had no visions of sugar plums. Sequestered in a Belgian farm house, they spent the dark hours of Christmas Eve redistributing ammunition and reviewing the plan of attack. Petersen covered their sign/countersign and they synchronized watches. After that, Petersen directed them to eat. What they had was cold, but it was important that they eat and save up their energy for the attack. While his men ate, Petersen moved among them, checking their equipment, asking them questions about the attack plan and offering words of encouragement. 'Davis,' he said, crouching beside his first squad leader. 'Keep an eye on things here.' He tapped the face of his watch. 'If I'm not back by midnight, go ahead without me,' he winked. Davis chuckled 'Sure, John.'

By 2200 hours, Petersen was back carrying a large pasteboard box. He staggered under its weight and let it drop to the floor of the farm house with a loud thump. 'All right boys,' Petersen said just loud enough for all to hear, 'gather round.' He pulled back the flaps of the box and began pulling out white woolen underwear. 'Courtesy of your friendly division quartermaster!' he smiled. Immediately several of the men began

215

to disrobe. 'Hold it boys,' Petersen held up his hand. 'These go on the outside.'

'The outside, sarge?' George Fagan asked.

'Yep, we're going across a mile of snow covered ground and these babies,' he tapped the box, 'are our camouflage!' Smiles broke out as 2nd platoon realized Santa Claus had made a totally unexpected visit.

Chapter 61

The hour between midnight and 0100 was cold but quiet. John lay with his long arm draped over Lisbeth's tiny frame. Over the last few days, she had seemed to relax more, the debates over the relative merits of firing squads and hangmen fortunately behind them. She had been more affectionate, more like the Lisbeth of the previous winter and spring. John snuggled closer to her and felt her stir. He fell back to sleep.

A loud pounding. John didn't know where he was, only that there was a loud pounding noise coming from nearby. He realized he was still in bed, in the darkness, Lisbeth beside him. The noise continued and he realized it was coming from the main room, more specifically from the front door. He dragged himself out of the bed, trying not to disturb Lisbeth, but wondering how she was sleeping through the racket. He pulled on his robe and closed the door to the bedroom behind him.

By the time he reached the front door, his head had cleared sufficiently to realize that no one came calling at this time of night to deliver good news. He took a deep breath and opened the door. There, in the dim illumination of a flashlight was man in a dark overcoat and fedora.

'LT Petersen? Forgive the interruption,' said the man. Petersen knew he had seen him before, but could not remember when or where.

'What is it? I know you, but I can't remember how,' Petersen was confused, and concerned.

'I'm sorry!' the man exclaimed, 'I should have introduced myself immediately,' he said reaching into his breast pocket and pulling out a wallet. He flipped it open revealing some sort of badge. 'Dan Nealy, Criminal Investigation Division. We met at your Colonel Gaffner's Christmas party last year. Can I come in?'

'Sure, sure, sorry,' Petersen apologized stepping back and opening the door wider. 'Listen Mr. Nealy, what's this all about? What time is it anyway?'

'Unfortunately, I'm here on business, but I guess you already figured that out,' Nealy smiled as John switched on the overhead light. 'And it's about,' he looked at his watch, 'about 0230.'

'Here,' John gestured at the table, 'have a seat.'

Nealy took off his overcoat, looking around at the house as he did. He took in the phonograph and the radio. He made a mental sketch of the layout, noticing the four chairs at the table, the small sofa and the closed doors leading to the two bedrooms. 'Nice place you got here LT Petersen.'

'Thanks,' John said. 'LT Simmons gets the credit.' He regretted his words immediately.

'Yeah,' Nealy said, taking a seat opposite John at the table. 'Yeah, actually I'm here to ask you about LT Simmons.'

'Look Mr. Nealy,' John began, trying to delay and compose a strategy at the same time, 'I'm happy to help you however I can, but can't this wait until morning. I'm sure I would be a little more clear-headed in the daylight,' John attempted a small laugh.

Nealy plowed ahead. 'Sorry LT Petersen. As I said, I'm here on official business and unfortunately it won't keep until morning. I am investigating a crime involving LT Simmons and, frankly, I need some help. I'm hoping you can provide some information.'

John was now wide awake and very concerned for his friend's welfare. 'OK, Mr. Nealy. How can I help the CID?'

Nealy went back to his pocket and dug out a small notebook and pencil. 'Can you tell me when and where you first met LT Simmons?' Petersen duly replied to this and half a dozen other harmless questions. Nealy was a methodical questioner, working in a predictable, but effective order. John knew harder questions were just moments away and that he would have to be careful how he answered, for Robert's sake and his own. 'Did you know LT Simmons was involved in the black market?'

'C'mon Mr. Nealy. Name one GI in Germany who's not involved in the black market.'

Nealy lifted his pencil to his lips and looked toward the ceiling. 'Well let's see, there's me, that would be one. And so far, we haven't been able to pin anything on General Eisenhower, that's two.' He dropped the pencil on his notebook and fixed John with a hard stare. 'Look lieutenant, I'm sorry I got you out of bed, but this isn't a game and I'm not here to play Abbott and Costello. I've got a job to do and I'd appreciate your help. But get this straight, I'm going to do it with your help or without it. What'll it be?'

'Sorry,' John said and indeed he was, for he saw no way out for Robert.

'Do you know who Simmons' colleagues are?'

'No.'

'Have you ever met any of his contacts?'

'Only once. No names or anything, but I saw Robert meet with a German guy once,' John admitted.

'When and where,' Nealy asked pencil poised.

'Gosh, it was right after I got here, back in August or September of last year,' John recalled, leaning back in his chair and rubbing his hand across the top of his head.

'Anything more recent?'

'No, that was the only time I went with him.'

'What happened at that meeting?'

'Well,' John wrinkled his brow, trying to remember back over 14 months. 'He gave this German guy a satchel full of cigarettes. It was up near the Grand Hotel at a little plaza up there.'

'What did the guy, the German look like?'

'He was short, lean, wearing a *Wehrmacht* greatcoat. I remember it had bloodstains on it. I wondered if it was his blood.'

'Lieutenant, I know it's late, but I need you to work a little harder. You've described about 200,000 German men. Can you remember anything else, hair, eyes scars, speech, spectacles, anything?'

'He had dark eyes, short hair, dark face, like a 5 o'clock shadow, but no real facial hair. I'm sorry, it was getting dark and it's been over a year.'

'Besides cigarettes, what else did LT Simmons trade?'

'I really don't know Mr. Nealy. I told Robert, LT Simmons, that I didn't want to be involved and he respected that.'

'Good decision on your part lieutenant. Did LT Simmons mention any names or where his partners worked?'

'No sir,' John lied.

'Did he mention meeting places or shipments, anything like that?'

'No sir.'

'Did he ever have large amounts of cash?'

'Look Mr. Nealy, I've told you all I know. I'd like to be helpful, but if you want to know more, you really need to talk to LT Simmons,' John said with a tinge of exasperation in his sleepy voice.

Nealy looked up and closed his notebook. 'I'd like that LT Petersen, I really would. But you see,' Nealy paused, 'he's dead.'

Chapter 62

At 0100, 3rd platoon on the left and 2nd platoon on the right began to move out. Dickens looked enviously at his ghost white comrades on the other side of the road. In the darkness, they blended in to the snow blanketed field. Knowing they were only yards away, Dickens could rarely fix them in his vision.

Petersen was half way back as 2nd platoon, crouching low, crept across the frozen field. For hours they moved forward, fingers, toes, cheeks and noses painfully cold. Their breath condensed and froze on their mustaches and whiskers. Petersen was pleased with his men's discipline. They were quiet, stealthy in their advance. When they reached to within 50 yards of the wood line, they halted and hunkered down in the snow. The sky to their left front was beginning to turn dark gray. Petersen could make out the green clad men of 3rd platoon to his left. Their advance had also been skillfully completed, but they would soon find themselves at a serious disadvantage as the morning sky brightened. At a predetermined time, 0700 hours, with the sky still dark except for a thin sliver of pink near the horizon, the first of the mortar rounds began to fall. They were close to Petersen and his men and they felt the uncomfortable concussions as the rounds detonated, scattering snow and frozen clods of dirt. Slowly the mortar rounds marched across the remaining open ground toward the wood line. The German soldiers were shouting and running for cover. Petersen signaled to his men and they crept forward slowly, their movements masked by their camouflage and the smoke and noise from the exploding shells. The mortars walked their rounds into the trees, Petersen and his platoon scarcely 50 yards behind. A round of yellow smoke exploded among the trees, the signal for the ground attack to begin.

'George, Frank! Base of fire!' Petersen shouted above the cacophony of small arms fire. The Germans were firing on 3rd platoon's visible attackers when 2nd platoon's snow ghosts opened up. Petersen and Lincoln dashed the last few yards under covering fire from their platoon mates. Reaching the relative safety of the tree line, they laid down a base of fire to allow their comrades to

move forward and join them. By watching the muzzle flashes, the Americans determined the layout of the defenders' positions. With greater freedom of movement, the Americans dashed in between the German gunners, upsetting their forward oriented fire plans. Petersen positioned two squads to the right and directed the BAR gunners to lay on heavy fire. He dispatched Lincoln and the third squad to attack the Germans' flank. Petersen crawled forward twice, lobbing hand grenades into enemy machine gun positions and knocking the guns out of action. He crawled over the lip of the second dugout and tumbled down into a little parcel of hell. A mangled body sprawled across the top of a red hot barrel of the machine gun, cooking the exposed flesh of the gunner's arm. The sizzling sound and the horrid smell sickened Petersen. He knelt down and looked out of the muddy hole, his knee landing on a Luger pistol. He quickly snatched it up and jammed it into the pocket of his jacket. He turned his attention toward the next German position, just as a German grenade landed in the hole. Petersen jumped as it exploded, sending a hot shard of metal slicing across the top of his left arm. He lay stunned, his eyes burning and his ears ringing, unable to hear anything but a loud fuzzy rush. He looked to his right as Lincoln fell beside him spraying the remaining German positions with his Thompson. Frank Allen plopped into the snow on his left, his BAR stitching the back of a German soldier fleeing into the woods. Petersen closed his eyes and laid his head in the snow.

Chapter 63

Nealy looked across the table. 'I'm not here investigating the black market lieutenant. I'm here investigating a murder,' he said as gently as he knew how. 'We found LT Simmons with a hole through his chest about 2000 hours. He was about a block from the Stork Club, near the Opera House, but we haven't found anything. No shell casings, no weapons, no witnesses. We don't even know if the murder is related to the Black Market or if it was a random shooting. Are you sure you don't know anyone else who might be able to help us?'

Petersen shook his head. 'I'm sorry Mr. Nealy,' he said. 'I don't know who his associates were. There was a pretty, young woman in the PMO's office that came to court with him a couple of times. You probably know her, but I never met her. She might be worth talking to.'

Nealy watched Petersen. He was experienced enough to detect the shock wearing off and the initial stage of grief coming on. 'I'm sorry about your friend lieutenant,' he said. 'Really, I am.'

John looked up. 'Yeah. Thanks.'

Nealy stood and put his coat back on. He stuck out his hand. 'Thanks lieutenant.' John was struck by the coldness of Nealy's grip. 'If you think of anything, you know how to reach me and I would appreciate any help.'

'Of course,' John said, walking Nealy to the door. 'Good night.'

Nealy walked down the steps and turned north on the wet, deserted street. Petersen watched him fade into the night. He pushed the door closed and turned off the light. He sat down at the table and stared into the darkness. He felt Lisbeth's hand on his shoulder. The ticking of the clock echoed through the room.

Chapter 64

'Merry Christmas, sarge!' Pete Whaley's voice echoed around inside his head. Petersen rolled over in the snow and looked up into Whaley's cherubic, red face. The sun was up now, burning through a light fog, and promising the first clear day in over a week. Petersen watched, detached, as Whaley, Baker Company's medic, clipped away at his left sleeve. The medic jabbed a small syringe into Petersen's arm. Petersen wondered why he couldn't feel it. He knew Whaley though and he knew Whaley would take care of him. He still couldn't hear very well. It was as though he was at the seashore and someone was holding shells over both his ears. Petersen watched silently as Whaley wrapped a bandage around his left bicep. Whaley's lips were moving and he was looking at Petersen and smiling.

'What?' Petersen asked, his own voice sounding strangely muffled.

'I said it looks like you boys really kicked Hermann's ass!' Whaley shouted. 'And it looks like you are going to get a well-earned rest,' he said tying off the ends of the bandage. 'Don't worry though sarge. The only lasting damage from this little nick will be a handsome scar!' Whaley patted Petersen on his helmet. 'Feel like standing up?' Petersen nodded. Whaley helped him to his knees and then to his feet. 'Steady now!' he shouted in Petersen's ear. Whaley handed Petersen off to Lincoln who helped him to the newly established company command post in yet another farm house, this one closer to the scene of the recently completed action.

Petersen's head was beginning to clear by the time Captain Allgood returned. 'How's your shoulder?' he asked offering Petersen a canteen cup of hot, black coffee.

'OK sir, thanks.' Petersen took a swallow and savored its warmth. He held the canteen cup in his red, cold hands, enjoying the heat.

'Good work Sergeant Petersen. I don't think the Krauts had any idea you and your men were anywhere near them, even after

the shelling started.' Allgood sat down on an ammo crate facing his sergeant. 'Where'd you get the idea for your snow suits?' he asked pointing to Petersen's blood stained woolen outerwear.

'Well sir,' Petersen said, sneaking another sip, 'I was cold and I was thinking it was Christmas Eve and I wanted to get the men something and it just hit me. So I went over to the quartermaster and did a field expedient requisition,' Petersen winked, 'if you know what I mean.'

'I read you,' the captain laughed. 'Good thinking and good work. Second platoon suffered only one killed and two wounded, you and Grambling. He's a little worse off than you, but he'll be all right.' Allgood stood and stretched. 'Sergeant Petersen, you've done a good job with 2nd platoon. Taking over after the action at Lindern, you did an admirable job of rebuilding the platoon. In a relatively short period, you got it combat capable again. Your leadership under fire has been exemplary on several occasions, including today. Your attack knocked a hole in Fritz's line. Second battalion was able to punch through. The Germans are on the defensive for the first time since their offensive began.'

'That's great, sir. Thanks for the coffee,' Petersen said, leaning forward as if to stand.

'Hang on Sergeant Petersen,' Allgood smiled and waved him back to his seat. 'The last week has seriously depleted the division's complement of junior officers. Company commanders have been ordered to recommend for battlefield commissions NCOs who have demonstrated exceptional leadership under fire. I have forwarded your name to Division G1.'

'Yes sir,' Petersen responded, uncertain what to say or even what to feel.

Allgood laughed again. 'Try to contain your excitement sergeant. For now, get back to the battalion aid station and have that shoulder fixed up. Once you're released for duty, report to division for reassignment.' Allgood stepped over and helped Petersen to his feet. 'Congratulations sergeant and well done. You're a good soldier and a fine leader. You'll make an excellent lieutenant. I'm sorry you won't be coming back to Baker

Company, John, but I know you'll be a welcome addition wherever you end up.' Allgood shook his hand. 'Oh, and Merry Christmas!'

Petersen blinked at the glare of the sun off the snow as a trio of P-47's thundered overhead. A jeep rolled slowly by, a wounded soldier lashed across its hood on a stretcher. Petersen hopped on the back, his arm beginning to throb. He had no doubts about his abilities to lead. He had been leading since he was 14 years old at Gatesville. But, he had no idea how to be a gentleman.

Chapter 65

Emmy Sonnemann was a film star when she first met Hermann Goering. Goering, a widower since the death of his Swedish wife in 1931, was captivated by the beautiful and vivacious actress. Together, they formed the most handsome and popular couple in the Third Reich. Emmy, who married Goering in 1935 in what was the second marriage for each of them, enjoyed a lavish lifestyle, moving between mansions, estates and castles in Germany, Austria and Poland. Her husband surrounded her with stunning works of art, most of them looted from the great museums in Germany's conquered territory or stolen from private Jewish collectors. When Emmy gave birth to their daughter Edda in 1938, Goering ordered 500 aircraft to fly over Berlin in jubilant celebration.

By the time of her visit to the prison on the first Saturday in October, Emmy Goering had been reduced to living in a two room cottage without electricity or running water. Her once extensive wardrobe had been pared to two dresses. At 53, even without her accustomed finery, she still possessed the charisma of a movie star. She moved with a graceful fluidity that still caused men's heads to turn and their eyes to stare.

Petersen escorted her into the family interview room in which Goering already waited. When she saw him, her hand went to her mouth and her eyes widened. She started for him, reaching out with her arms. PFC Seleck, as ordered, stepped in between them. Emmy stopped short. Goering fumed. Turning to Petersen he asked with annoyance, 'May I at least be allowed to kiss my wife?'

'Of course, *Reichsmarschall*,' Petersen answered, nodding to Seleck who retreated to his position behind the visitor's table. Petersen watched Emmy's hands as closely as he could to ensure that nothing was passed between husband and wife.

'You look wonderful my dear,' Emmy said as her eyes filled with tears. Petersen figured Goering was about 60 pounds lighter than when Mrs. Goering would have seen him last.

'As do you my darling,' Goering smiled stepping back. 'Let me introduce you to my American friend here, LT Petersen. He is from the great state of Texas!'

'How do you do, LT Petersen,' Mrs. Goering offered her dazzling smile and her right hand. Petersen shook it gently.

'LT Petersen has been my best American friend here,' Goering continued, with a wink at Petersen. 'Here, sit,' he said to Emmy indicating the chair on the side of the table opposite where he would sit.

Emmy, in her frayed dress, and Goering in his now too large uniform, chatted like young lovers, gazing with obvious longing at each other through the wire screen rising from the center of the table. Petersen watched vigilantly, but he tried not to listen. His German was not strong to begin with, but even so, he found it awkward to listen in on what was likely to be the last conversation between this man and his wife.

Only when Goering began to laugh did the conversation recapture Petersen's attention. Emmy was telling Goering about Edda, their eight-year-old daughter. Petersen detected a wistfulness in the *Reichsmarschall*'s expression. Soon, he was laughing again and Emmy was dabbing at her eyes with a lace handkerchief. Petersen watched the clock on the wall as it passed the 30 minutes allotted for the visit. He was reluctant to interrupt. Finally, at 40 minutes, he cleared his throat and nodded to Goering. Goering nodded back, acknowledging that his time was rapidly drawing to a close. He leaned forward, resting his forehead against the screen. Emmy stretched forward as well, so that only the screen separated them. Goering whispered softly, words that Petersen could not discern, 'They will not hang me.'

Chapter 66

Army headquarters in Nuremberg assigned a newly arrived second lieutenant as the survivor's assistance officer and detailed him to catalogue and ship home Simmons' personal effects and property. Lieutenant Godley slowly went through the items in Simmons' bedroom, making a list on a yellow notepad of what was to be shipped home and throwing the rest, like the box of condoms, into a pile on the floor. Uniforms and clothing, official papers, books, and personal possessions like alarm clocks, razors and toiletries were itemized on the pad, line after line, in Godley's tight, neat script.

'Sir, if you will hand me that last book,' Godley said, 'I think that will wrap it up.'

'You don't have to call me sir. I'm a lieutenant like you,' Petersen said again, handing over a copy of *For Whom The Bell Tolls.*

'Yes sir,' Godley answered without looking up from the pad. 'Well, all these things on the bed here will be boxed and shipped to LT Simmons' next of kin. Is there anything else here that belonged to him?' Petersen thought of the record player and the radio, the beer under the back step and the half case of champagne Robert had given Lisbeth. 'No LT Godley, that's pretty much everything. Thanks for your help.' Petersen had liberated the Christmas Luger, rationalizing that he had more right to it than some rich, fat New York banker who had spent the war growing richer and fatter.

'Very well, sir,' Godley said walking to the front door of the house. 'Thank you for your cooperation.' As he reached the top step, Godley turned and saluted. Petersen was caught off guard, but only for a second. He saluted back.

Chapter 67

On Wednesday, October 9, the Allied Control Council, meeting in London, considered the appeals filed by the attorneys for Goering, Hess and the other men judged guilty by the Tribunal. For over three hours, representatives for each of the four powers discussed, debated and deliberated, before finally denying all appeals.

Without the distractions provided by the daily sessions of the Tribunal, the languorous pace of life in the prison slowed to glacial. The prisoners were still allowed to visit Petersen's library, but the small parties they had been allowed during the Tribunal's deliberation period had been terminated. Tempers grew shorter as the hours dragged by. The prisoners weren't the only ones affected. The guards grew increasingly listless, disinterested and dazed, as though the endless hours of watching caged men had dulled their senses. Only during meal periods was there any collective personality evident in the population of the ground floor prisoners, and then, only for the relatively brief duration of the meal period itself.

On Sunday, following the morning chapel service, Colonel Gaffner visited C Wing. Captain Stevens summoned LT Petersen and LT Langley to his office, where the colonel stood nursing a mug of black coffee.

'Good morning, sir,' the two lieutenants said as they entered.

'LT Petersen, LT Langley,' Gaffner nodded. 'Take seats.' The two junior officers sat on straight backed wooden chairs. Stevens edged through the narrow gap between the wall and the corner of his desk and fell back into his chair. Gaffner set the mug down with a shaky hand and brought his hands to his hips. 'Well, men,' he began, looking from the lieutenants to the captain and back, 'we're just about to the end of our mission.' This captured the full attention of the three officers. 'General Watson's office has informed me that the Allied Control Council has denied all of the prisoners' appeals. Now, what that means to us is pretty simple. It means that pretty soon, I don't know how soon yet, but pretty soon, we are going to have eleven less prisoners to worry about. The sentences handed down by the Tribunal will be carried out. The condemned men will be hung.'

'Sir, do we know where that will happen?' Langley ventured to ask.

'Plans are being made even as we speak LT Langley,' Gaffner replied evenly. 'We are still working out the details. My recommendation to General Watson is to use the gym here. It's big enough for the construction of gallows and it has the great advantage of proximity to the prisoners. The less movement involved the better for everybody, them and us.'

'What will our role be, sir?' Stevens asked.

Gaffner nodded, 'Good question. The answer is that we will continue to do pretty much what we've been doing: house, feed and safeguard. We will be responsible for securely transporting the prisoners to the place of execution. That's where our responsibility will terminate, pardon the pun,' Gaffner smiled at his morbid joke. 'I will inform the prisoners this afternoon that their appeals have been denied. LT Petersen,' Petersen's brain jerked to full alert status, 'you will accompany me through the first floor cell block.'

'Yes sir.' Petersen hoped there was no special significance to the colonel's directive. 'Sir, will you tell the prisoners when their sentences will be carried out?'

'I can't,' Gaffner shook his head. 'First of all, I don't know myself just yet. Even when I do find out, I want things to stay as normal around here for as long as possible. I see no reason to tell them until it is time to take them away.'

After lunch, which Petersen observed from the back of the dining room, he met up with Gaffner and Sergeant Barnes to begin the painful task of telling the condemned men that their last hope for clemency had been extinguished. The military men, Keitel and Jodl, received the news stoically, standing ramrod straight and clicking their heels together as Gaffner and Petersen exited their cells. Several of the others trembled. Streicher and Sauckel wept.

Petersen dreaded the confrontation with Goering. Despite the villainy in which Goering had engaged, despite the evil done at his command or with his acquiescence, Petersen had found him to be a likeable rogue, a charming, cultured, intelligent scoundrel. He also feared Goering might put him in an awkward position with Gaffner. He was anxious that Goering not treat him with the same friendly deference he had shown with Mrs. Goering the previous week.

'Well, well, the chief jailer!' Goering smiled and rose from his chair as his cell door swung open and Gaffner strode in. 'To what do I owe the pleasure of your company,' the *Reichsmarschall* said with the familiar twinkle in his eye. Petersen stayed behind the colonel. He could not determine if Goering was genuinely happy for company or if he was hiding behind a thin veil of sarcasm.

'Goering,' Gaffner began abruptly, 'I have come to officially inform you that the Allied Control Council has denied your appeal.'

Goering's smile faded as he digested the news. 'And as to my request that I face a firing squad rather than the hangman, colonel?'

'Your appeal has been denied in all respects, Goering.'

'I suppose it's just as well,' Goering said an angry sneer on his face. 'I hear you Americans are lousy shots!' Petersen looked down at the floor and bit his lip to keep from laughing. But Goering wasn't finished. 'Colonel,' the smile and twinkle reappeared, 'why is it that you consistently fail to show me the respect of my rank and office?'

'You have no rank and no office here Goering,' Gaffner responded coldly.

'Why then do you not address me as *Herr* Goering, in keeping with the most common courtesy?' Petersen fidgeted nervously, fearful of where the conversation might lead.

'Well, you see Goering,' a thin smile spreading across Gaffner's thick face, '*Herr* is a German word and I don't speak German.' Gaffner turned suddenly causing Petersen to dodge to the left as the colonel swept by him and out of the cell.

Petersen nodded to Goering as turned to exit the cell. Goering winked and nodded back.

Chapter 68

Monday morning found LT Petersen sipping coffee with Sergeant Goodman in his basement kitchen. They were discussing food requisitions, trying to figure out when they should reduce the quantities of food ordered to offset the reduction in the number of 'customers.' As they struggled to determine the most likely scenario, Captain Stevens' clerk appeared in the doorway.

'Captain Stevens' compliments, sir,' he said to Petersen. 'The captain would like to see you.'

Petersen gulped down the rest of his coffee and stood up. 'Be back soon,' he said to Goodman who just grunted.

Petersen knocked on the open door and walked in without waiting for a second invitation. 'What's up, sir?' he asked.

Steven's set aside the book he was reading, something by Zane Grey, and said, 'It looks like Wednesday night.'

'What looks like Wednesday…, oh. I understand, sir.' With the date set, the executions were no longer abstract, floating ahead somewhere in the mists of the future. Now they were real and only two days away.

'The mission will be carried out about midnight. I want you and Langley to shift to night duty effective tonight. I want both of you here Wednesday night. Sorry for the short notice, but I just got word myself,' Stevens explained. 'Go home and get some rest then come back here about 2000 hours.'

Petersen acknowledged the change. He informed Sergeant Goodman that, for planning purposes, he could plan on a reduction in the prison population effective Thursday. 'Not a word of this to anybody,' Petersen warned, 'not even to me.'

'Not a word, sir,' Goodman nodded, placing his index finger over his lips. He lowered his head and went back to his work.

Lisbeth was startled when Petersen opened the door to the house on *Gartenstrasse*. 'Oh! You surprise me!' she gasped when she realized it was John.

'Sorry darling,' he said, reaching his arms around her waist and pulling her close. 'I have the day off. I thought we could spend it together.'

Lisbeth looked at him questioningly, then smiled, the sparkle in her eyes returning. '*Ja*, that is nice,' she agreed.

They strolled to the market, where Lisbeth bought food for their supper. Robert had left them with plenty of cash. They had never had to spend any of John's salary. They stopped at a bakery, a small brick building with new glass in the windows and an oven heated by a wood fire. They purchased two small pieces of *Liebkuchen*, a sweet gingerbread-like wafer that was a Nuremberg specialty. They strolled through the old city with Lisbeth pointing out the mostly destroyed home of the famous painter Albrecht Duerer. She told John the story of Hans Sachs, Nuremberg's cobbler-poet, immortalized in Wagner's opera '*Die Meistersinger von Nurnberg*.' The cool, autumn air brought color to her cheeks and made her blue eyes seem bottomless.

As the sun crept past its zenith, they made love in the bedroom. Afterwards, John slept and Lisbeth stole away into the kitchen. At 5 o'clock, he awoke, washed his face and got dressed. The evening meal was served early, in anticipation of John's return to duty. They shared roasted chicken, black bread and asparagus, which John did not much like, but ate anyway.

'Lisbeth, I want to tell you something, but you cannot tell anyone else,' he began. 'Do you understand?'

'Yes.' She put down her fork and put her hands in her lap. John's tone of voice and solemn mood seized her full attention.

'The sentences will be carried out Wednesday night. That's why I've been moved to night duty.'

'And they will be hanged?' Lisbeth asked, but it was really more of a statement.

'Yes,' John replied staring into her blue eyes. 'There was nothing I could do. The Tribunal and the Control Council...'

'I understand,' Lisbeth cut him off. 'It is a tragedy. All of it. Killing to punish for killing.' Her eyes filled with tears which she brushed away with the back of her hand. She stood and placed her hand on John's shoulder. 'I need you to hold me,' she said. John drew her onto his lap and she laid her head against his shoulder. He stroked her blond hair and kissed her neck.

'Lisbeth,' he asked after a couple of minutes, 'what will happen to us when this is over?' She tried to smile, her tears flowing again, then leaned her head against his chest. 'I love you,' he said.

Chapter 69

It was already dark as Petersen reached the entrance to C Wing. He noted a couple of Army 'deuce and a half' trucks parked beside the gymnasium, along with a couple of jeeps. From inside, he could hear the sounds of a basketball game.

He reported to Stevens' office to find Langley already present. 'OK,' Stevens began as Petersen sat down, 'the next 48 hours or so are critical. Things must be done correctly. Remember this is not just an Army mission, this has the attention of the whole world. I want it to go smoothly and humanely.' Petersen and Langley nodded. 'First thing we're going to do is a surprise inspection. Every cell on tier one.' Steven's led the way and soon Langley and Petersen, with the door guards watching the prisoners, were inspecting and rechecking every cell, mattress, table, chair, bed frame and toilet in the eleven cells of the condemned men.

'Ah you are back!' Goering greeted Petersen with a smile. 'Tell me what you are looking for and I will help you find it!' he joked. Petersen returned his smile. 'Tell me, my young friend,' Goering probed, 'is the event at hand.'

'I'm sorry *Reichsmarschall*, I can't say.'

'Can't say or don't know?' Goering raised an eyebrow.

Petersen ignored the question, giving Goering his answer. The smile faded from his face. 'I see,' he said.

Langley and Petersen returned to Stevens' office with the results of their searches. 'Nothing, sir,' Petersen reported.

'Nothing for me either,' Langley echoed.

While the searches had turned up no contraband, they had clearly turned up the level of anxiety on the first floor. The prisoners were also concerned by the sounds of hammering and voices carrying across the 35 yards between the gym and C Wing. At this point, any departure from the routine caused new worries. With their appeals denied, the prisoners understood that their days were running out like the last grains in an hour glass. The unexpected visits by Langley and Petersen were unwelcome reminders of their fleeting mortality.

Chapter 70

'Tomorrow night,' Stevens instructed his lieutenants on Tuesday evening, 'the prison will be locked down. After 2000 hours, no one in and no one out. Only one phone line will be kept open. That means all guards have to be here on time according to the duty roster and no man who is not on that roster is allowed in. Colonel Gaffner is arranging for a press pool to cover the mission. He will bring them through and then lock them in a room in the Palace until it's time. Other than that, we should work to make things look normal. Third Army G2 is still concerned that some Nazi die-hards may attempt some kind of attack to delay or even prevent the executions, so the fewer people who know the schedule the better. Now, LT Petersen, you will select a detail to escort the prisoners to the gym. Your steadiest men for this. Four guards, plus the two of you,' he pointed to Petersen and Langley. 'You will escort the prisoners, one at a time, and turn them over to Master Sergeant Woods. He and his men set up the apparatus last night. I want you to go coordinate with him tonight so that everything is set for tomorrow. Any questions?' There being none, Petersen and Langley walked to the gym to find Woods.

Master Sergeant John Woods was the Third Army's executioner. In 15 years, he had 'dropped' over 300 men. He and his team had constructed two sets of gallows in the gymnasium, both hidden by long, black curtains. The lieutenants introduced themselves to Woods, a pot-bellied 43 year-old, and listened as he described the routine that would be followed the next night. 'Your colonel tells me you will bring them here under guard, one-by-one, right?' Woods asked with the casual air of a man accustomed to his job. 'My understanding is you will feed them like usual, put them to bed and then wake them up and bring them over here, right?'

'Right sergeant,' Petersen spoke up.

'You and your men bring them to right here lieutenant,' Woods said, stamping his right foot on a spot on the floor about ten feet from the steps leading up to the platform. 'Me and my boys will take it from here, right?' he cocked his head.

'Understood sergeant,' Petersen responded.

As they crossed the yard, headed back to C Wing, Langley spoke. 'John, did you notice how many steps there were leading up to the top of that platform?'

'No.'

'Thirteen.'

Chapter 71

Wednesday, October 16 dawned gray and overcast. John made it home before the rain began to fall. He ate eggs and sausage for breakfast, Lisbeth watching him intently. After breakfast, he headed to the bedroom. His body was still not completely adjusted to night duty. He undressed and laid down on the bed, pulling the blanket up to ward off the chilly air. The bedroom door creaked open and Lisbeth came in. John watched as she pushed the door closed and came to stand by the bed. She pulled off her sweater and her blouse, then unfastened her skirt and let it drop to the floor. She slipped out of her undergarments and slid into the bed beside him. Lisbeth sought out his eyes with hers. She reached between his legs and stroked him, never letting her eyes leave his. She crawled on top of him and rocked back and forth until he was spent. Then she gently slid off and nestled in beside him. When he began to snore, she crept from the bed and pulled the covers up around his shoulders to keep him warm. She gathered up her clothes and quietly left the room.

Lisbeth fixed *Bratwurst* with mustard and *Sauerkraut* for John's early supper. He intended to return to the prison early. He could not abide the thought of sitting and waiting with Lisbeth watching him as the clock ticked on. As he knotted his tie in preparation to leave, Lisbeth came up behind him and wrapped her tiny arms around his waist, leaning her head against his back. 'I love you,' she whispered. John turned around and held her for several minutes.

'I love you too,' he said finally. He looked down at her. 'I have to go now. I'll see you in the morning.'

'Yes,' she said, standing up on her tiptoes to plant a quick kiss on his lips, 'in the morning.'

Chapter 72

It was raining outside and Petersen had gone directly to Goodman's kitchen for an always available cup of hot coffee to ward off the chill. 'LT Petersen, Goering has been asking to see you,' PFC Rogers said as Petersen emerged from the basement. Petersen headed toward Goering's cell, trying to appear as though tonight was just another in a long line of evenings in Nuremberg.

'Good evening, *Reichsmarschall*,' he said peering through the wire screen on the door.

'Good evening LT Petersen,' Goering said. He had apparently been waiting, for he was already standing near the door, hands on his hips. 'I need a favor from you,' he said without preliminary.

'What can I do for you *Reichsmarschall*?' Petersen asked warily.

'My lawyer, Dr. Stahmer is to pay me a visit shortly,' Goering explained. 'I wish to make him a gift of a briefcase, something by which he can remember his most famous client.' Petersen saw a fleeting glint in Goering's eye as he tried to smile. 'It is in the baggage room with the rest of my belongings. The blue, leather case. About this big,' he said holding up his hands in a rough outline of the case.

'What time do you expect Dr. Stahmer, sir?' Petersen asked, thinking about the lock down.

'At six o'clock, which is any time now,' Goering replied consulting his wrist watch.

'Yes sir. I'll get the briefcase and bring it along with Dr. Stahmer when he arrives,' Petersen said.

Stahmer arrived just a few minutes later, bearing a letter signed by Sir Geoffrey Lawrence authorizing access to his client at any time. Petersen was grateful that he had come early, unsure of how he would have responded if the prison had already been in lock down. While Stahmer waited, Petersen unlocked the property room and shifted through Goering's enormous set of matched luggage. He found the blue, leather briefcase under a larger black one and dusted it off. From the heft of it, he judged it to be empty.

To be sure, he flipped up the twin brass clasps and raised the top. Inside he saw an expensive silk lining, but nothing else. He snapped the case shut and relocked the door. 'This way, sir,' he said to Dr. Stahmer and led him to Goering's cell. He nodded to the guard who slid back the bolt and opened the heavy door.

'Hello Otto!' Goering forced a smile. Stahmer, his thick white hair in sharp contrast to his dark overcoat, shook Goering's hand warmly. The two men exchanged pleasantries. Goering looked from Stahmer to Petersen and held out his hand. 'Thank you LT Petersen. You have been a good friend.' Petersen, still standing in the doorway, reached around Stahmer and handed the briefcase to Goering. The *Reichsmarschall*, in English, for Petersen's sake, said, 'Here Otto, hold this,' and handed the case to Stahmer. With Stahmer shielding him from Petersen's view, Goering popped open the case. 'You see,' he said to Stahmer, 'it has a pocket here and places here for files.' Goering continued to point out features as Stahmer looked down over the top of the open case he held. 'Your pens go here. It even has this pouch for a spare pair of glasses. It is my gift to you along with my sincere thanks for your friendship and counsel. I thank you,' he said, closing the lid and snapping the catches. He shook the elderly Stahmer's hand. Stahmer mumbled something that Petersen couldn't understand. The older man was clearly emotional as he turned back toward the door. Petersen stepped aside to let him pass. Goering put his hands in his pockets.

The prisoners' evening meal was served at 1830 hours. Goodman had cooked up some sausages and served them with fruit salad, potatoes and rolls. By 1915, the prisoners were back in their cells. At 2000 hours Gaffner guided his press pool through the cell block. He directed their attention to such high points as the property room, the library and the day room, where two soldiers along with Chaplain Gerrity were trying without success to pick up a broadcast of the World Series. The reporters, representing the International News Service, Tass, Pravda, Reuters and Le Monde, looked in on the prisoners. Some were smoking, some reading, a few pacing. Gaffner nodded at Petersen as his party passed out of the cell block and headed to their quarantine in the Palace.

As the members of the press disappeared up the covered walkway to the Palace, Stevens exited his office. 'Lock down begins now,' he said quietly to Langley and Petersen who had converged on him at his beckoning gesture. Guards were placed on each entrance to C Wing. Stevens had elected to forego firearms to avoid attracting attention, but each man was equipped with a billy club, a blackjack and a whistle with which he could summon help.

At 2100 hours, Petersen again descended the stairs, this time headed to the infirmary. Dr. Schuster had lined up his red and blue pills on his metal tray, along with twelve small paper cups half filled with water. With Petersen as his escort, Schuster climbed the stairs for his last round of dispensing pills. Petersen watched as each prisoner took the red pill to help him fall asleep quickly, followed by the blue pill for deep sleep.

Goering was uncharacteristically reticent as the doctor and the lieutenant entered his cell. He greeted Schuster and nodded to Petersen. He took the red pill and swallowed it with a sip of water. Goering opened his mouth for Petersen to ensure the pill was gone. Petersen nodded and said, 'Thank you *Reichsmarschall*.' Goering took the second pill and popped it into his mouth. He drank the rest of the water and again opened his mouth for Petersen's inspection. Schuster extended his bony hand, his eyes watery. Goering took his hand and said, 'Thank you my friend.' Schuster bowed slightly and left the cell.

'Sleep well, sir,' Petersen said.

'Good night lieutenant,' Goering said. The door closed and the bolt slid back into place. Goering turned his back to the door. He raised his right hand to his mouth and coughed theatrically, spitting the blue pill into his hand. In one fluid motion he dropped his hand into his trousers pocket and deposited the sleeping pill beside a longer, glass vial containing a far deadlier substance.

Chapter 73

The wind had picked up, joining the misty rain. A perfect night for an execution, Petersen thought as he peered out the window in the guards' day room. It was just like one of those Hollywood pictures: the dark, stormy night, the guards sitting around waiting, the chaplain sitting in the corner saying prayers. Of course this time, there would be no midnight call from the governor's office staying the sentences. And, truth be told, Chaplain Gerrity wasn't praying. He was still fiddling with the radio, trying stubbornly to pick up stray radio waves from Saint Louis, where his beloved Cardinals were battling the Red Sox in Game 7 of the World Series. Gaffner, in a rare concession, had allowed one phone call into the prison at the end of each inning. After seven innings, the Cardinals were up 3-1 and Gerrity was happy. He was swapping jibes with Sergeant Gamble, a rabid Boston fan. The phone rang and Gerrity pounced on it. He jotted some notes on a piece of paper on the table. When he hung up, he was frowning.

'Well, damn!' he said to no one in particular, assiduously avoiding Gamble's face, 'two pinch hits, two! What are the odds of that!' He tossed the pencil down in irritation.

'What's the scoop chaplain?' Gamble asked hopefully. Gerrity related that the Sox, after two pinch hits to lead off the eighth, had made two outs. Then, Dom DiMaggio had laced a double off the right field wall of Sportsman's Park to score two runs. Going into the bottom of the eighth, the game was tied at 3 all. 'How I hate to go on duty!' Gamble groused picking up his helmet liner and slapping it down on his head. 'I'm gonna be down there looking through a door watching a guy sleep and you're gonna be up here twiddling the dials on that radio. I bet you pick it up as soon as I leave. Let me know when you get the next call,' Gamble pleaded. He left the dayroom and headed down the spiral stairs to take up his post in front of Goering's cell. It was 2200 hours.

Petersen was reading the *Saturday Evening Post*. Actually, he was holding the *Saturday Evening Post*, but he hadn't read a word in several minutes. His eyes were fixed on an article about Broadway's resurgence following the end of the war, but he could not focus. He glanced again at the wall clock. Two minutes had passed since his last look. Half of him wanted the clock to move faster, to get this night over with. The other half wanted to avoid looking into the eyes of Goering and the others as they marched to the gallows. The ringing telephone startled him. Gerrity grabbed it. 'Yes,' he shouted into the handset, 'go ahead.' The chaplain scribbled a note. 'Praise God!' he said. 'Yes, thanks!' he hung up. 'Well, well, well,' he said gleefully, 'I must go inform Sergeant Gamble that the mighty Cardinals now own a one run lead going into the ninth!' Gerrity reported that the Card's Enos Slaughter had scored from first base on a Harry Walker double to left. According to his report, the ball had come back in to Sox shortstop Johnny Pesky, but Pesky held the ball, thinking that Slaughter had stopped at third. 'OK if I break the news to Gamble?' Gerrity asked Petersen.

'OK, sir,' Petersen agreed, 'but keep quiet out there. And chaplain,' Petersen added with a smile, 'be gentle.' Gerrity chuckled and headed toward the door, but he stopped, a puzzled expression on his face. Then Petersen heard it: running footsteps, followed by shouts. It was Gamble, charging up the spiral steps and yelling. 'LT Petersen! Something's wrong! Something's wrong with Goering!' Petersen was on his feet, dashing for the door, where he collided with Gerrity, who had stopped short, and Gamble who had barged in. Petersen pushed Gerrity out of the way and spun Gamble around.

'Go!' he shouted. Together, the two thundered down the stairs. Petersen shouted at the first guard he saw, 'Quick, fetch Dr. Schuster!'

Gamble and Petersen skidded to a stop outside of cell 5. Petersen ripped aside the bolt and yanked the door back. 'Turn on the lights,' he shouted to Gamble as he knelt next to Goering. Goering was in obvious distress. He was on his back, his face a sickly green with bubbles forming at the corner of his mouth. His breathing was harsh and labored. One eye was open, staring vacantly at the ceiling; the other was closed.

Schuster arrived wearing a tattered bathrobe. He gently pushed Petersen aside, kneeling and examining Goering, whose breath rattled in his throat and then stopped. Schuster pressed his fingers against Goering's flabby neck. 'There is no pulse. He is dead,' he said without emotion. Gerrity stood just outside the cell, having followed Gamble and Petersen on their mad, but futile, dash.

'Step back please doctor,' Petersen began to assert control over the situation. He knew a bunch of shit was about to hit the fan and that he and every other soldier on duty at the prison would be standing right in front of it. He turned to Gerrity. 'Chaplain would you please find Captain Stevens and tell him his immediate presence is required. Sergeant Gamble, no one is to enter this cell until further notice. Dr. Schuster and I will wait outside with you until Captain Stevens arrives.'

'Yes sir.'

Stevens arrived within five minutes, a very long five minutes to Petersen. Stevens immediately telephoned Gaffner's office and told the colonel an emergency existed in the cell block. Gaffner, leaving the press pool under armed guard, ran the entire way and was winded when he arrived.

'Good God Almighty!' he moaned when Stevens ushered him into cell 5. 'What happened?'

'Sergeant Gamble was on guard sir,' Stevens replied sheepishly.

Gaffner turned on Gamble. 'What happened sergeant?' he demanded.

'Sir I came on duty at 2200 hours and everything seemed normal. He,' Gamble pointed at Goering's body, 'was asleep. I could hear him snoring lightly. About 2245, he rolled over and I saw him bring his arm up to his face like this,' Gamble raised his right arm up to his face with his right hand clenched. 'Then he let his hand fall back down. A couple of minutes later, he starts making this strange sound, like he's gagging or something. That's when I ran to get LT Petersen.'

Gaffner turned to Petersen. 'You next,' he said, strangely calm.

'Chaplain Gerrity and I were upstairs in the dayroom,' Petersen began. He recounted the moments between Sergeant Gamble's initial alert and their arrival back at the cell. He continued through the arrival of Dr. Schuster and the determination that Goering was dead. 'At that point sir, we left the cell to preserve it for further investigation.'

'Good decision,' said Gaffner, who apparently had not been drinking on this particular night.

'Dr. Schuster?' Gaffner asked.

'It is as you have heard sir. There is nothing more to say until the body has been examined.'

Gaffner shook his head. He walked over to Goering's body, stretched across the bed. He stared down into the lifeless face. He slapped his gloves against his thigh. Then, without warning, he swung the gloves down in a ferocious slap across the corpse's face. Petersen and Gerrity started.

'What did you do that for?' blurted Gerrity, his face pale.

'You can't not flinch,' Gaffner muttered. 'The son of a bitch is really dead.'

Chapter 74

It was Gaffner's unenviable duty to inform his commanding officer, General Watson, of Goering's suicide. Gaffner recommended that the remainder of the executions go forward as scheduled, a suggestion that Watson embraced. It was time to close this chapter. Shortly after 2300 hours, Gaffner ordered the ten remaining condemned men to be awakened. While Gaffner made final arrangements in the prison, Watson appointed a panel of three officers, one from Gaffner's staff and two from his own, to conduct an immediate investigation.

Von Ribbentrop, Hitler's incompetent foreign minister, wearing a khaki shirt and dark gray trousers, was the first prisoner to be marched across the yard to the gym, flanked on either side by two guards. Petersen walked behind him, impressed by his composure. At the agreed upon spot, the detail halted. Sergeant Woods stepped forward and bound Ribbentrop's hands behind him with a leather strap. At the foot of the stairs, Captain Stevens asked him to state his name, an Army stenographer recording the event. Woods and one of his men, helped the disgraced diplomat up the thirteen steps to the platform. Once positioned over the trap door, they turned him toward the small press pool and the official witnesses from each of the conquering powers as well as Germany. Captain Stevens, standing on the gym floor in front of the gallows, read the official order of execution handed down by the Tribunal. He looked up at Ribbentrop. 'Do you have a statement, sir?' he asked.

The little man looked down at Stevens and nodded. 'I wish for understanding between East and West,' he said. 'I wish for peace.' Then he raised his eyes and stared straight ahead as Woods lowered a black hood over his head. His feet were bound together by an Army web belt. The noose was positioned over the hood and tightened. Gerrity mounted the platform, fighting his emotions long enough to deliver a short prayer in his rough Midwestern German. The chaplain stepped back and Woods pulled the handle, releasing the trap and dropping Ribbentrop to his death.

By the time the last prisoner had been pronounced dead and his body loaded into a pre-positioned coffin in the rear of the gymnasium, Petersen was back in the day room, fielding questions from the investigating officers.

'We've spoken to everyone else lieutenant,' said Colonel Duncan, General Watson's chief of staff, from a chair beside the table where Petersen had first met Robert Simmons. Duncan was joined by two other officers, Colonel Collins, Watson's adjutant, and Lieutenant Colonel Morehead, Gaffner's executive officer. 'We'd like to hear your story from the time you arrived for duty until Captain Stevens' arrival in the cell after Goering's suicide.'

'Yes sir,' Petersen replied and launched into his story. He didn't get far.

'You mean to tell me that Goering had a visitor tonight?' Colonel Collins asked.

'Yes sir, his lawyer, Dr. Stahmer. He had a letter authorizing access from the president of the Tribunal, Sir Geoffrey Lawrence,' Petersen explained.

'Incredible!' Collins shook his head in disbelief.

'Should I have turned him away, sir?' Petersen asked.

Collins shook his head. 'It doesn't matter now. Go ahead.'

Petersen continued, but again did not get very far.

'Did you inspect this briefcase before you turned it over to Goering?' asked Lieutenant Colonel Morehead.

'I did sir. I opened it and looked inside. It was empty. Weren't all those bags inspected when they first went into the baggage room?'

'Good question lieutenant, but how about you let us do the asking, OK?' Morehead responded. He, like the others, was peeved at having been rousted from his comfortable quarters in order to conduct a middle-of-the-night investigation that could have no happy ending.

Petersen described Stahmer's visit, providing as much detail as he could recall. 'Did he give anything to Goering, hand him anything, a package, letter, anything?' Morehead asked.

'No sir, nothing. I had them both in clear view the whole time. They only came in contact twice: once, on Dr. Stahmer's arrival when they shook hands and the second time as he was preparing to leave.'

'Could he have handed Goering anything, a capsule maybe?' Collins picked up the questioning.

'I don't think so sir. I just don't think so. What killed him sir?' Petersen risked another question.

'The doctors say it was a cyanide capsule. He must have put it in his mouth when Sergeant Gamble saw him raise his arm up. After that, all he had to do was bite down on it and the rest is history,' Collins said. 'He left a suicide note; did you know that, lieutenant?'

'No sir, after Dr. Schuster said he was dead, we left the cell. We didn't look around or disturb anything. If you don't mind me asking sir, what did the note say?'

Collins, Morehead and Duncan looked at each other. Duncan nodded and said, 'He wrote that none of those who searched his cell were to be blamed, that there was no way they could have found the capsule. He wrote some other stuff to his wife and to the chaplain, but none of that has any importance to our little investigation here. Tell me lieutenant,' Duncan resumed the questioning, 'did you accompany Schuster when he gave out sleeping pills tonight?'

'Yes sir.'

'And did you verify that the medicine was ingested?'

'I did sir.'

'Did you know that we found a blue pill in the pocket of his pajamas?' Duncan asked.

Petersen sat for a moment. 'I checked his mouth sir,' he reiterated. 'I did not see the pill. I believed that he swallowed it.'

'Apparently he did not,' Duncan said. He glanced at his colleagues. 'Any more questions?' Morehead and Collins shook their heads and stood up. Petersen stood. 'If we come up with any more questions, LT Petersen, we know where to find you.'

'I'm really sorry sir,' Petersen said to the three colonels. 'I'm sorry it happened and I'm sorry it happened on my watch.'

'Yeah, well, I'll tell you what lieutenant,' Duncan said cocking his head. 'The way I see it, he was going to be dead one way or the other by the end of tonight. One more dead Nazi can't be all bad.'

Petersen saluted and walked back down the spiral staircase.

At the bottom of the stairs, Petersen turned right, stepping into Stevens' office where this long night had started only a few hours earlier. 'John,' Stevens looked up at his arrival, 'you all right? Did the three stooges work you over?'

'No sir, no worse than I deserve anyway.'

'Don't be hard on yourself, John. According to Goering's suicide note, there were two more cyanide capsules hidden in his luggage, one in a jar of cold cream.'

'Where do you think he got the one that killed him?' Petersen asked.

'Who knows? Maybe it was in that briefcase or maybe it was up his ass the whole time,' Stevens speculated. 'He's dead. It's done. You've had a stressful night. Clock out early if you want. Check in with me this afternoon.'

'Yes sir, I will,' Petersen said, leaving the office.

'John!' Stevens called after him.

'Yes sir?'

'The Cardinals won 4-3.'

Petersen smiled to himself. At least the chaplain would be happy. He walked down the middle of the empty cell block, his footsteps echoing off the concrete walls. No sentinels stood guard. The doors to the cells stood open, all of them vacant for the first time in sixteen months.

Petersen pulled on his overcoat and pushed out the door of C Wing. It was early, not yet 0500, and he longed to crawl into bed and pull Lisbeth's warm body close to his. The rain was heavier than before and Petersen lowered his head as he turned up the collar of his coat. In the darkness, he ran squarely into Gaffner's thickset frame, colliding with a grunt. Realizing what he'd done, he jumped back and saluted. 'I beg your pardon sir!' he stammered. 'I wasn't paying attention to where I was going!' he apologized as droplets streamed from his cap and down his shoulders.

Gaffner's voice was menacing in the darkness. 'Well, lieutenant,' he snarled, 'I *have* been paying attention. I know how you cozied up to Goering and the others. I know how you've been friendly with that scum. You think I don't know what's going on in my own command? You think you're pretty damn slick, don't you boy?' Gaffner's words were slurred, his face a wet, unreadable mask in the darkness of the yard. 'I'll tell you what hotshot. You just cost the United States of America a great deal of prestige, prestige we're going to need to face down these Russian bastards. You made me look like an incompetent fool, boy. I ought to rip you to pieces right here and right now.' Gaffner took an unsteady step forward. Petersen stepped back. 'What's the matter, Petersen? Scared? You weren't scared when you helped that fat bastard Goering cheat justice. Why are you scared now?'

'Sir,' Petersen thought fast, trying to devise a way out of this unpromising conversation, 'I think maybe now isn't the best time for this discussion.'

'I reckon the hell you do,' Gaffner replied sarcastically. 'But you know what? I don't give a rat's ass about what you think.' He stepped forward again, his foot splashing into a puddle. Petersen flinched, and Gaffner noticed with delight. 'Yeah, you are scared aren't you? You ought to be. But I'm not going to beat the shit out of you. That would be too easy and it would be over too fast. Besides, there's nobody here to see it.' Gaffner's eyes were smoldering in the darkness. He pointed his stubby finger at Petersen's chest. 'I'm going to ruin you, boy. I'm going to expose you for the incompetent, ass-kissing suck-up you are. When I get finished with you, everybody's going to know what I know. You'll be lucky if they don't throw *you* into C Wing!' With that, Gaffner pushed Petersen to the side and staggered into the darkness. Petersen stood in the darkness, trembling from pent up anger, the cold rain dripping down the back of his neck.

Chapter 75

The rain somehow managed to fall harder as he walked through the inky darkness, keeping his head down in a futile attempt to see and avoid puddles. He pushed the door to 22 *Gartenstrasse* open and ducked in. He stood for a moment on the door mat, letting the water run off his overcoat and his eyes adjust to the unlit interior. He took his overcoat off and hung it on the rack along with his now soaked cap.

'Lisbeth,' he called out, but not too loudly for fear of startling her. He loosened his tie and began unbuttoning his shirt as he walked toward the bedroom. The door was open, the bed empty. He turned back to the main room.

'She's not here,' came a man's voice from the darkness. Petersen started. He saw the orange glow of a cigarette hovering above the sofa, its holder invisible in the unlit room.

'Who are you and what are you doing here?' Petersen said, trying to keep both fear and anger out of his voice. He moved slowly toward the glow, feeling along the wall for the light switch.

'Nothing to fear, lieutenant,' the voice said. 'I'm a friend.' Petersen reached the switch and flicked the lights on. A familiar man in an expensive, tailored suit sat leisurely on his sofa. Petersen recognized Erich Greinke, the younger of Goering's attorneys.

'*Herr* Greinke? What are you doing in my quarters at 5:30 in the morning?' Petersen paused. 'Was anyone here when you got here?'

'No,' Greinke replied. '*Frau* Bichler is not here.'

'You know about her?' Petersen asked, with a growing apprehension.

'Of course,' Greinke replied nonchalantly. 'We know lots of things. Some of the things we know, you should know too. That's why I'm here,' he smiled, putting out the cigarette and leaning forward with his elbows on his knees.

'Well, by all means, let's get right to the point *Herr* Greinke,' Petersen said snatching one of the wooden kitchen chairs from the table and dragging it toward the sofa. His temper was rising as he sat down four feet from his visitor and leaned forward. 'I've had a pretty shitty night and I'd like to know what the hell is going on around here. My girlfriend is missing, everybody I've been taking care of for the past sixteen months is now dead and in a pine box, I've just had my Army career snuffed out and now I come home to find a stranger sitting in my house in the middle of the night. No offense.'

'None taken,' Greinke smiled.

'I'd like to know what you know,' Petersen snapped.

'Where to begin?' Greinke asked rhetorically, looking around the house. It began to sink in that Greinke was speaking English without hint of an accent. 'I'm not really a lawyer, nor am I a protégé of Dr. Stahmer and I wasn't exactly hired by *Reichsmarschall* Goering.' Greinke looked Petersen in the eyes. 'I'm with the OSS,' he paused savoring the drama of the moment. 'The Office of Strategic Services, lieutenant.'

'I know what the OSS is, *Herr* Greinke. I even met Donovan.' Petersen snapped, growing angrier, more apprehensive and more curious, all at the same time.

'Donovan was impressed with you, Lieutenant Petersen,' Greinke leaned back and made a tent with his fingers.

Petersen cocked his head, 'Wait a minute. I thought the OSS was out of business.'

'Well, technically,' Greinke smiled. 'What if I told you that you had done your nation a great service tonight?'

'I don't think my commanding officer shares that view,' Petersen said with a rueful shake of his head.

'Don't worry about Gaffner,' Greinke said with assurance. 'We'll handle all that. The fact is lieutenant, the United States needed things to transpire pretty much as they did. Do you recall during the trial that *Reichsmarschall* Goering repeatedly protested that he had done all he could to avoid war?'

'Yes,' Petersen replied. He felt himself being drawn more deeply into Greinke's web.

'Well, a lot of it was true. What he didn't say, what he couldn't say, was that he had tried to broker a peace deal after D-Day, when he knew the game was up for Hitler and the Nazis.'

'Why didn't he say that during the trial?' Petersen asked, his curiosity piqued.

'Like I said, he couldn't. We, well, we cut a deal with him so to speak.' Greinke paused, searching for the right words. 'You see, the *Reichsmarschall*, though eager to save Germany from total destruction, only wanted to deal with us and the Brits. His proposal was that we all join up to drive the Russians back to the Stone Age.'

'I don't get it *Herr* Greinke,' Petersen interrupted. 'Why is this such a big deal? We turned him down didn't we? Unconditional surrender and all that jazz.'

'Have you been around any of the Russians?' Greinke asked.

'No, but I've seen some of them around,' Petersen answered. He thought back to Simmons' descriptions of the Russians and how unsophisticated he made them out to be.

'Let's just say they're different: uneducated, savage and suspicious. Like us, they have intelligence people snooping around and they had them inside the Third Reich too. They got wind of Goering's overtures and immediately suspected their allies, us, of going behind their backs to cut a deal for a separate peace.'

Petersen leaned back. 'Thanks for the history lesson, but what's this got to do with me?'

'You were at the hangings this morning. What happened before each man was dropped?'

'He got to make a final statement. I'm sorry, *Herr* Greinke, I still don't get it.'

'We couldn't take the risk of Goering standing up there and pretending that there was some kind of secret, unholy alliance between us, the Brits and the Germans. The Russians would have gone berserk and they're dangerous enough already.'

'Why didn't we just deny it?' Petersen asked, confused.

'Because they already believe it! They have a pretty significant inferiority complex that tends to cloud their perspective,' Greinke explained. 'So,' he continued, 'we cut a deal with Goering back when we had him at Mondorf. We knew there was no way the Russians would ever let him off with just prison time. Neither would the British or the French. I doubt we would have either. We also knew the Tribunal's method of execution was hanging. So we offered him an option: his silence for a dignified, more heroic death. That hero stuff really appeals to his sense of theater,' Greinke said, referring to Goering in the present tense. 'He preferred a firing squad, as he told you, but we couldn't make that happen under the authority of the Tribunal's charter, so we had to go with Plan B.'

'Suicide.' Petersen stated flatly.

'Right. Once we realized the firing squad wasn't going to pan out, we switched to the cyanide capsule option. It had been there all along. He let you find one on the initial inspection back in August. That was our test to see how thorough your security was going to be. But, your property officer, Rose, slipped up by never checking all the luggage the prisoners brought with them. As far as we know, there was no methodical check of the bags. We still had two more capsules hidden in addition to the one you delivered last night. Like I said, you did your country a real service. Goering too. He didn't want to hang.'

'Gee, I feel all better now,' Petersen said caustically. 'Just like a puppet with no will of my own.'

'Oh don't take it hard, lieutenant,' Greinke smiled again. 'It's a lot like combat. Somebody else is always pulling the strings.'

'What would you know about combat?' Petersen asked with an icy stare.

Greinke's smile took on a hard edge. 'More than you might guess.' He put his hands on his knees and pushed himself up. 'Well, lieutenant,' he stuck out his hand, 'I can't say it's been a pleasure, but I do appreciate your time.'

Petersen stood, ignoring the outstretched hand. 'I still have questions. Where is Lisbeth?'

'She's not here,' Greinke said, head down, heading toward the front door.

'I can see that. Where is she?'

'She's gone.'

'Where?' Petersen caught Greinke by the elbow, spinning him around in the doorway.

'Gone.' Greinke stared into Petersen's face. He sighed. 'OK, listen, I'm sorry. She's gone. She's not coming back.'

'Wrong, pal,' Petersen snapped, but he wondered if maybe he was the one who had it wrong. 'We're in love. We want to be together.'

'Not going to happen, *pal*,' Greinke responded in kind, gently pulling his arm free. 'Lisbeth, as you call her, was doing a little job for us. She was here to back you up, to help you make the right decisions. Job's over. She's gone.'

Petersen tensed up, balling his hands into fists, ready to spring at Greinke. 'She can't be working for you,' Petersen felt his voice catch.

'I'm sure there were certain aspects of the job she really enjoyed,' Greinke said, a cynical note in his voice, 'but it was still a job. Let's just say we were assisting her with some legal problems of her own. We gave her a chance to work them off,' Greinke said with a level gaze.

Petersen swallowed, a lump rising in his throat as the bleak reality descended upon his heart, 'I want her back and I want her back now.'

'You'll have to take that up with her,' Greinke said. 'And her husband. And their son.' Greinke paused, his hand on the door handle, and turned back toward Petersen. 'It's time to move on lieutenant. It's over. Don't worry about your Colonel Gaffner. We'll take care of things.'

'One more question, *Herr* Greinke,' Petersen said, shoving his arm across the doorway to block his guest's departure. 'Did you have Simmons killed?'

Greinke stared for a moment into Petersen's angry face. Then he smirked and shook his head. 'Of course not, lieutenant. What kind of people do you think we are?' He pushed Petersen's arm aside and stepped out into the gray dawn. Petersen watched him vanish into the thick fog. Petersen closed the door and wandered back through the house, the silence assaulting his sadness. He sat at the table, scene of so many pleasant evenings, and listened to the ticking of the clock.

Chapter 76

At 1630 hours, after a lonely day of bitter self-recrimination, Petersen reported back to the quiet C Wing. Stevens, looking freshly shaved and rested, sat at his desk thumbing through his paperback. 'Hey lieutenant!' he said as Petersen trudged in to his office. 'I hope you got some rest. You still look pretty beat.'

'I haven't adjusted to the new circumstances yet sir,' Petersen responded obliquely.

'Yeah, quite a night last night, wasn't it? Oh, I've got a package for you,' Stevens remembered, pulling a sealed manila envelope from the top of the cluttered desk. Petersen opened the package and removed a set of orders. He read them as Stevens stood peering over his shoulder. 'Well, I'll be,' Stevens whistled. 'I've never seen the Army operate so efficiently,' he said. 'Mission accomplished at 0300 and new assignment twelve hours later. Never seen anything like that.'

'No sir, it's not like the Army at all,' Petersen said.

1LT John Petersen looked up at the damaged archway which led into the main gallery of Nuremberg's *Hauptbahnhof*. In sixteen months, the Germans, working with generous assistance from the American government, had made miraculous progress in rebuilding their city. The trains were again running on time. The business of commerce was rejuvenating in Nuremberg and throughout occupied Germany. He now saw nearly as many businessmen in suits as he saw soldiers in uniform. Maybe, he thought, Goering hadn't been so wrong after all in wanting to unite Germany with the west.

He had crammed as much stuff as he could into his over/under bag, weighing down his left side. In his right hand, he carried the multiple copies of his orders which he would need to travel from Nuremberg to the Army's main port facility at Bremerhaven. He had been assigned to the personnel depot there pending stateside reassignment. He was 'moving on,' but far faster than he desired. His heart ached. He had laid in bed for most of two days just to smell her scent, just to be in a place they had shared. His head ached. He had not slept for more than ten minutes at a time since Greinke's visit. His stomach growled, but he had no appetite.

He threaded his way through the crowded terminal, searching. In every direction he saw men and women walking together, talking together, laughing together, holding hands. He looked into every face desperately searching for Lisbeth's laughing blue eyes. But it was only in his dreams that he would find them. And his dreams would not come.

Acknowledgments

The War Widow is my first novel, but it's not the product of a single mind. Many friends were gracious with their time, their encouragement and their advice, all of which helped create the story you've read. Dr. Troy Terry of Furman University was the first non-family member to read the manuscript and offered valuable suggestions as well as encouraging words. Dr. Scott Walker of Mercer University's Institute for Life Purpose shared his experience in dealing with agents and publishers. Dr. Don McKale, emeritus professor of history at my alma mater Clemson University, invested hours reviewing the manuscript for historical accuracy and saved me from embarrassing errors. Dean Kay Wall of Clemson University's Cooper Library, and her staff, opened their resources to me and were free with their encouragement as well. In an effort to present the most accurate depiction of the Nuremberg Trials, quotes from the trial sessions were taken from the transcripts of the Avalon Collection at the Yale Law Library.

I am grateful to my business partner Joe Turner who tolerated my sometimes singular focus on writing and who has enthusiastically supported this effort. Finally, no one has had greater support and encouragement on the all-important home front. Thanks to my parents, Harry and Ina; to my children for understanding when Dad wanted to write rather than watch TV; and to my wonderful wife Yvonne, who doubles as my CEO— chief encouragement officer.

William Kelly Durham
Clemson, SC
June 2010

About the Author

William Kelly Durham lives in Clemson, SC with his wife Yvonne, their daughters Mary Kate, Addison and Callie and their dog, George Marshall. A graduate of Clemson University, Durham served four years in the US Army including assignments in Arizona and Germany before returning to Clemson and entering private business. *The War Widow* is his first novel.

27374392R00147

Made in the USA
San Bernardino, CA
12 December 2015